A Good Book

JEWEL E. ANN

USA Today & Wall Street Journal
BESTSELLING AUTHOR

A GOOD BOOK

SUNDAY MORNING SERIES

JEWEL E. ANN

Cover Design: Boja99designs

Photo: © Jessica Rockowitz

Formatting: Jenn Beach

IYKYK
For all the young women who did not know.

You know you're in love when you can't fall asleep because reality is finally better than your dreams.—Dr. Seuss

Chapter One

U2, "I Still Haven't Found What I'm Looking For"

1989
Gabby

IT WAS my second week at the University of Michigan, a college I chose because my sister discarded her perfectly good boyfriend, and someone needed to scoop him up. I fell in love with Matthew Cory before she did. Sure, I didn't have boobs yet, but my heart was mature beyond its years.

Somewhere on the three-thousand-acre campus, my future husband was studying for a law degree, and I was officially an adult and ready for him to fall in love with me.

Ben, my best friend, ripped open a pack of Pop-Tarts and handed one to me on our way to freshman English. A group of young women gawked at Ben, then giggled after we passed them. He pulled back his shoulders and lifted his chin, bringing himself to his full six-foot-two, basking in the glory of the attention.

"Don't get your hopes up. Once they find out you're a music major, the fantasy will die."

Ben blew his shaggy brown hair away from his forehead before biting into his Pop-Tart. "I think it's far more attractive and *honorable* to attend a particular college because: A) it fits your career path, and B) you got a scholarship."

"You got a *music* scholarship," I said.

"Gabby, you took out student loans because you're a stalker and your parents didn't save for out-of-state tuition. *And* you're a psychology major. Those are a dime a dozen. The only people who study psychology are those who need to cure themselves of something like an unhealthy infatuation for a guy who has never given you a second look."

We cut right toward the Roman-style building where we had our only class together.

"Or a career in criminal justice—dang it!" I fumbled my Pop-Tart.

"Five-second rule," Ben declared, plucking it off the ground for me.

"Ew ... I'm not eating it."

Ben blew on it, took a bite, and handed me the remaining portion of his.

"What would I do without you?" I nudged his arm.

"I realize that's a rhetorical question," he shot me a quick side-glance as we continued toward Angell Hall, "but I'm going to answer anyway. You'd still be in Devil's Head, Missouri, with your nose in a book because the only reason your father let you attend an out-of-state college is because I'm here and he trusts me. Or you might have been in jail for stalking. I imagine it could have gone either way."

"Stop. You make me sound incompetent."

We passed another group of girls who smiled and blushed at Ben.

"You act like Matt doesn't know I exist. He's given me lots of looks and used to play Uno with me when Sarah wouldn't. He taught me how to throw a baseball. Plus, he said, and I quote, 'Gabriella will be a heartbreaker.' My mom talked to his mom, and he's going to show me around campus."

We climbed the concrete stairs.

"I've shown you around campus. You've been going to classes for two weeks. Don't you think it's a little late for a tour?"

"You're such a dork. Of course, I don't need a tour now, but it's okay for him to think that I've been getting lost if that's what it takes to reunite with him."

"Reunite?" Ben snorted and sang the lyrics to "Reunited" by Peaches & Herb.

"Stop!" I giggled. "Shh ... you're embarrassing."

"I'm embarrassing? You should be embarrassed of your-self, Gabriella Grace Jacobson. Do you think a guy four years older than you is going to find your infatuation romantic? Ya think he's looking for a girl who has never uttered a single swear word, never missed a curfew, and has an untouched vagina?"

"Oh my gosh, stop!" I hissed, mortified that he said "untouched vagina" so loudly.

"Never been kissed," he whispered in my ear before opening the lecture hall door. Ben was on his way to becoming my *ex*-best friend.

I don't know why my dad trusted him. Ben was far from a saint. Our senior year, he dated three girls and had sex with all of them. This past summer, he and his family spent two weeks at a cabin in the Ozarks, where he met a woman ten years older than him. Ben wouldn't give me all the details because he said he didn't want me to judge him. But leaving me to guess only made me judge him more. Still, my parents loved him because they didn't know he was such a sinner. He was a "ma'am" guy, so my mom adored him for respecting women with his "Yes, ma'am. No, ma'am. Thank you, ma'am."

Ben dragged me to the third row from the blackboard because he liked to record all of his classes to relisten to the lecture before bed. So I had to actually pay attention instead of scribbling poems in my notebook, which should have been fine since it was a creative writing class.

I wrote a message on my notebook and slid it toward him.

How many times have you done it?

Ben squinted at it before peaking his eyebrows at me.

The professor removed several books from her bag and glanced up to survey the rest of the students making their way to their seats.

Ben retrieved a pen from his backpack and scribbled:

DONE WHAT?

He knew darn well what.

IT!!!

Ben smirked. He loved getting me riled up.

I DON'T KNOW.

How could he not know? He was on the verge of turning nineteen, not twenty-nine. If I knew I'd had sex zero times, then he had to know if he'd had it five or ten times.

8?

Ben shook his head and bobbed a thumbs-up.

10?

Again, he signaled up.

15?

The professor cleared her throat and asked everyone to take a seat and quiet down.

I frowned at Ben, so he scribbled on my notepad again.

30+

My jaw dropped, and Ben returned a muted laugh while pressing his finger below my chin to close my mouth.

Ben needed more Jesus in his life.

Chapter Two

Lisa Lisa & Cult Jam, "Head to Toe"

Gabby

"DOES your mom know you have a crush on this guy?" My roommate Olivia asked as I applied a little blush and cherry ChapStick in the full-length mirror behind our dorm room door.

I knew nothing about makeup because my parents frowned upon me wearing it, but I wanted Matt to see me as all grown up.

"Who said I have a crush on him?" I rubbed my lips together. "He's a friend. Our families go way back. He dated my oldest sister."

She reclined in her desk chair, hair-sprayed bangs the size of two sausages and the rest of her red permed hair pulled into a banana clip. She pushed her glasses up her nose. Olivia always wore electric blue eyeshadow and thick mascara with dark red lipstick, and she did so with confidence.

"Matt plays baseball," she crossed her arms over her chest, "and he's in law school. And he has good manners. He rarely missed a Sunday in church. He's smart. His family owned most of the land in Devil's Head. Dude ... I feel like I *totally* know this guy because you've not-so-casually mentioned him a hundred times. I don't talk about my family's 'friends' or my sister's ex-boyfriend because that would be weird. So you totally have a crush on him. Just admit it so we can *really* talk about him. Like do you think about kissing him? Would you have sex with him or would your sister be mad? What about a girlfriend? Does he have one? How far would you go on a first date?"

Those were good questions, but did I know her well enough to share the answers? We would be roommates until summer. Aside from her, Matt, and Ben, I didn't have any other friends yet.

"Fine." I zipped my makeup bag. "If you must know, Matthew Cory has not only been the muse for my poetry, I imagine he's the one who I will be with on my wedding night. We'll be in a white canopy bed with Roberta Flack's 'The First Time Ever I Saw Your Face' playing, and he'll whisper in my ear, 'It's always been you, Gabriella.' After we finish," I cleared my throat, "doing *it,* we'll spoon the entire night, and I'll wake with perfect hair and minty breath. And if you ever tell anyone I told you that, I will have to kill you, which means I'll also go to Hell. So please give me something to hold over your head. It's only fair."

Olivia cupped a hand over her mouth and snorted. "Oh my gosh, Gabby!"

Embarrassment worked its way up my neck and settled in my cheeks.

"Are you a virgin?" Her eyes bugged out.

"I'm serious, Olivia. Tell me your darkest secret."

"Fine. Whatever." She tapped a finger on her chin. "I have a crush on someone too."

"That's not good enough. I need to know who, and you have to tell me something embarrassing about it that would make you want to slit your wrists if anyone found out."

"I can't tell you."

"Why not?"

"Because you'll tell him."

"If I don't know him, how can I tell him? And I'm a good friend who can keep a secret."

"You won't tell Ben?"

I shook my head, feeling mostly sure that I wouldn't tell Ben. I usually told him everything. My messed-up reasoning made sense of it because he was a boy and therefore exempt from secrecy rules because he rarely interacted with my girl-friends.

Olivia's leery gaze studied me through her thick glasses. "Since he's a lot taller than me, I've imagined sixty-nine with him."

"Sixty-nine what?" I parked a hand on my hip.

She laughed. "Like ... you know. *Sixty-nine.*"

"Is it a movie?"

"Gabby! I'm talking about the sex position."

I nodded slowly then shook my head. "No. I uh, don't know what you mean."

Olivia gaped at me. Total crickets.

"I'm a preacher's daughter from a small town," I said

because it was the number one reason I wasn't prepared for real life outside of Devil's Head.

"Well," she pressed her lips together for a beat, "that explains why your fantasy involves Roberta Flack and spooning."

"What's sixty-nine?" I ignored her jab at my limited sex knowledge.

"It's basically oral sex at the same time, like six and nine are the same shape just inverted. You do him and he does you simultaneously." Olivia waggled her eyebrows.

A little bile worked its way up my throat. "That's ..."

"Hot?"

I shook my head. "Weird."

"Why do you say that?"

"Well," I tried to envision it, "his thingy points up, so that's probably fine, but if he does that to you, then his nose is awfully close to your uh," I wrinkled my nose, "butt."

"Don't knock it 'til you try it. Listen, if you look at sex from the standpoint of body parts and an exchange of bodily fluids, it's totally repulsive and disgusting. But it's also *so* amazing. Don't ask me how both things can be true at the same time, they just are. You'll see."

"Stop. This conversation is going in the wrong direction. Now that I know more about this 'sixty-nine' thing than I wanted to, who is this tall guy?" I loved that we were bonding over cute guys.

"Ben." Olivia trapped her lower lip between her teeth.

"Who's Ben?"

"Your Ben."

"*My* Ben. What do you mean by that? You have a crush on my best friend?"

"Yeah. Is that okay, or is that weird?"

"He's a music major."

Olivia laughed. "That only makes him hotter. He runs, swims, and lifts weights several times a week. Ben has a schweet bod and hella good hair. And he's a big-time gentleman. When our resident assistant asked him to help her carry a box to her car the other day, he said, 'Yes, ma'am.' Why does that make me want to jump him? What eighteen-year-old says ma'am?"

The "ma'am" thing again. Did Olivia grow up around a bunch of ill-mannered people? Why was that a sought-after trait?

"Well, I don't know if he likes you. And even if he does, I don't want him to hurt your feelings because that would make things uncomfortable between us. I'm not saying that I'd take his side if things didn't work out, but he's been my friend for so long, and—"

"Gabby, take a chill pill. I don't want to marry him. I just think he's tall, dark and hot. He looks thirty with those thick whiskers and strong jaw. Maybe we could have some fun together. Ya know?"

Yes. I knew what Olivia meant, but I wasn't sure how I felt about it. She caught me off guard.

"Yeah. Sure. If you're not worried about getting hurt, then whatever." I pulled on my black Chuck Taylors and slid my keys and student ID into my purse.

"It would be major cool of you to put in a good word for me," she suggested.

I glanced at my watch. Matt was meeting me out front in less than five minutes. "If you're only wanting to use my friend for weird-positioned sex, what kind of good word could I possibly put in for you? That you're flexible?"

Olivia snorted. "Duh. You're such a nerd. You know what I mean."

After opening the door, I smiled as if I knew, but I didn't, nor did I enjoy imagining Ben having upside-down oral sex with her. "Later," I said, shutting the door.

As soon as I exited the dormitory, I spotted Matt in the grass, watching his feet as he walked in a slow circle, hands tucked in his jeans pockets. His once wavy, dark blond hair was shorter, not a full buzz, but close, and those blue eyes still made me weak in the knees. Matt seemed taller, and his shoulders were definitely broader, he had thicker defined muscles and a mustache, not like Ben's *thick,* unkempt whiskers. I giggled at the thought.

Matt was a god. Not my God, but *a* god.

"Look at you, Gabriella Jacobson," he said as I booked it down the stairs, straight into his brawny arms for a hug. "All grown up."

Yes!

I wanted him to see me as all grown up. A woman. *His* woman.

When he released me, I felt the heat of Mercury in my face. Why did he have to be so handsome?

"You've done some growing too. Ya big jock." I squeezed his bicep.

Matt laughed, and I realized how silly I sounded calling him a jock. Other people, like Olivia, sounded cool saying things like that, but I felt silly.

"Four years of baseball training will do that," he said.

I clasped my hands behind my back to prevent them from squeezing anything else. "I heard you got injured and you're done. I'm really sorry."

"Yeah, it was a labral tear. I didn't see my career ending in college, but ..." he shrugged.

"But law school."

"Yeah." Matt chuckled.

"Well, we never know what God has planned." I berated myself for bringing up God. It was habit, but I didn't want Matt to only think of me as his preacher's youngest daughter or the little sister of his high school sweetheart, who obliterated his heart. Every cell in my body wanted Matt to see me as his destiny.

"Yeah, God's full of surprises." He nodded slowly, eyeing me.

Like really *eyeing me*.

"I appreciate you taking the time to show me around campus. I feel like I know the way to my classes, but that's about it. Ya know? Where are the best places to eat or get photocopies? Ice cream. Stuff like that."

"For sure. Well, the dining hall is not at the top of the list for food, but if you have a food plan, you should grab what you can from there." He offered his arm, and I nearly died from my heart bursting with excitement.

How chivalrous.

I hooked mine around his (like I'd do on our wedding day), and we walked around campus. Matt knew all the buildings and a lot of the history behind them too; he had always been smart. After showing me the hot spots for food, entertainment, and photocopies, we grabbed cans of pop and bags of chips near the campus bookstore and found a bench to watch the squirrels.

"Do you like your roommate?" he asked, popping a ranch-flavored chip into his mouth.

"Yeah, so far. Her name's Olivia. She's from Ohio, just outside of Akron, and she wants to be a lawyer too."

And she wanted to do weird sex positions with my best friend, but Matt didn't need to know that.

"My mom said you had a friend from school who's here as well." Matt tossed a chip toward the squirrel near our bench.

I sipped my Sprite, then nodded. "Ben. He wants to be a conductor."

"Boyfriend?"

"Nope. Just a friend. You've met Ben, but you probably don't remember. It's been years."

"Yeah, I think I remember him. He sounds like Sarah, a music lover."

I wondered if he'd mention my sister's name. It had been over four years since their breakup.

"Sarah's more ..." I twisted my lips, searching for the right word as a group of students walked past us, leaving a trail of cigarette smoke in their wake.

I coughed and Matt laughed. His older brother used to smoke, but I hated cigarette smoke.

"Sarah likes country and pop music. Ben salivates over Beethoven. They're not at all alike." I waved my hand at the residual smoke.

"Well, who doesn't get a hard-on from Beethoven?"

I tried to act unaffected by hearing Matt say the word "hard-on," but it was difficult. My dad's godly voice always in my ear, so my laugh was a forced *tee-hee*.

"What about you? Do you have a girlfriend?" I asked, unsure if my heart was ready for the answer.

He squeezed his empty pop can until it crushed and tossed it into the bin a few feet away. "I'm not sure."

I laughed. "How can you not know if you have one?" My brain short-circuited into a dreamy monologue:

"Oh, Gabriella, the reason I don't know is because I haven't asked you to be my girlfriend yet. For four years, I've thought nonstop about you. And now you're here like a dream. Say you'll be mine."

Who needed drugs? Nothing had me tripping like my infatuation with Matthew Cory.

"There's this girl I've been seeing, but she's thinking of transferring to UCLA because her parents just divorced, and that's where her mom's moving. I guess her mom is having a hard time. I'm not excited about a long-distance relationship, and neither is she. So I feel like we're coming to a slow end if she transfers at the semester."

"Do you love her?" The words were out before I gave my common sense a second to ponder them.

Matt grinned, rubbing the back of his neck. "I mean, I would have said yes a month ago. We've been dating for over a year. And I'm bummed that she's leaving, but I'm not brokenhearted. So maybe that's the answer. She thinks baseball is my greatest love, so I've clearly done a terrible job of making her feel special."

I restrained my enthusiasm. "Hmm, maybe God—"

Ugh!

Was I really on the verge of saying, *"Maybe God has other plans for you?"*

Yes. I absolutely was.

"I mean," I cleared my throat. "Maybe it's a sign. Not necessarily from God. Just like uh ... you know, a sign."

"That's what I've been thinking too," he said.

My back straightened. Were we on the same page? I hoped so.

Matt was so rad, casually leaning back on the bench with his outstretched legs crossed at the ankle. I was a lame, fidgeting mess, having fiddled with the pop can tab until it broke, and my half-eaten bag of chips was nothing but crumbs because I kept channeling my nervous energy into my hands, relentlessly squeezing the bag.

He basked in the autumn breeze, warm sun, and the silence between us while I bounced my leg and gnawed the heck out of my lower lip because the silence killed me. Every passing second felt like the last before he would suggest we head back to my dorm.

"We should grab pizza sometime. We don't have to talk about Sarah or your parents," I said. "I could catch you up on all the Devil's Head gossip. Or you can tell me about playing baseball, before you got hurt, of course. Not like a date or anything, because you have a girlfriend. And—"

"Most definitely." Matt saved me from myself.

I froze, unblinking, as if his answer hadn't registered. "Yes?" I confirmed just above a whisper because anything more would have been an all-out squeal.

"For sure." He sat up straight, laced his hands behind his head, and stretched side to side. "And just so you know, I've talked with my brother and Sarah. Everything's good. You don't have to tiptoe around talking about them. And I'm on good terms with my parents too. It's been four years, Gabby. Time heals."

"Thank goodness." I grinned, wiping invisible sweat from my brow.

Chapter Three

George Harrison, "Got My Mind Set on You"

Gabby

"THERE YOU ARE," Ben said as I ran up the dormitory stairs after Matt walked me home.

"Jeez, you scared me!" I pressed a hand over my heart, cheeks flushed as if he caught me doing something wrong—like thinking inappropriate thoughts about Matt.

"Where ya been?" He pivoted and followed me to the second floor; Ben's room was on the fourth floor.

"I told you. Matt gave me a tour of the campus." I kept my chin tucked to hide my grin.

"Oh, yes," he said. "How'd that go? Think you'll be able to find your classes now? Wait, you already knew where they were. So this must have been a date." He grabbed my left hand. "Hmm ... no ring yet."

I pulled my hand from his and pushed through the door to my hallway. "You need a shower."

"No duh. I just worked out. How far did he get? First base? Second? I hope he didn't accidentally call you 'Sarah' in the throes of passion."

Only my dorky best friend said things like "throes of passion."

"If you must know, we had an awesome time. And we're going to get pizza Friday night."

"A date?"

I shoved my room key into the lock. "Kinda. Yeah." I *kinda* lied.

"Kinda. Yeah. Doesn't sound like a date. Sounds like he doesn't know you're stalking him yet."

"Stop." I laughed, opening the door. Thankfully, Olivia wasn't there, so I didn't have to worry about her giving Ben hungry eyes. I tossed my keys onto my desk as he sat on Olivia's bottom bunk bed.

Ben was too tall to sit there without hitting his head on the top bunk, so he leaned to the side and propped himself up on his elbow.

Olivia's dad made the bunk beds out of two-by-fours. The Def Leppard posters. The boombox. The milk crates hung on the walls as shelves. The mini fridge. It felt like everything was hers.

"Speaking of *kinda*, Matt has a girlfriend, but she's probably transferring to UCLA. Good timing." I smirked.

Ben slowly shook his head. He was tired of hearing about Matthew Cory, but that was too bad. It went with the territory of being my best friend.

"And he said things are fine between Sarah and him. And I know she said that too, but it's always the one who does the breaking up that makes it sound like everything is good. So I was glad to hear it from Matt too. It's not like I want to spend a lot of time talking about their relationship, but totally avoiding it is awkward. After all, they lost their virginities to each other."

"Aw yes. The infamous condom fiasco." Ben picked at a thread to Olivia's comforter.

"Shh..." I giggled, hiking one knee up and hugging it to my chest. "You've been sworn to secrecy about that."

"Gabbs, you swear me to secrecy about everything. You start every sentence with 'this stays between us.' I'm afraid to speak my own name, let alone anything about your family."

"Speaking of things staying between us, Olivia likes you, and she wants me to put in a good word for her."

Ben's eyebrows shot up his forehead. "Oh? So what's the word?"

"Ha ha. You know what I mean."

The word was sixty-nine. But how was he to know the word was a number? Unless I told him. Which I would never do.

"I haven't really taken a long look at her, but she's not ooglay. Right?"

"Duh. No. She's not ugly. She's fine if you're into makeup and big hair."

"Big boobs? Smart?"

"You're such a doofus. How can you ask about her boobs and if she's smart in the same breath? You've seen her *breasts*. I haven't asked for her GPA yet. Besides, I don't think she's looking for a boyfriend. Just someone to ..." I rolled my lips together. Ben and I were well-practiced at finishing each other's sentences. Surely, he could read between the lines.

His lips parted, eyes flaring a bit. "She just wants to mess around? She's looking for a boy toy?"

"I don't know." I averted my gaze to the window.

"Oh, you know. I'm not stupid. Having a girl as a best friend has given me exclusive access to Chick World. And I know chicks tell each other everything. So spill. Is this what she wants?" He gestured his hand up and down his body like one of Barker's Beauties showcasing a new refrigerator.

I snorted. "You're a dork. Girls are not chicks. And I don't know why she'd want," I mimicked his gesture, "all of that, but she seems to think she does. However, I don't like the idea. She's my roommate, and as much as she pretends it would just be casual, I fear you could break her heart."

Ben scratched his chin. "Of course I could break her heart. It's not my fault that when they fall, they fall hard."

I stuck my finger down my throat. "Gag me. Could you be more arrogant?"

"I'm the right amount of confident, and you know it."

"Shut up." I wadded a piece of paper from my desk and threw it at him.

He caught it and laughed. "You're so tough."

I jumped out of my chair and lunged at him because I was tough. He fell flat on the mattress as I landed on him, our faces inches apart, grinning as far as our ears as we laughed.

"Now you're just asking for it," he said, tickling my sides.

"Stop! You need a shower." I giggled, trying to wriggle out of his hold. "S-stop ... I'm gonna pee my pants!"

He didn't stop, so I flailed my arms and legs, trying to break free from his hold.

"Tell me I'm a stud, and you're the nerd," he demanded.

"You t-think"—my sides hurt from him digging his fingers into them and laughing so hard—"'Chopsticks' is a ballad."

"Take it back," he said with his mouth at my ear as we rolled one way and then the other, making a tangled mess of Olivia's bedding. "Say it."

My joking about wetting my pants turned into a real possibility, so I had to say "uncle" first. "Fine! You're a stud."

"I can't hear you."

My body jerked to get away, but he was too strong. "AHH!" I squealed. "YOU'RE A STUD!"

In the next breath, he released me, and I rolled to sit up, only to find Olivia at the door with her mouth agape. "Sorry, I didn't mean to"—she shook her head, confusion stealing her face—"I can come back later, if you need to finish."

"What?" I jumped to my feet and straightened my clothes before combing my fingers through my hair. "No. There's nothing to finish. Nothing going on."

Olivia's gaze ticked between Ben and me. "Well, just so you know, everyone on the floor has their heads poking out of their rooms because it sounded like you were getting nailed pretty hard, if you know what I mean. You're lucky our RA left for dinner. Dude, I could hear you with my Walkman on." She set her yellow Walkman and headphones on her desk.

I slapped a hand over my mouth, and Ben had the nerve to snicker. It wasn't funny. I had never been so much as kissed by a boy, and thanks to my obnoxious best friend, all the girls on my floor thought I was a loud hussy having sex in my dorm room with a real stud.

"I want to die," I whispered, dropping my hand from my mouth.

Ben stood, tightening the drawstring to his sweatpants as if we had done something. I cringed, meeting his unaffected gaze before shifting my attention to Olivia, who tucked her hands into her hoodie pocket. Her expression was hard to decipher, so I didn't read into it.

"He was tickling me because he's mean and he's an idiot. That's why he doesn't have a girlfriend, and he'll most likely die alone as an eighty-year-old conductor."

"Why do you have me only living to be eighty?" Ben asked.

I groaned and grabbed his arm, dragging him out of my dorm room. As soon as we stepped into the hallway, a cascade of doors clicked shut. Olivia was right; we'd attracted a crowd.

"If you ever embarrass me like that again, I swear I will find a new best friend." I rubbed my hands over my face and shook my head. When I peeked at Ben between my spread fingers, he beamed with a goofy smile.

"Gabbs, you were the one who was screaming. And I have to admit, I never imagined you'd be a screamer, but it oddly fits you."

"Shut up!" I shoved him.

Ben cackled while hugging me so I wouldn't shove him again. "Should I warn Matt?"

I wriggled my way out of his hold. "Go shower. You will never be in the same room as Matt." I crossed my arms over my chest. "You can't be trusted, Benjamin Ashford. You know too many embarrassing things about me."

He crossed his arms over his chest, mirroring and towering over me. "I'm the keeper of all your secrets. That's like saying Fort Knox cannot be trusted."

"Trusting you with my secrets is not the same as trusting you to preserve my dignity."

"Dignity is overrated, homegirl. See ya for breakfast." Ben sauntered past me, riding his usual wave of confidence.

I wanted a fraction of such self-assurance. He never cared what anyone thought of him. Boys in school called him Cro-Magnon because of his size and the full beard he grew our senior year. But the comments never phased him. He brushed them off like a horse, swatting its tail at a fly.

Matt would surely fall for me if I could muster Benjamin Ashford's level of confidence.

Olivia pinned me with a hard gaze the second I stepped back into the dorm room. "So that's how this is going to go, huh? I'm interested in Ben and you suddenly decide to show interest in him too?"

"Stop." I waved her off. "He's obnoxious. The brother I never had. And I'm feeling grateful that God didn't give me a brother because being pestered all the time is exhausting."

Olivia changed into shorts and a tee, her go-to pajamas, and pulled her hair into a ponytail. "So you put in a good word for me then, right? Is he down with the idea of us going out?"

"Of course I put in a good word. But I don't know if he'll ask you out," I mumbled, finding my favorite baby-blue nightshirt with pink hearts and a pair of white sweats to wear from our room to the shared bathrooms down the hallway.

"What did you say?"

"I said you were interested in him, but not in anything serious."

While I changed into my pajamas, Olivia inspected me. I could feel the distrust without even making eye contact.

"What did he say?"

"I don't remember for sure. It gave him a big head. I didn't want to feed his mega ego, so he tickled me until I said what you and everyone else heard."

"That he's a stud?"

I laughed. "Believe it if you want, but I've known him too long. I knew him before he had his growth spurt and grew facial hair. I knew him when his voice was squeaky like a little girl's."

Olivia tucked her toiletry bag under her arm and opened the door. "And he knew you before you had boobs or knew what sixty-nine was. Oh wait ..." She twisted her lips. "That was today."

"Shut up." I laughed, following her to the bathroom. "I had boobs before today."

Both she and Ben knew too many embarrassing things about me. I couldn't let either of them around Matt.

Chapter Four

Brenda K. Starr, "I Still Believe"

Gabby

If hope were a color,
it would be blue like your eyes
and shine like your smile.
Hope is eternal,
like my love for you.

AFTER A TWO-YEAR HIATUS from writing poems and affirmations about Matt, I was at it again. His recent presence in my life rekindled my creativity.

My life.

Not Sarah's.

Not the girl on her way to UCLA (hopefully).

Matt was mine—well, I was working on it.

He deserved someone who put him first and wanted him

more than anyone or anything. Patience was a rare trait, but eternal love was the ultimate gift bestowed upon those who truly believed and kept the faith with little regard for time. And no one had been as faithful as me.

I drew hearts next to my poem, gently placed the ribbon down the spine, and closed my journal—my first journal. When I'd lived at home, I wrote my poems in the margins of my Bible or novels where I knew my parents' prying eyes wouldn't think to look, not that they would have. I was the favorite child (or so I told myself), the youngest of three girls. Sarah thought she was the pleaser child, but she proved otherwise. Eve hid alcohol by the creek and came home without her panties. I had never been grounded. All my dad had to do was give me a look, and I fell in line.

The knock on my door wasn't unexpected, but it still felt like my heart might explode from my chest. Matt was here to pick me up for our pizza date. In my imagination, it was a date; manifestation started with imagination and lots of prayer.

After a calming breath, I buttoned all but the top button of my jean jacket and curled my hair behind my ear on one side and then uncurled it.

Curled it.

Uncurled.

"Stop it," I whispered, fisting my hands to quit fidgeting while briefly closing my eyes. "Hey," I said, opening the door.

"Ready?"

I bobbed my head, pretending that Matt wasn't out of my league because he was older, smarter, talented, and gorgeous. "You look handsome," I said.

He chuckled, glancing down at his gray Michigan T-shirt

and navy unzipped hoodie. "I don't think I tried hard enough to deserve that compliment, but thanks. You look nice too."

"Nice" felt like wholesome's slightly prettier cousin. I wanted to be beautiful in his eyes.

"Everything cool?" he asked.

My smile rebounded from my slight disappointment that he didn't shoot for a higher compliment. "Yeah. Let's go."

Matt opened all the doors for me, including the passenger door to his red 1972 El Camino.

"Thank you."

After he slid into the driver's seat, I put on my seat belt. "I wondered if you still had this car. I've always loved it."

"Oh, hell yes. I'll buy other cars someday, but I won't sell this one."

For a few seconds, I thought it was cool that he wasn't selling it, since it had been a graduation present from his grandparents. But then it hit me; my sister lost her virginity on this very bench seat. I slowly peeled my hands from it and folded them on my lap.

"How are your classes going? If you ever need help with anything, just ask." He shot me a sideways glance and a killer smile.

"Thanks."

"How are your parents?"

"Good. Dad's still preaching. Mom's still organizing everything from funerals at the church and fellowship dinners to baby and wedding showers. She's been bugging my dad to take some time off to travel, but he thinks the town will fall apart without him. His best friend Fred has offered to fill in at the church if my parents want to go out of town for a couple of weeks to visit Sarah or Eve, but my dad can't bring himself to do it."

"Your dad has always been dedicated."

"You mean a workaholic?"

Matt laughed. "I was trying to be nice since I imagine when I'm an attorney, I'll have to work long hours and take minimal time off. Hopefully, I find a wife who's as understanding and supportive as your mom."

I folded my hands, squeezing them hard to keep from raising one to volunteer to be said wife. As a school counselor or something like that, I'd have normal hours and could be home to have dinner ready. And when we had kids, I'd stay at home to raise them.

Garden.

Sew.

Clean the house.

Bake bread.

"I'm sure if you're a true romantic, you won't have trouble finding a good woman."

"A true romantic?" He pulled into the Pizza Hut parking lot.

"Flowers. Love notes. Perhaps a necklace with her birthstone. Help with dishes after dinner. You know, make her feel appreciated and it will go a long way to her understanding and feeling okay about you working long hours."

"Love notes?" He wrinkled his nose while unbuckling.

I giggled. "Don't panic. You don't have to be a poet or anything like that. A simple 'Have a good day. I love you,' is sufficient. And flowers don't have to be bouquets. A single rose or a few spring tulips are just as special."

He made funny duck lips and nodded. "I see. I guess I need to find someone like you who feels content with such simplicity."

"Well," I unbuckled, "I need to get through school, but

you can check back with me. I might be available." I didn't have Sarah's confidence or Eve's quick wit and practiced humor, but I did my best to feign that I did.

Matt opened the door and gave me a conspiratorial grin. "Can you imagine? That would make our families talk for sure."

"But we wouldn't care, because we are the babies of our families. The favorites." I stepped out of his car and shot him a flirty smile and a wink. At least it was supposed to be a wink. I didn't have the genes for bodily functions like tongue rolling and winking, so it must have looked like I had something in my eye.

"Favorites, huh?" Matt perked up as we met at the front of the car and headed into the building. "You might be right."

"The only ones who went to college and didn't start a war between our parents," I said.

"You're cutthroat." He playfully nudged me while we waited to be seated.

My heart soared higher with every innocent touch and flirty grin. It's how I had always imagined we'd fall in love. Well, it's how I'd imagined he would fall in love with me. I'd been in love with him for years. I didn't want him to see me as a sexy, short fling, blinded by physical passion. Those didn't last. But admiration and respect were foundations that could withstand the test of time, and I wanted him to be mine forever.

A server grabbed two menus and seated us at a booth.

"Pepperoni?" Matt asked before I had a chance to look at the menu.

"Absolutely."

"Pan or thin?"

"Thin," we said at the same time.

"A Pepsi or Slice?" He set our menus on the edge of the table.

My grin swelled.

"Slice?" he asked.

I nodded.

"And garlic bread of course," he added.

I couldn't have dreamed of a more perfect first date. Matt was confident and right about all of it, like someone told him my favorites ahead of time.

"With extra sauce," I said.

"Duh." He rested his crossed arms on the table, the gleam in his eyes shining brighter than ever.

I don't know why my sisters made falling in love so complicated. Why they had to battle unimaginable grief and so many tears to find their happily ever after.

"Was that all a good guess, or did you call my mom?"

Matt shook his head. "Just a good guess. I assumed your family ordered the same kind of pizza. And Sarah liked Pepsi, so I figured you liked Slice because there's no way you're going to be like your sisters."

I inspected him for a few seconds before relinquishing a guilty grin. "And you like Coke."

"Yes. But now I prefer a cold beer with my pizza. Don't tell your dad."

The server grabbed our menus. "Looks like you're ready to order."

"We are. We'll start with an order of garlic bread, extra sauce. Then we'll have a medium thin pepperoni, a Pepsi, and a Slice."

"You got it." She smiled.

"Thanks," he said.

"You could have gotten a beer." I played it cool, like I hung out with people who drank beer all the time.

"Nah. I'm driving precious cargo."

We shared a look, and I knew he was referring to the drunk driving accident that shook our little town four years earlier. And while it still stung, I felt special for being considered precious cargo. The girl in the booth behind Matt walked over to the jukebox and selected, "I Still Believe." I loved that song.

"So what kind of lawyer do you want to be?" I asked instead of belting out the romantic ballad.

"I'm leaning toward criminal law, but I have a friend who's interested in tort law, and he thinks we should open our own firm someday."

I nodded slowly.

"Do you know what tort law is?"

Again, I nodded. Then I grinned and shook my head. "I have no idea."

"Tort is a civil wrongful act. Like harm to someone or their personal property. It can either be from an intentional act or negligence such as car accidents, medical malpractice, vandalism, defamation."

"I see. Sounds exciting."

"I suppose. It's not as exciting as studying the brain or why humans behave the way they do, but it's interesting and challenging in other ways."

The server delivered our drinks. I stirred my Slice with the straw. "My mom thinks I'll end up changing my major. She said that most students do."

"Why did you choose psychology?" Matt set his straw on the table and sipped his Pepsi straight from the glass.

"Honestly?" I rolled the straw between my fingers.

Matt nodded.

"Two incidents led me to consider this path. There was this boy in my class whose parents were having marital issues, and my dad counseled them. But I overheard that boy talking to one of his friends about how ridiculous it was for them to let my dad get involved since he's not a real therapist. But the couple stayed married, and I thought it was pretty cool my dad played a part in it. Then after the accident four years ago, a lot of students visited the school counselor, including me because I wanted to talk to someone who wasn't my dad. That's when I knew I wanted to help others in that way too."

"That's awesome, Gabriella."

Matt's compliment gave me a warm, tingly sensation all over. I loved when he called me by my full name. Just him. When my parents or sisters said it, it sounded condescending.

"So tell me about Ben. How long has he been your boyfriend?"

"What? No. I told you he's not my boyfriend. What did you say your girlfriend's name is? Oh, that's right, you didn't tell me."

The server delivered our garlic bread. Matt nodded for me to take one first.

"Her name is Julianne."

"What's she studying?" I blew on the garlic bread before taking a bite.

"Engineering."

I blotted my mouth with my napkin. Of course he would be with an ambitious, smart woman. I imagined she had long hair, defined arms, perfect cheekbones, and flawlessly applied makeup.

Pierced ears.

A collection of high heels.

And she probably knew sixty-nine.

How was my offer to bake bread and pop out babies while counseling married couples or troubled kids supposed to compare to a Julianne who would go on to design things like bridges or rocket ships?

Ugh!

"Sarah was never going to be an engineer." I let her be the sacrificial lamb instead of pointing to my own short-comings.

Matt barked a laugh. "From what I've heard, she's doing just fine. Have you seen her perform?"

I pressed my lips together and nodded. Sarah wasn't the favorite child, but she was well on her way to being a very successful performer. She had the voice and charisma that bled talent when she stood on a stage with a guitar in her hands.

Again, I thought of ironing clothes and breastfeeding babies while my dream husband wore a suit and tie, winning cases in a courtroom. Were my standards too low?

"Sarah's going to be a big star," I murmured.

"How's Eve?" Matt asked.

"She's no longer hiding alcohol by the creek."

Matt chuckled. "Well, I suppose that's good."

I loved making him smile and laugh. "Eve followed Sarah's lead and fell for an older guy. If you think Sarah and Isaac caused a commotion, you should have been there to witness Eve's dramatic fall from grace."

"Well," he sipped his Pepsi, "I wouldn't have expected any less from Eve. But she's doing good now? Happy?"

"Yeah. Very happy. What doesn't kill you makes you stronger."

He lifted an eyebrow.

"It's a long story."

"Sounds like it," he said.

As we ate our pizza, Matt let me know he was planning on visiting his parents in North Carolina over Thanksgiving. He shared his excitement of winning a conference title and national championship playing baseball for the Wolverines. I swore he had tears in his eyes, reminiscing about the bittersweet ending to his baseball career.

I had no comforting words that didn't involve "God has other plans for you," so I stuck to a sympathetic smile and a gentle bob of my head.

"I've got it," he said when I pulled out my wallet at the register to help pay for dinner.

Yep, it was officially a date.

"Are you sure?"

Matt grinned, handing the cash to the employee. "Of course."

"Thank you." I tucked my wallet back into my purse.

Matt fished change from his pocket and stuck a nickel into the gumball machine and turned the knob. It spit out a blue gumball which he offered to me.

I wrinkled my nose. "Not blue."

He laughed and popped it into his mouth, then he slid another nickel into the machine. "Boring white." He handed it to me.

I took it. "White is not boring. It's classic. White is just as sweet without feeling the need to show off." I chomped down on the gumball and grinned at him.

"Is that so?" He held the door open for me.

"Mm-hmm," I mumbled, stepping past him.

"Did you know that while you had your nose in a book, Sarah and Eve suspected you were going to be the biggest rebel, stealthily flying under your parents' radar?" Matt asked.

"Did you know that while my sisters thought I had my nose in a book, I heard them talking about your senior prom night mishap?" I took two steps, feeling triumphant with my comeback, but when my brain caught up, I realized I just confessed to knowing the details of Matt's fumbled attempt at losing his virginity with my sister.

Four years.

It had been *years* since I'd seen Matt, and I, Virgin Gabriella, brought up sex on our first date.

"W-what?" Matt coughed, opening my car door.

"Nothing. Never mind." I ducked into the car without making eye contact.

His gaze covered me like a suffocating cloud of smoke, but I focused on the seat belt.

"Stupid," I whispered after he shut my door.

He walked around the car and slid into his seat while I laced my fingers together and prayed for God to erase the previous thirty seconds from his brain.

"Well, that's pretty fucking embarrassing," he mumbled as the engine roared to life.

I briefly closed my eyes. "I mean, the first time is totally awkward. Right? Not to mention if the first time is in a car."

Shut up, Gabby!

He shoved said car into reverse and opened his mouth,

but quickly clamped it shut. At least five minutes passed before he broke the silence with a soft chuckle. "Did she throw me under the bus? Or did she take a little credit for the mishap?"

"Um ..." I rubbed my hands along my jeans. "I don't remember."

"Liar."

I squirmed in my seat. "It was a long time ago."

"Was it because the condom landed on the floor or that I only had one?" he asked, and I could tell it was bugging him.

Our date was taking the worst possible turn.

"Um ..."

"It's okay." He shot me a sidelong glance, but I kept my head bowed. "If we can't laugh at our mistakes, then life will be pretty miserable. Right?"

Perhaps one day I'd look back at this conversation and laugh that I made a big mistake by bringing up the subject, but I had no laughs to spare at that moment.

Matt pulled into the dormitory parking lot. "So how has *your* sex life been?" He laughed while parking the car. Was he making fun of me? Surely, he knew I was a virgin. But how? Did I look like one? Had my mom told his mom that I was saving myself for marriage like a faithful lamb?

"I'm joking."

I could barely muster a smile past the wave of panic that left my heart racing and palms sweaty as I stepped out of his car. "Ha. Ha," I managed to say.

"I would never expect you to kiss and tell." He walked beside me toward my dorm's entrance.

Had I been kissed, I would have told someone. Ben, of course. Maybe Olivia too, since she was slowly gaining my trust.

"Thanks for dinner."

We stopped at the sidewalk as a group of guys entered the building.

"I'll pay for the next date," I said.

Matt's lips parted, eyes unblinking.

Oh my gosh.

I said date. It wasn't a date. I knew it wasn't a date, but my silly little mind enjoyed thinking it was. And that innocent thought rooted and grew into a full illusion to where I blacked out reality for a few seconds.

I was mortified.

"Dinner. Not a date." I faked a yawn. "Stupid brain. I'm tired. Olivia snores so I haven't slept well. Of course this wasn't a date because you have a girlfriend."

Matt's silence *killed* me. With my hands tucked into my front jeans pockets, I rocked back and forth on the balls of my feet, eager to run into the building and never see him again. I blew it big time.

He narrowed his eyes. "So it *was* true."

I stopped rocking. "What was true?"

"Sarah used to say that you had a crush on me."

I coughed a laugh. "What? Oh my gosh! Leave it to Sarah to assume that everyone wants what she has. She probably thought I wanted to be a singer in Nashville too."

Matt studied me with an unreadable expression as his head cocked ever so slightly to the side. I tried to hide my visible squirming by rubbing my arms as if I wasn't wearing a jacket. He stepped closer, forcing me into an audible gulp.

"Would you?" he asked.

My eyes couldn't hold his gaze, so I stared at his chest. "Would I w-what?"

"Kiss and tell?"

Sweat formed between my breasts and soaked my armpits as his words turned me into an inferno. He was going to kiss me.

My. First. Kiss.

Oh gosh.

No. *Oh GOD!*

Matthew Cory, on the verge of kissing me, wasn't a gosh moment. It was a full-on Lord's-name-in-vain-moment. The single greatest moment of my life. Only ... I didn't know how to kiss. I mean, everyone knew how to kiss. I had kissed my mom and animals that I'd loved, not a romantic kiss on the lips. But Matt had kissed his girlfriend, my sister, and probably a bunch of girls in between.

I trapped my lips between my teeth, making them unavailable to him. They weren't ready to be kissed. I'd saved my first kiss for him, but who wanted someone's first kiss? I would proverbially fumble the condom like he had done with Sarah.

"It's been fun. We'll have to do it again," he said, taking a step backward. "Maybe Julianne can join us. You'd like her."

Keeping my lips hostage, I nodded several times.

"Maybe you can bring Ben."

I kept nodding, but I wasn't bringing Ben with me on a real or imaginary date with Matt. Well, Matt and his girlfriend.

"Goodnight," he said, leaving me with a smile as he pivoted and sauntered back toward his car.

I sprinted inside the building, all the way to the fourth floor, and down the hallway, weaving past groups of guys laughing and chatting. After a half dozen hard knocks, Ben opened his door.

I craned my neck to see past him, looking for his roommate. When I didn't see anyone, I shoved his chest so I could step inside and shut the door behind me.

"Please, come in," he said with a slight laugh.

"I don't know how to kiss!" I stabbed my fingers into my hair.

Chapter Five

Michael Jackson, "The Way You Make Me Feel"

Ben

LOVING GABRIELLA JACOBSON WAS EASY.

Being her best friend? Pure torture.

When we were in elementary school, she brought injured animals like cats, rabbits, and birds to my house because her dad said it was God's plan for the animals to die in nature, and that's where she needed to leave them. But Gabby thought that finding them was a sign from God for her to save them. And because she was the pastor's daughter, my parents said I needed to be nice to her and help her nurse the animals back to health in the barn.

By middle school, Gabby taught me to braid her hair because it relaxed her. And in return, she listened to me play my saxophone, clarinet, piano, cello, and trombone. She danced, swayed, and snapped her fingers with a huge smile and enthusiasm in her eyes, whereas my parents used to say, "That's nice, Ben," without even looking at me.

Gabby wrote her first poem for me, and I wrote my first cello piece for her.

In eighth grade, her friend, Michelle, told me that Gabby liked me more than a friend, but just days earlier, Susie had asked me to "go with" her, so I called Gabby to tell her that we could only be friends because I had a girlfriend. She gave me a "duh" like it was ridiculous for me to think that she liked me more than a friend, and she swore Michelle had lied.

By the following year, I had grown over three inches taller, a few zits appeared on my forehead and chin, and the chemicals in my brain made me see Gabby in a new light. I was in love with my best friend and always had been. When we were younger, I didn't know my desire to spend all my free time with her was actually my first crush. Though, by the ninth grade, I knew I'd never love another human being the way I loved her. If only I hadn't been scared out of my mind to tell her.

"What do you mean you don't know how to kiss?" I asked as she covered her face with her hands and shook her head.

"Ugh!" She dropped her hands to her sides. "Matt was going to kiss me. I just know it. But I freaked out because it suddenly hit me that my efforts to save myself for him have only made me really inexperienced. Who saves their lips? He's a real man who's had real sex. What was I thinking?"

I tried not to laugh, but my best friend had been in love with the idea of falling in love for as long as I could remember. And for whatever reason, she fell for her oldest sister's boyfriend. While she shelved her infatuation long enough to pine for a few other guys who were not real options either, she always came back to Matt.

"Don't think that I'm not going to demand you explain 'real man' and 'real sex' to me later, but for now, let's just think about this logically. Are you *sure* he was going to kiss you? Because I swear he turns you into a space cadet."

She flipped out her hip and crossed her arms over her chest. "I'm not stupid. I know when a guy is about to kiss me."

"How?"

"Don't be a jerk."

I laughed. "I'm not being a jerk. But whatever. We can pretend that you're right. The last time Matt saw you, you were fourteen. Sarah had demolished his heart. And after a walk around campus and a pizza, he suddenly wants to kiss you. Makes total sense."

She stuck her tongue out at me.

"If you do that, then I'll be forced to tickle you. And I'd hate for you to get a reputation on your floor *and* mine." I twisted my lips for a few seconds. "Never mind. I'm fine with the other guys on the floor thinking I'm expertly giving a girl an orgasm."

Gabby blushed, and she never looked as beautiful as she did with pink cheeks. Even the top of her ears were red as she curled her light-brown, shoulder-length hair behind them.

She turned her back to me, fiddling with the zipper to my backpack on my desk chair. "You have to show me."

"Show you what?"

"How to kiss."

"Real funny. Don't girls use the back of their hands or something like that to practice?"

She kept her back to me and shrugged. "Maybe. But the back of my hand can't tell me if I'm doing it right."

"Gabbs, no one goes to kissing school. You just do it and figure it out in the moment. There is no right or wrong."

She turned, nose crinkled. It was another one of her adorable expressions. "But there's good and bad. I want Matt to think I'm good at it."

I was still ninety-nine percent certain that Matt had no plans of kissing his ex-girlfriend's youngest sister. But friends didn't dash other friend's dreams.

"I thought you said he has a girlfriend."

"Who's probably leaving for California."

"Still. Did they break up yet?"

She shrugged.

"Do you think he'd cheat on her?"

Gabby averted her gaze while fidgeting with her jacket's buttons. "I mean, is it cheating if they know they're not staying together?"

"I don't know. Why don't you ask Matt if he thought Sarah cheated on him when they knew they would not stay together at the end of that summer."

"Benjamin," she frowned, "why must you always do that?"

I leaned against the door and crossed my arms. "Do what? Make sense?"

That earned me a dramatic eye roll.

"If he's the dream guy you think he is, then he'll find your inexperience endearing. He'll want to be your first kiss. And he won't judge you for how you kiss because all his brain will think is 'I can't believe this amazing girl is letting me kiss her.'"

She returned a blank expression and several slow blinks.

"Fine. It's like licking peanut butter off a spoon."

"No way." She giggled.

"Yes way."

"I've never kissed a spoon. You're so warped. You're just trying to embarrass me."

"That's because you're only thinking of puckering your lips and making a smacking noise like kissing your dad's cheek. But when you kiss someone you're attracted to, it's like you want to devour their lips and taste the inside of their mouth. But it's not quick like a spoonful of cereal, it's slow like sticky peanut butter that you have to suck and lick over and over. And if it's really good, you might even hum a little."

"I'm not going to make out with him. I'm talking about a kiss like a goodnight kiss."

"Fine, then." I shook my head and raked my fingers through my hair. I hated talking about this with her. "Just mirror whatever he does. If it's slow, go slow. If it's fast, let it end. If he gives you a little tongue, give him a little tongue back."

"I'm not sure how I feel about French kissing."

"You're right. And you don't want to catch mono, so maybe just stick to a kiss on the cheek or even just a handshake or a tip of the hat. He probably always has a baseball hat on, right?"

"Stop." Laughter bubbled up her chest. "He wasn't wearing a hat. And I'm not shaking his hand."

"Then maybe a high five."

She snorted. "I'm being serious. If you show me how to be a good kisser, I'll be at the dining hall when they open tomorrow and get you like five or six of the bear claws you like."

Kissing the girl that I loved beyond reason and five bear claws. What kind of idiot passed that up?

Me.

"It would be like kissing my sister. Too weird," I lied. I was a fraud and an idiot.

"Tillie is super cute. I bet she's a good kisser."

"Gross, Gabby." I rubbed my eyes with the heels of my hands. "Don't say that about my sister."

"What about Jason?" She sat on the bottom bunk bed, which was mine.

"Jason? My roommate?"

She nodded.

"What about him?"

"Maybe *he* could teach me how to kiss. He's not my type, but he has a nice smile, and it looks like he brushes his teeth, so—"

"Gabriella, I'm calling your dad."

"What? No! Are you crazy? This is not what a best friend does. So help me, Benjamin, if you leak any of this to my dad, I will never speak to you again."

I stepped away from the door as it opened behind me.

"Yo," Jason said, his gaze focused on Gabby for a second before looking at me. "Bad timing?"

"No. It's fine," I grumbled.

"Hi, Jason," she said and then bit her lower lip to suppress her ridiculous smile. "That orange backpack is pretty gnarly."

"Gabby and I were just heading out to get ice cream." I grabbed her hand and pulled her to standing.

Jason adjusted his baseball cap over his short blond hair and grinned at Gabby. "Later."

"Bye." She barely got the word out before I had us in the hallway with the door closed.

"I'm full from the pizza. I don't want ice cream," she said.

"I'm tired of you losing your mind over Matt Cory. So we're going to have a little chat, and *I* do want ice cream." I held open the door to the stairwell.

She scowled at me before proceeding down the stairway. "I'm not losing my mind. And even if I were, isn't that what love is supposed to be?"

"You don't even know him." I followed her down the stairs, our steps echoing off the concrete walls.

"I do too. I've known him for as long as I can remember." She pushed through the front door as the cool evening air enveloped us.

"Your family has known his family. Sarah knew him because she dated him. You were just there like an old lamp. You blended in, but he never thought about turning you on."

"Ben!" She slapped my arm.

"You know I'm right." I led her north toward Baskin-Robbins.

"Why are you so grumpy? Why can't you just be happy for me?" She swatted a swarm of bugs.

"I'm grumpy because my best friend is willing to kiss my roommate because she's so desperate to be something she's not. Sorry that doesn't make me happy."

"If you were a girl, you'd be happy for me. You'd squeal and jump up and down with me because the guy I have a crush on almost kissed me."

"He did not!" I stopped walking.

Gabby halted, too, but not until she was a few steps ahead of me. On a long sigh, she turned.

"I love you," I said because my heart couldn't take it any longer. Whatever she thought she felt for Matt, I felt that for her times a million. I should have said it four years earlier.

All I wanted was for her to love me back because no other guy would see her like I did. They wouldn't have years of Gabriella Jacobson woven into every memory worth remembering. They wouldn't see themselves as a product of being her friend.

But I did. I saw her, and I couldn't let her infatuation with Matt go any further.

Gabby returned a pouty face. "Aw. I love you too." She took two steps and wrapped her arms around me, resting her cheek on my chest. "I know you're just looking out for me. I'll stop talking about Matt. Maybe Olivia is a better choice if I need to discuss boy problems."

I couldn't bring myself to hug her back because my bold declaration of love backfired. With the utmost bravery, I had set my heart at her feet, and she treated it like a speed bump. To my knowledge, we had never said those words to each other. It wasn't like my mom telling me ten times a day how much she loved me. Did girls do that? Did they say "I love you" to their friends? Guys didn't.

"Come on." She looped her arm with mine. "I'll buy the ice cream. So, did you get your short story grade back?"

I glanced over my shoulder and took a mental picture of the crime scene, where she unknowingly shot me down with an arrow dipped in the poison of unrequited love.

Gabby was my Matt.

Chapter Six

Madonna, "Like A Prayer"

Gabby

My life was over.

It had been three weeks since the near-kiss incident with Matt. I had no reason to call him. God hadn't blessed me with allowing our paths to cross on campus. And no mutual friends or family members died, so I could have a reason to call him and suggest we go to the funeral together.

To make matters worse, Olivia and Ben had been on three dates, and she wouldn't stop talking about what a good kisser he was, his broad chest and bulging biceps, or the way he smelled like pine trees, and was just so "bad to the bone."

Ugh! He was a music major which was the opposite of bad to the bone.

As I studied for my Developmental Psychology test and ate Wheat Thins, the phone rang. I didn't bother to get up to answer it. No one called me, except for my parents. But it was Thursday, and they only called on Saturdays.

Olivia hightailed it off her bed to answer it. Her Walkman crashed to the floor. Luckily it landed on the hot pink rug. "Hello? Oh, yeah, she's right here. Gabby, it's for you." She held her hand over the receiver and whispered, "It's a guy."

"Ben?" I said, stopping short of rolling my eyes.

She shook her head, handing me the phone.

"Hello?"

"Hey, Gabby, it's Matt."

I sucked in a breath like a newborn baby, and I wanted to scream like one, too, as I mouthed, "It's Matt," to Olivia.

Her eyes widened.

"Hey," I said without losing it.

"My two roommates and I are having a party at our house tomorrow night. Do you have plans? If not, you should come."

I slapped a hand over my mouth and jumped up and down.

Olivia giggled. "What? What did he say?"

I shook my head and pressed a finger to my lips to shush her, then I cleared my throat. "Um, yeah. That sounds fun."

I was *dying*.

"Great. Do you have something to jot down my address?"

I scrambled, pulling on the phone cord to snag a pen from my desk. "Okay," I said, uncapping the pen with my teeth and writing his address on my forearm. "Got it," I mumbled, spitting the cap out of my mouth.

"Bring Ben and your roommate, if you want."

"Um, okay." I turned in one direction and then the other, trying to pace the room while the phone cord tangled around me.

"It starts at seven, but you can come anytime."

I nodded as if he could see me.

"See ya."

"Bye." I hung up the phone. "Oh my gosh! Oh my gosh! OH MY GOSH!" I jumped up and down, sending the phone flying to the floor as the receiver dangled from my arm.

"Dude, take a chill pill." Olivia untangled me and hung up the phone.

I grabbed her arms. "Matt is having a party tomorrow night, and he invited ME!"

"Oh my god! Schweet!" She joined in my jubilant celebration with a squeal and manic jumping up and down. "What are you going to wear? Do you think his girlfriend will be there? Oh my god, Gabby! What if she's not? He's going to kiss you. No, he's going to do more than kiss you." She threw open the closet door and rifled through my things. "We have to find something for you to wear. You have to look fantabulous." She stepped back and deflated. "But it's none of this crap. Why do you dress like Holly Hobbie?"

"Okay. Okay. Okay." I blew out a long breath. "You and Ben are invited too, but I don't know if I want you there. No offense."

She frowned.

"It's just that if you're there, then he'll know I have someone to talk to, but if you're not there, then he'll probably keep me at his side and introduce me to all of his friends."

"Unless his girlfriend is there."

I nodded, biting my thumbnail. "Yeah. Maybe I should call him back and ask."

"No! You can't do that. Ben and I will go, and if she's not there, we'll make up an excuse to leave. But if she is there, we'll stay until you're ready to leave."

Keeping my nail trapped between my teeth, I nodded several more times.

"Now. Let's find something in my closet that might fit you."

"My knees have to be covered, and I can't show cleavage."

Olivia blinked several times. "Oh sweetie, this year is going to be life-changing for you." Pity dripped from her words.

What could I say? Nothing. So I smiled, excited and fearful of the life changes headed my way.

"I don't dress like Holly Hobbie," I snorted as her previous comment finally registered.

"Okay, maybe not the bonnet," Olivia said. "But the long dresses and brown shoes are a match. All you need is a pair of bloomers."

As much as I wanted to feign offense, I couldn't stop giggling because at home, I had at least four Holly Hobbie dolls in a box on the top shelf of my closet.

Two hard knocks vibrated our door. Olivia opened it.

"Ready?" Ben asked.

"No. Sorry." She rested a hand on his chest. "I got distracted by Gabby's big news. Let me run down and use the bathroom and fix my makeup." Olivia grabbed her bag and headed down the hallway.

Ben stepped into the room and closed the door. "What news?"

At the same time, I asked, "Where are you two going?"

"Subway for dinner," he mumbled, sitting in Olivia's desk chair as I snatched my box of Wheat Thins. "Wanna come?"

"On your date? No thank you." I popped a cracker into my mouth.

"It's dinner, not a date. But I suppose you still don't know the difference."

I stuck my tongue out at his little jab.

"What's your big news?"

"It's about Matt, so I don't think you want to hear it."

He perked up. "Matt, huh? Haven't heard his name in weeks. Do tell."

"He's having a party at his house tomorrow night, and he invited me." I fished out another cracker. "He invited you and Olivia too."

"No thanks."

"Olivia said you two would go, then stay if I need you or leave early if I'm good."

Ben chuckled, lacing his fingers behind his head, which made his shirt creep up just far enough that I could see his abs. I tried not to look at them because it made me think about him and Olivia doing things that involved numbers.

"For your information," he said, "Olivia doesn't speak for me. She's not my girlfriend or my secretary."

"Well, I'm still your best friend, so you'll go for me."

"You haven't asked me to go." He smirked.

"Will you go?" I mumbled while chewing my cracker.

"I have no interest in watching you fawn over Fumble Fingers."

"Don't!" I snorted and cracker crumbs flew from my mouth onto his lap.

Ben frowned, wiping them from his jeans. "Thanks for that."

I covered my mouth and finished chewing. "Sorry." I swallowed. "But you can't call him that. I don't want it coming out that I told you. It's bad enough that he knows I know."

"What do you mean?"

I shrugged. "I may have let it slip that I knew about the prom night incident."

"Gabbs, how do you let that slip? This fantasy of yours is over. He's never going to be anything more than a family friend now that he knows you heard about the most embarrassing moment of his life." He leaned forward and plucked the box of crackers from my hand.

"How is that the most embarrassing moment of his life?"

"Oh, Gabriella," Ben slowly shook his head while shoving his big hand into the cracker box, "you have so much to learn. The pinnacle of manhood is sex. A fumbled attempt is about as gut-wrenching as running over the family dog."

That was ridiculous.

"I'm sure he's recovered just fine," I said. "If he has a girlfriend, he must have figured it all out."

"Maybe he revirginized and is saving himself for marriage." Ben dumped the last of the cracker crumbs into his mouth.

"You think?" I straightened my back with a jolt of hope.

Ben fisted his hand at his mouth and shook in silent laughter. "No, Gabby. I'm just kidding."

"You're mean."

"Honest."

"Well, you're going with me tomorrow. Olivia's not asking. I'm asking. And you can't say no to me."

Ben got a funny expression on his face. I hadn't seen it before, so I couldn't decipher it. But after a few seconds, he nodded and muttered a soft, "Yeah."

"Okay. Let's go," Olivia said, bursting through the door and tossing her makeup bag onto her bed. An overwhelming perfume scent filled the room, and I coughed.

"Is your roommate in or out tonight?" she asked Ben as he stood.

"Out. Why?"

Olivia batted her mascara-laden eyelashes. "Since Gabby's doing homework, I thought we could go up to your room after dinner."

Ben looked at me, and again he had that weird look on his face.

I fiddled with my sleeves, not comfortable knowing that my roommate planned on doing dirty things with my best friend, and they were all but saying as much with me hearing everything.

Then I thought of Ben's exposed abs, and I wondered if he was good at sex. Was he better than Matt? Did Ben ever fumble a condom? As I got a little hot, I cleared my throat and offered a smile. "Have fun," I managed with a slight squeak to my voice.

"Need any help with homework tonight?" Ben asked, nodding toward the pile of books on my desk.

Olivia was offering him "the pinnacle of manhood," and he wanted to know if I needed help with my homework.

My gaze shifted to my big-haired roommate standing just behind Ben. She gave me a quick headshake and prayer hands while mouthing, "please say no."

"I'm good." I smiled.

Ben continued to study me for a few more seconds.

"Okay. Goodnight, Gabbs." He tossed the empty cracker box in the trash while Olivia took his other hand and led him out the door.

"Don't wait up," she said.

I flinched when the door closed. Why did the two of them make me so uneasy?

Chapter Seven

The Escape Club, "Wild, Wild West"

Gabby

FRIDAY NIGHT, Ben impatiently waited in the hall for Olivia and me to finish getting ready for the party.

"I look like a hooker," I said, standing in front of the full-length mirror after Olivia borrowed her friend's Clairol Benders to use on my hair.

She finished the look by giving me mall bangs with her singed curling iron and a half bottle of hairspray. Then she painted my face in shades of blue, purple, and hot pink makeup, and dressed me in a short denim skirt with black tights, leg warmers, heeled boots, and a Van Halen T-shirt tied at the waist.

"Gee thanks, Gabby. I was going to say you look like me with shoulder-length brown hair. But now I know how you really feel." She pulled on her tan, suede fringed boots.

It wasn't fair that she got to wear jeans.

"You know what I mean. You can pull off this look. I can't."

"You won't know until you try." She relentlessly sprayed me down with her heavy, musky perfume.

"Stop!" I coughed and waved my hand in front of my face.

She giggled. "Let's see what Ben thinks." She opened the door.

He lumbered to standing and brushed off his backside while glimpsing at me. "What the fuck, Gabbs?"

I froze.

Ben rarely cursed in front of me. Maybe the occasional "damn" or "shit," but I honestly couldn't remember hearing the F-word come from his mouth.

"Doesn't she look hot?" Olivia gushed.

"She looks like—"

I interrupted him by clearing my throat. "I look like Olivia, only not as pretty."

"Oh, stop." Olivia accepted the compliment while swatting my shoulder.

My attention remained glued to Ben, daring him to say another word that might offend her, make me cry, or all-around ruin the night.

I looked like a whore; he didn't have to say it. Had my dad seen me, he would have dragged my butt home to Devil's Head, locked me in my room, and arranged for the rest of my higher education to take place at an all-women's college.

"Here." Olivia pulled on the neck of my shirt.

I jumped as she planted a condom in my bra.

"Always be prepared." She winked at Ben, but he looked ready to murder someone.

"Let's go, kids." Olivia strutted toward the stairs.

I closed the door as Ben waited for me. "I'm not going to use it. And you don't need to tell my dad. This wasn't my idea, and you know it." A tiny yelp escaped as I took my first step in the heeled boots and my ankle buckled.

"This is ridiculous," Ben grumbled, catching me before I ate it.

I adjusted my skirt that wanted to ride up my ass, and Ben peeled away the stray hair that was stuck to my makeup.

"*My* Gabby is stunning—always the most beautiful girl in the room. I don't know who this Gabby is."

"Except Olivia. She's prettier," I murmured, because I not only believed it, I knew it.

Ben wrapped my arm around his so I wouldn't fall again. "*No* exceptions."

"Come on, you two," Olivia called.

I gazed up at Ben, not sure I heard him correctly, but he kept his focus on Olivia as we made our way to her.

Since Olivia was the only one who had a car, she drove us to Matt's house. His address was still on my arm, but the bangle bracelets that Olivia loaned me made the inked area less noticeable.

"If his girlfriend is there, you need to be nice. Nobody likes a catty person. If you're nicer than his girlfriend, you'll be the one he thinks about in the morning." Olivia delivered her pep talk while parking along the street near his house.

Sitting by myself in the back seat, I pulled at my skirt. It was awfully short.

"Gabby's always nice," Ben said, getting out of the car and opening my door.

I stepped onto the curb and adjusted my skirt again, but it wouldn't go any lower. Then I shot him a nervous smile and whispered, "Thank you." I appreciated his vote of confidence.

Again, he wrapped my arm around his so I didn't fall on my face. "Just take off those stupid boots when we get inside."

"She needs the practice," Olivia said.

I nodded nervously. Yes, I needed the practice. Yes, I needed to remove them if I didn't want to kill myself.

Before we reached the driveway filled with cars, the rhythmic bass of "Wild, Wild West" thumped, reverberating through my body. Inside, people were packed shoulder to shoulder. Cigarette smoke filled the air, along with deafening music and people yelling over it. Olivia clasped Ben's hand, pulling him toward the kitchen. He glanced back at me. I smiled and mouthed, "I'm fine." As I bent over to remove my boots, someone bumped into me, sending me to the floor on all fours.

"Whoa. Careful, that's my friend," Matt said, sliding his hands into my armpits to bring me back to my feet where I wobbled in the boots.

Oh my gosh!

The denim miniskirt slid above my butt. Thankfully, black tights covered it, but I was nonetheless mortified. As I shimmied it back into place, Matt pulled a chunk of hairsprayed bangs out of my face.

"You okay?" he yelled over the music.

"I uh, was trying to take off my boots."

He shook his head. "No need. It's better if you keep them on so no one steps on your toes."

Was it better to risk spraining an ankle while falling on my face or have someone step on my toes? It felt like a toss-up.

"Glad you made it. Come on, I'll introduce you to Julianne."

So much for hoping she couldn't make it.

"You look different," he said as we weaved through the crowd.

I gripped his arm for support like when I learned to roller skate and needed to hold on to Ben because he was great at it and never let me fall.

"Olivia loaned me this outfit and did my hair and makeup."

"It looks good on you. And I'm not just saying that because I'm drunk. But I'm pretty fucking drunk." Matt laughed, shooting me a grin before opening the sliding door to a weathered deck filled with people huddled around two kegs of beer.

I released him, and he hugged the back of a long-haired brunette, burying his nose in her neck and wrapping his arms around her.

My heart tripped like it, too, wore wobbly heels and could fall and get injured at any moment.

She turned, planting a big kiss on Matt's lips.

"This is Gabriella," Matt said with a slight slur to his voice as he stole her beer and took a long swig. "Gabby, this is Julianne."

She looked like Brooke Shields with her big hair, striking blue eyes, and chiseled jawline. I died a little.

"Oh, the preacher's daughter." She offered her hand. "It's so nice to meet you."

Yep, preacher's daughter. That was the reputation I was going for in college.

I shook her hand and accepted my lot in life with a slight nod that matched my tiny smile. "You too."

"Can I get you something to drink?" she asked. "I know you're not twenty-one, but I won't tell anyone if you have a beer. There's also pop in the kitchen. Whatever you feel comfortable having. No pressure. Oh, and snacks. We ordered twenty pizzas or more. *Please* eat something."

Ben was correct; I was nice. But dang it! Julianne was nice, too. It wasn't her fault I loved Matt. Nor was it her fault that I took on thousands of additional dollars in debt to go to college out of state. Still, I had no intention of feeling bad for loving her boyfriend.

"Pop and pizza sound awesome. Thanks."

"Can I get you anything, babe?" she asked Matt, pressing her hand to his cheek.

He leaned into her touch. "I'm good. Thanks." Then he grabbed her butt and kissed her at the same time.

I blushed with envy.

She pulled away and rubbed her lips together. "Let's go." Julianne led me into the house.

With the help of a couple of walls, and briefly leaning into a few strangers along the way, I made it without incident.

"I don't know how you walk in those boots. I've never been comfortable in heels," Julianne said, handing me a plate, then opening the lids to pizza boxes. She stacked the empty ones in a pile, then tossed abandoned red cups into the trash bin.

Her aversion to heels and her tidiness immediately earned my respect. I would have done the same thing in her shoes. But I wasn't in her cute white canvas sneakers, as she pointed out.

"They're my roommate's boots, along with the rest of my outfit. She thought I needed to fit in tonight." I set one piece of pizza on my plate and lifted a second to my mouth.

Julianne opened a can of Sprite for me. "I bet you don't drink a lot of caffeine." She handed it to me after I set my pizza on the plate.

"Did Matt tell you that?"

Guys didn't talk with their girlfriends about other girls who they almost kissed. That made me reevaluate our date night. Was Ben right? Did Matt *not* almost kiss me?

"My father isn't a preacher," she said, "but I was raised in a strict house, religiously speaking. No caffeine. No unclean meat. No swearing. No sex before marriage. No using the Lord's name in vain."

My heart sank. We were bonding. I wasn't allowed to bond with Matt's girlfriend *and* steal him from her. Why couldn't she be awful and catty so I could be the nice one who he wanted to take home to his family?

"Right?" I didn't wait a second to solidify our connection. "How's the no-sex-before-marriage thing going?" Yep. I basically asked her if she'd had sex with my future husband.

It obviously wasn't a deal-breaker. After all, my oldest, slutty sister took the honor of robbing his virginity. Still, what if Julianne was saving herself? And what if that wasn't as appealing to Matt? And what if I was willing to give him say ... second base, all in the name of manifest destiny or a good old case of God's will?

Julianne laughed. "By the end of the night, I'll be so drunk I can hardly stand. I've already had unclean meat." She looked around at the people in our vicinity and leaned in closer to my ear. "And I'll be screaming God's name with Matt balls deep in me by midnight." She fanned herself and giggled.

I pretended to wipe my mouth with the back of my hand, but I was really hiding my gasp. She wasn't like me after all. Matt made the same mistake of falling for another heathen like Sarah.

"Oh my gosh, I'm going to miss so many things about him, but the sex is very close to the top of that list."

I cleared my throat. "W-what do you mean?"

Julianne frowned. "I'm moving to California. Transferring to UCLA at the semester. My mom's moving out there, and since she and my dad split, she hasn't been doing so well."

"Sorry to hear that," I said before taking several gulps of my Sprite.

She held a hand to her ear. "What?"

It was *so* loud.

With a jerk of her head, she turned, and I followed her back outside.

"I said—"

Before I could repeat my condolences for her situation, Matt grabbed her face and kissed her. There was so much tongue involved, I nearly lost the contents of my stomach. They were experts at licking peanut butter from a spoon.

"Baby, you're so drunk." She giggled as he moved his lips to her neck.

"Just so fucking horny," he mumbled over her skin.

It's like I wasn't there, but I was there. Right there. Yet, they ignored me and everyone else on the crowded deck as they groped each other. So I took another bite of my pizza, slowly chewing it while watching them. How could I turn away? And why wasn't everyone else watching them?

Oh yeah, they were all drunk.

I wasn't trying to be rude, but I had nowhere to go, so I

took notes on how he liked to be kissed. How she touched him. And what noises she made that drove him wild. When his hand snaked up her red sweater, I stopped mid-chew. His other hand gripped her butt while she kissed his neck. That's when he made eye contact with me.

ME!

Could I have been a bigger freak, just gawking at them?

She whispered in his ear, and he removed his hand from her shirt. Then they laced their fingers together and brushed past me toward the door.

"It was nice meeting you," Julianne said. "Get more pizza. There's plenty."

Before I could respond, Matt pulled her into the house. When I craned my neck to look for Olivia or Ben in the crowd, something wet penetrated my shirt.

"Oh shit," a tall guy wearing a baseball cap said.

I looked down at his beer soaking into my top and right through to my bra as well. Everyone could see the outline of said bra, so I quickly set my plate and pop can on the railing and pulled the material away from my skin.

"I'm so sorry," he said with a laugh that didn't feel as apologetic.

I offered a fake smile. "It's fine." I stumbled again in the stupid boots as I stepped toward the door, but thankfully I recovered without landing on the ground. Most everyone ignored me and my drenched shirt as I wormed my way through the throng of drunk people.

"Hey, how's it—" Olivia cringed when she saw my shirt.

"Where's Ben? It's time to go."

She shrugged with a Diet Coke in her hand. "He found some guy who's a music major, too, and I think they went out front because it's so loud in here," she yelled. "Go get

cleaned up while I look for him. The bathroom is upstairs."
She pointed toward the split-level stairs.

At the top of the stairs, there was arguing coming from the room next to the bathroom. It was Matt and Julianne. Despite it being none of my business, I leaned toward the door to hear better.

"Maybe your mom is only thinking of herself," Matt said. He dragged out each word.

"You're drunk," Julianne replied.

"So are you. Maybe if you'd sober up, you'd see that putting yourself first isn't always bad."

"I hate it when you get like this."

"Well, I hate that you're fucking leaving me!"

I jumped at Matt's outburst.

"Grow up! Not everything is about you."

They were just making out. What happened?

"I thought *we* wanted this. If you loved me like I love you, it would be about us, not just me. Christ, Jules ... you're making me into the enemy so you don't feel guilty about ending things."

"I'm done. This is over. You can try to make me feel bad for taking care of the person who raised me, but that's on you. Go find someone who thinks you're the only person who matters in the whole world."

"Good riddance, babe. Don't call me when you figure out your mom is fucking messed up."

"Screw you."

I stumbled onto my ass when Julianne suddenly flung open the bedroom door and stormed out. She stopped for a few seconds, eyeing me with confusion while she wiped her tears. Then she ran down the stairs.

"FUCK!" Matt yelled.

Before I could find my feet, he stepped out of the bedroom, stabbing his hands through his hair. And just like Julianne, when he saw me, he paused.

"I uh ..." I scrambled to my feet, tugging at my skirt. "I was, um ... on the way to the bathroom and she came out and I fell back. But not like it was her fault. And I totally didn't hear anything ..."

Matt squinted at my shirt, so I glanced down, forgetting about the beer. I pulled the wet cotton away from my chest. "Someone spilled their beer on me. I was just going to clean—"

"Come on," he said, grabbing my arm and pulling me into the bathroom, then kicked the door shut behind him. "Take off these fucking boots," he said like he was mad at me or the boots.

I gasped when he lifted me onto the vanity. His blood-shot eyes met mine for a second before his gaze homed in on my wet T-shirt. I pulled the material away from my skin again. He lifted one of my legs and unzipped my boot, slowly removing it while staring at my chest. "We broke up," he murmured before removing my other boot.

"I'm sorry."

Matt let my boot drop to the floor. "That's life," he murmured.

"She uh ... she was really nice." My voice shook.

"I'll get you a clean shirt," he replied just above a whisper, but he didn't move. Instead, he lifted my shirt above my head so quickly, I didn't have time to think, let alone stop him.

Ohmgoshohmygoshohmygosh!

I covered my bra with my arms, and his drunken gaze

returned to my face. He had the saddest expression I had ever seen. "I have the worst luck with women."

What was I supposed to say? Even fully clothed, I would not have had a suitable response.

"You're the prettiest one," he said before wetting his lips.

Not only were my arms covering my breasts, they were preventing my heart from breaking through my chest. Matt was intoxicated, and I should have skedaddled, but the man of my dreams had me ensnared.

"Sarah and Eve were pretty like," he twisted his lips, "conventional pretty, but nothing special. But you have this tiny mole on your cheek. And from a distance, it looks like a cute dimple." He smiled. "And your eyes are mesmerizing and full of ..." He blinked heavily. Yes, he was *so* drunk, but I pretended he wasn't.

"Lashes so long." He tried to touch them, but he nearly poked my eye. That made him grin. "And another tiny mole" —his thumb caressed along my cheek toward the corner of my eye—"right here. You're just so very, like a lot ... really pretty without all this stupid makeup."

I was embarrassed by our close proximity with my shirt off yet amused by his fumbled and uncensored words.

I withdrew from his touch, looking for space, clarity, and an escape route. "You're drunk," I said with a nervous chuckle.

He bobbed his head in contemplation while curling my hair behind my ear on one side. "I'm not *not* drunk." He laughed. "But I still know what I'm fucking talking about." His gaze dropped to my chest, and he narrowed his eyes for a second before stepping backward and pinching the bridge of his nose while bowing his head. "Shit. I took off your shirt.

That was wrong. I'll get you one of mine. God, what was I thinking. I'm uh ..."

"Nope, um ... it's fine. Well, I know I have to go. My ride is waiting for me. You're not in a good place or sober. And uh ..."

Matt ran his hands through his hair. "I'm sorry. I've had way too much to drink."

I hopped off the counter, but as I bent over to pluck my shirt from the floor, the condom fell out of my bra. I quickly snatched it and my shirt from the floor. When I stood, Matt gave me a look. He saw the condom.

My eyes were ready to pop out of my head.

The corner of his mouth quirked into a tiny smirk. "Gabriella Jacobson." He clicked his tongue and slowly shook his head. "Aren't you just full of surprises?"

I tossed the condom into the garbage by the toilet and pulled on my shirt in record time before grabbing Olivia's boots and running out of the house.

"Whoa! Where are you going? Olivia just went back inside to look for you," Ben said, grabbing my arm to stop me. He narrowed his eyes, giving me a full body inspection. "What the hell, Gabby?" Anger strangled his words while his Adam's apple bobbed. "Your shirt is on inside out and backward."

I pulled at the neck and dipped my chin to look at it. Sure enough, the tag was in front and facing out.

Worst. Night. Ever.

Chapter Eight

Great White, "Once Bitten Twice Shy"

Gabby

"Ready to talk yet?" Olivia asked as I stared at the ceiling the following morning.

I turned my head, and she grinned. She wore pink sweats hiked up to her knees, white tube socks scrunched at her ankles, and her wet hair had dripped onto her Michigan T-shirt. She sat at her desk while gulping Tropicana straight from the bottle.

The previous night, I gave her and Ben the silent treatment on the way home from the party, washed my face, and went straight to bed.

"If you were raped—"

"What?" I sat up. "No. I wasn't raped."

She capped the bottle. "But you could tell me—"

"Olivia, I wasn't raped." I climbed down and put on my

robe and slippers while squinting against the sun cutting through the window.

"Did you have anything to drink? We were there less than an hour, but after you went out back, I lost track of you."

I cringed at my reflection in the mirror of my rat's nest hair and raccoon eyes from the residual mascara that survived manically washing my face the previous night.

"You don't have to tell me, but Ben was in a lame mood after you went to bed without telling us what happened. Be prepared for the third degree."

Nothing felt real, which was saying a lot since I had a vivid imagination that often felt like reality. Oh my gosh, last night really happened.

"I need a shower." I gathered my things and headed to the bathroom.

When I returned, Ben was in my desk chair, drinking a cup of coffee while fisting Olivia's red and white hacky sack in his other hand.

"Where's Olivia?" I hung my towel on a hook and stuffed my pajamas into the laundry bin.

"She went to the library to study. If you don't tell me what happened last night, I'm calling your father, but not before I beat the crap out of Matt."

I squinted, wondering if he would win that fight. He was a little taller than Matt, but Matt had put on a lot of muscle since he moved away from Devil's Head.

"I wasn't raped. And I didn't have sex. Happy?"

"Young lady, you're better than this."

I turned my back to him and brushed my hair in the mirror, fighting so hard to keep from laughing. Ben had perfected my dad's favorite guilt trip. Even his voice resembled my dad's when he dropped it an octave.

"Why was your shirt on backward?"

"Because someone spilled their beer on me."

"So your fix for that was to turn it backwards *and* inside out?"

"Yes."

"Liar."

"You're the liar." I turned and pointed my brush at him. "You tried to make me think I was delusional for thinking Matt wanted to kiss me. But I wasn't. And I know this because he took off my shirt in the bathroom after his girlfriend left in tears because they broke up. And it wasn't my fault, so before you go pointing any fingers at me, just keep that in mind."

"Gabbs," he mumbled, setting his coffee on my desk then leaning forward to rest his elbows on his knees. His fingers rubbed circles on his temples. "This time I'm being serious. You're better than that."

I deflated. "It's not like that." My words lost all their fight because I felt so guilty for what happened, even though nothing really happened. I liked Julianne. And even if I hadn't liked her. I wasn't that girl.

"I had beer on my shirt. And on my way to the bathroom, I heard something. They were fighting. The next thing I knew, she flew out of his room, in tears, and I stumbled onto the floor because of those stupid boots. Matt helped me to the bathroom. He seemed a little heartbroken, but also like a different person, maybe because he'd had too much to drink. He said things that made me feel seen and wanted. But I didn't want it to go anywhere. Still, I liked that he looked at me the way he did."

Ben folded his hands in front of him. "You know when a guy is seeing things clearly? When his heart is most pure? When it's the best time for him to make big decisions like making a move on the preacher's daughter?"

I already didn't like where this line of questioning was going.

"Mere seconds after dumping his girlfriend."

I could have done without his sarcasm.

"Nothing happened." Again, I waved my brush at him. "He took off my shirt because I had beer on it. All I'm saying is that he no longer sees me as Sarah's little sister. Can't you just be happy for me?"

"No. You deserve better. He had no business taking off your shirt. And you deserve a guy you don't have to chase. You're the prize, Gabby. Wait for the guy who pursues you. Don't forget what your Grandma Bonnie said."

I had a love-hate relationship with Ben because he knew everything about me and my family. He knew that my Grandma Bonnie told me (and my sisters) to find men who we loved with our whole hearts, but who loved us just a little bit more.

"Ben, why do you think it's called 'falling in love?' It's because love blossoms into a beautiful garden of intertwined emotions. I don't think all love is love at first sight. Just because I fell first doesn't mean he won't fall harder."

Ben opened his mouth to speak, but I cut him off.

"And if we end up together, married with a family, we'll look back on this time as part of our journey. All journeys have trials. But we'll be glad we didn't give up."

He scratched his chin while worry lived deep in his brown eyes. "Can I play devil's advocate?"

"That's all you play."

He crooked a finger at me, and after a few seconds of stubbornness, I sulked toward him.

"Sit."

I sighed and handed him my brush before sitting on the floor between his legs. He brushed my hair like old times, then he braided it. My eyes drifted shut, and I melted into his touch.

"Do you have a Plan B? Is your whole heart invested in Matt, or is your brain stuck? Do you have tunnel vision? Have you shrunk your dreams into this one guy and the life you envision with him, or will you be okay if this doesn't work out? Because I can support that. I can be happy for my friend, Gabby, who wants something (someone), but isn't pinning every hope and dream and reason for existing to this one person. It's okay to imagine a day when you look back feeling grateful that you kept fighting the good fight, but I also need you to imagine a day when you look back and see how letting go of this dream led you to a better place."

I turned on my knees and rested my arms on his legs. "You don't get it. Is this just what girls do? You never talk about a girl like I talk about Matt. It's kind of a downside to being best friends with a guy. Are you crushing on Olivia? I promise I won't tell her if you are."

"Crushing?" he laughed. "No." Then his smile simmered into something akin to sadness. "Gabbs," he leaned forward and threaded his fingers through my hair, slowly undoing the braid, "I only get one heart. I'm going to protect it for as long as I can."

"You're afraid some girl will break it?"

"Undoubtedly."

I stood and leaned past him to snag the brush from the

desk. "Well, if someone ever breaks your heart, she can bite me. I'll have a few words to say to her."

Ben lifted his eyebrows. "Is that so? What will those words be?"

I grabbed my hair dryer from the basket on the floor of my closet. "I will tell her that Benjamin Ashford is ..."

Ben's posture straightened.

"I'm not doing this." I giggled.

"What? Why not? Throw me a bone or give me a boner. Come on. I need something."

"Stop." I snorted.

"You'd tell her that Benjamin Ashford is hella smart?"

I nodded, untangling the dryer cord.

"Kind?"

Another nod.

"Handsome?"

When I glanced up at him, he lifted his chin and stroked it while pursing his lips.

I bobbed my head. "Sure."

"Sure? That's your answer to me being handsome?"

"What's wrong with sure? It's kind of a yes."

"Kind of a yes? Gabbs, where's the conviction?"

"Sorry. I don't look at you that way anymore."

Before he responded, I plugged in my hair dryer and quickly turned it on. Then I flipped my hair upside down and dried it while combing my fingers through it.

My dryer stopped, and I glanced back at the wall. Ben was next to the outlet, holding the unplugged cord in his hand.

"Hey, why'd you do that?"

"You don't look at me that way *anymore*?"

I squirmed for a few seconds under his scrutinizing gaze

before I snagged the cord from his hand. "You misunderstood. I meant I don't look at you that way any more than I look at my"—my mind scrambled for the right comparison—"than I look at my dad as handsome. Like when I was really young, I wanted to marry my daddy, but now *my father* is old and gross."

"So when we were young, you wanted to marry me?"

"Go." I pointed toward the door. "I have to dry my hair, grab breakfast, and study."

Ben's smile swelled into a triumphant grin. "When you dreamed of marrying me, did your dad officiate? Who was your maid of honor? One of your sisters? Probably Eve, huh? Were the bridesmaids' dresses green like the off-the-shoulder dress you wore for your senior pictures?" He shook his head and whistled. "Damn, I loved that dress. And I'll never forget how upset your dad was that your mom encouraged you to get something that showed so much skin."

"Benjamin, get out of here." I opened the door and waited for him to take his smug grin out of my room.

He stopped at the door, gazing down at me, but I kept my focus on his chest.

"I remember what your face looked like before your acne went away," I said as if I thought it was a pointy enough pin to deflate his ego.

It wasn't.

"I remember when you started your period, and I let you wear my sweatshirt tied around your waist for the rest of the day so no one would see the blood spot."

I *had* loved him so hard for that, but I hated that he wouldn't let that memory die in the past like I did that day when one of my girlfriends whispered in my ear, *"Don't panic, but you have blood on the back of your shorts. You must have started your period."*

I pushed him into the hallway with the ease of moving a two-hundred-pound dresser three feet. "You promised never to mention that again."

"Well, yes." He chuckled. "But everything has an expiration date. A statute of limitations. Right?"

"Yep. Including our friendship. Nice knowing you." I closed the door.

As I bent down to plug in the cord, the phone rang. I set the dryer aside and answered it. "Hello?"

"Hey, it's Matt."

I slapped a hand over my mouth to keep from squealing. "Hey," I mumbled behind it.

"I can't hear you. Must be something wrong with the connection."

I dropped my hand. "Sorry, is this better?"

"Yeah."

There was an awkward silence.

"Listen, about last night, I had too much to drink. And I went upstairs with Julianne, thinking things were going in one direction, but she casually mentioned how much she was going to miss what we had, and for some reason that made me mad. I couldn't watch another relationship slowly die. And everything went south. Again, I had way too much to drink. Then I saw you, and you're always so positive. You always have that big smile on your face. And I wanted some of that joy. But my intoxicated brain took off your shirt before getting you a clean one, and I know it was disrespectful and unforgivable. I'm embarrassed and disappointed with myself. And just so *so* sorry."

I sat in my desk chair and twirled the phone cord around

my finger. "Don't apologize. It's fine. I uh ..." I bit my lip for a second, as if I needed to hide my grin from him. "I know you had too much to drink. And I was obviously a mess in those boots, and uh ... well, that thing that dropped on the floor was from my roommate. She gave it to me. Like, you know, as a joke." Heat settled into my cheeks, and I was so glad he couldn't see me.

"So you're not mad?"

"No. Of course not. I was just surprised. Julianne ran past me, clearly upset and hurt. But then you were obviously upset and hurting too. And I never imagined it happening like that. But—"

"Wait, you imagined something happening between us?"

"No. I mean, well, what I meant was, uh ..." I pinched my eyes shut. "I didn't mean it literally. Like more figuratively."

Matt chuckled, and I couldn't tell if he was laughing at me or laughing from the joy of finding me so endearing. I feared it was the former.

"Well, I didn't mean for anything to happen. I hope you know that. And I want to make it right. Okay?" he asked.

"Make it right?"

"Yeah. Nothing involving a party, alcohol, my girlfriend crushing my heart, or close quarters in a bathroom."

My girlfriend crushing my heart.

"I don't know. Maybe since you just broke up with Julianne, you need time to grieve and get over her."

"You're right. I should sit around and feel sorry for myself, listen to sad songs, and rent a breakup movie and eat a whole tub of ice cream."

I snorted. "Don't forget to call her a dozen times and hang up as soon as she answers."

"Boom box over my head, standing outside her window begging her not to leave me?"

"Now you're talking." My grin was so big it hurt.

"The question is, do you want to do all of this with me? I'll buy two tubs of ice cream."

"Do I want to grieve with you?" I asked.

"Sure. Like a friend. You and Ben are just friends. Maybe you can be my friend, too."

I didn't want to be that kind of friend to Matt, but I also didn't want to wait for him to properly grieve Julianne before seeing him again.

"Fine," I said with fake exasperation in my voice. "I'll be your friend. But I get to pick the movie because *The Terminator* is not a breakup movie."

"I disagree. It might be the ultimate breakup movie. It's *The Terminator*. The end. But I was thinking something like *Aliens*."

"Oh jeez. I'd better bring the ice cream. You're obviously the kind of person who would get a flavor with nuts in it."

"Gabby, please don't tell me you're not a fan of rocky road."

I grinned. There was a lot I knew about Matt. But one of his least attractive traits was his love of rocky road ice cream. I hated nuts in anything. Peanuts by themselves or peanut butter was fine, but not nuts in cookies, ice cream, or candy bars.

"Rainbow sherbet," I said.

"Noooo!"

I giggled.

"Gabby, that's not even real ice cream."

"It is too."

"Yuck. But that's fine. I'll get you fake ice cream and real rocky road for me. I'll meet you out front at seven."

Chapter Nine

Terence Trent D'Arby, "Wishing Well"

Gabby

MY BRAIN WAS MUSH. After breakfast, I spent the afternoon trying to study, but I couldn't focus on anything but Matt. He said we'd be friends, but he also saw me in my bra. So what if, in the middle of the movie, he decided we should be friends who kissed? With Terence Trent D'Arby's "Wishing Well" playing on my alarm clock radio, I felt like anything was possible.

Since Olivia went out with some of the other girls on our floor, I was left to my own devices to pick out my clothes, style my hair, and apply makeup. I kept my hair straight and my makeup was nothing more than cherry ChapStick, so I got adventurous and wore jeans that were a little tighter and rolled them up at the bottom to show a little bare leg. And I wore a V-neck sweater instead of a more conservative crewneck.

Of course, I was ready an hour early with nothing to do but dream of being alone with Matt on a sofa, maybe under a blanket, for as long as I wanted because I no longer had a curfew. What were the chances of him kissing me? Who could resist cherry ChapStick?

I looked around, even though I knew I was alone, and kissed the back of my hand. It was fine. Yummy cherry. But my hand didn't kiss me back. Was I going too slow? Too fast? Not hard enough? Would tongue be involved? And who would initiate it? The movies made it look so easy, but those were actors with experience in kissing. I had no experience.

Hopping off Olivia's bed, I wiped the back of my hand on a towel and ran up to the fourth floor. After two knocks, Ben answered.

"Where's Jason?" I stepped past Ben to give his room a quick inspection.

"Bowling or something. I don't know. What's up?"

I turned toward him as he closed the door. "Do you love me? Like I'm truly your very best friend in the world?"

He squinted for a few seconds before nodding slowly.

"I'm going to Matt's tonight to watch a movie. He says we're just friends, but I don't know if that's true. And I'm so scared that he's going to kiss me."

"Then tell him no. It's your right to say no. And for God's sake, he just broke up with his girlfriend." He crossed his arms over his chest.

"No duh. But what if he doesn't want to grieve his breakup? What if I don't want to say no if he tries to kiss me?"

"Fuck, Gabbs." He rolled his eyes like I suddenly annoyed him, and I must have since he dropped the F word again. "Then suck face with him. Whatever. What is your deal?"

"I don't know how to kiss!" I balled my hands, then relaxed them when Ben gave me a look that confirmed my outburst lacked any sort of sanity.

What was happening to me?

Why had my desperation smothered all dignity and instinct for self-preservation?

"If you really love me, you'll kiss me." I scraped my teeth along my glossed lower lip. "Please."

Ben planted his hands on his hips and gazed at the ceiling.

"I won't tell Olivia or anyone. I promise. And we'll never speak of it again after tonight."

He remained stock-still. Maybe he was saying a brief prayer while looking to God. Something like: "Dear Lord, please let Gabby flunk out of school so I can gain a higher education in peace."

"No way, Gabbs."

"Way, Ben. *Way!*" I added prayer hands to my pathetic, desperate whine.

"Fine," he grumbled.

"Yes?" I perked up.

"I didn't say yes. I said fine. Yes implies consent. Fine implies submission as a result of emotional coercion."

"Eek! Thank you!" I blew out a slow breath to calm down, then I laced my fingers behind my back and closed my eyes while tipping my chin up.

"What are you doing?"

I peeked open one eye. "I'm waiting for you to kiss me."

"You look like a three-year-old who's just been instructed to give her grandma a kiss."

I let my hands fall to my sides. "Fine. Then what am I supposed to do?"

He stepped closer. "Look at me."

"The whole time?"

"No."

"How long do I wait to close my eyes?"

Ben chuckled, pinching the bridge of his nose. "You'll just ... know."

"What if I don't?"

"You'll close them when leaving them open feels too weird. Think of it like a blink. If I do this," he crept his finger toward my eye, "you blinked because my finger was so close it was hard to keep your eyes open. Well, a kiss is the same, but instead of blinking, you just close your eyes and keep them shut until the kiss is over."

"How will I know when the kiss is over?"

"When your lips are no longer touching, it's over."

"Duh. You know what I mean."

"No. I don't."

"Ben, you have to tell me things, step by step. Like when I had a loose baby tooth, my mom tied floss around it, and there was a countdown to her yanking it out. She kept me calm by telling me each step."

"Oh yeah?" He squinted.

I nodded.

"Lucky you. My mom used to tie floss around my teeth, too. And she'd count down, but before she reached zero, she'd yank the thing out."

I flinched. "Oh, that's terrib—"

Ben kissed me.

No talking it through.

No countdown.

Just his palms gently cradling my jaw, fingers teasing the nape of my neck, and his lips pressed to mine.

It was my first kiss, so without a comparison, I couldn't say if it was slow or fast. And I couldn't remember closing my eyes, but they were shut. And somehow my lips knew exactly what to do. I didn't have to think about it.

My heart beat a little faster.

A tingle of warmth spread along my skin.

And I didn't want to stop.

That's how I knew I not only loved kissing; I was really good at it.

Then it was over, and I realized I wasn't the one who ended it. Ben was. But that was okay. Someone had to end it.

He was the greatest friend in the history of best friends, and my grin said as much. However, he didn't look as pleased as he averted his gaze and wiped his mouth with the back of his hand.

"What? Did I do something wrong? Was it bad? Too much ChapStick? Is that why you wiped your mouth?"

With a slight headshake, he brushed past me and turned on his desk lamp while lowering into his chair. "It was fine. Don't you have a date tonight?"

"You're mad."

"I'm not mad."

"Frustrated?"

"Gabriella." He rested his elbows on his desk and dropped his head, stabbing his fingers into his hair.

I hated feeling like I was annoying him. It reminded me of my sisters when we were younger. They were too busy or too cool to deal with me and my stupid questions. That was one reason why I loved Matt. When he and Sarah were dating, he never made me feel like that, and he even told

Sarah to "be nice" when she'd try to brush me off like a pesky fly.

"Whatever." I spun toward the door.

As I reached for the handle, Ben's hand slid around my waist, fingers splayed along my stomach, and he hugged me from behind, pressing his lips to the top of my head.

I closed my eyes and covered his hands with mine. "I'm sorry I'm so annoying."

He chuckled. "You're just you, Gabbs. Innocent. Honest. Kind. Don't ever be anything you're not. If he kisses you, don't worry about what he thinks. It doesn't matter."

I turned toward him, burying myself in his embrace and the way his body cocooned me. My safe place.

Chapter Ten

Belinda Carlisle, "I Get Weak"

Gabby

"Hey!" I skipped down the stairs toward Matt waiting for me, again with his hands in his pockets while walking in a slow circle. I knew if we lasted, I'd always think back to how innocent he looked and the smile he gave me.

"Hey, yourself. You look nice."

"Thanks."

"Well, let's go, *friend*," he said with a smirk while keeping his gaze in front of us as we headed toward his car. That grin said he was still thinking about the previous night; the *friend* felt like another apology for it happening.

I was okay with being friends for the time being because I liked Julianne, and I couldn't imagine being opportunistic like Matt's brother had been with my sister, swooping in like a vulture to take the body while it was still warm. However, I just found out I was really good at kissing, and it was better than having my hair braided, reading, writing in my journal, Air Supply, and rainbow sherbet *combined*.

While I had no plans of making the first move, I wasn't going to object to being friends who kissed. That silent confession gave me a jolt of excitement, a taste of the unfamiliar. Was I on the verge of being a rebel? Or was I on the verge of stealing the love of someone else's life?

We grabbed Subway sandwiches, a movie from Blockbuster, rocky road, and rainbow sherbet. Then we went to Matt's house to watch *Die Hard*.

"Where are your roommates?" I asked as Matt pulled our sandwiches from the plastic bag.

"Beats me. They're only here to sleep for a few hours or they're throwing a party." He handed me my sandwich and drink.

I sat on the faded brown leather sofa that faced the TV while Matt put the movie into the VCR. When he turned, our gazes locked. He seemed to study me for a few extra seconds.

"What?" I asked with a nervous laugh.

"Nothing. It's just you feel so familiar."

"Is that a good thing?" I popped a pickle into my mouth that had fallen out of my turkey sandwich.

He sat next to me and unrolled his sandwich from the paper. "It is now. I couldn't wait to get out of Devil's Head, but seeing you is a reminder that most of my memories from living there and going to school were good."

"Does Julianne know I'm Sarah's sister? I mean, did you tell her about you and Sarah or just that I'm a preacher's daughter?"

He bit into his sandwich and chewed it slowly as the previews played on the TV. "Let's not talk about Julianne or Sarah. At the moment, I find you far more interesting."

I wrapped my lips around my straw to hide my grin.

"What's your thing?"

"My thing?" I asked, setting the drink on the floor between my feet.

"Yeah. Eve ran cross country. Sarah was into music. What do you enjoy doing?"

Planning our wedding.

"I love a good book."

He chuckled. "Everyone reads. What else?"

No. Everyone didn't read. Eve read road signs and recipes. That was about it. Sarah read music. I read two to three books a week in high school.

I searched my brain for something besides reading. Clearly, I hadn't ever given it much thought. Then I realized I had nothing. Was I the world's most boring person? Was there nothing special about me?

"Well," I mumbled over a bite of sandwich that I slowly chewed to give myself more time to think. "I write poetry. And I have a good imagination."

"That's cool. What else?" He dipped his head to eat his sandwich.

What else? Jeez. Was it a job interview? Did I need a dating resume? Five special talents and three references?

"I'm pretty good at croquet."

Matt fisted a hand at his mouth and laughed. "I love that about you, Gabby. No one else would say croquet."

"Well, some of us aren't singers, cowboys, bakers, baseball players, or future engineers."

"Oh, no ..." He shook his head and cleared his throat while wiping his mouth. "Sorry. That came out all wrong. I wasn't trying to put you on the spot like that. I'm just trying to get to know you more than just as Sarah's sister."

With a shy smile, I glanced over at him. "I'm okay with a hacky sack, but not as good as Ben. Oh! I'm good at Chinese jump rope."

"Now that's what I'm talking about. I suck at that."

"Have you ever even done it?"

Matt cleared his throat. "Sadly, no."

"Well, I'm pretty good at macramé and latch hook too because we did it with the kids in vacation Bible school."

"Latch hook ..." Matt shook his head and chuckled. "You win."

I loved his laugh. Matt didn't hide his feelings, and maybe that came out as impulsive behavior, but it was honest, too.

We finished eating and watched the rest of *Die Hard,* pausing it halfway through for an ice cream intermission. He didn't hold my hand or kiss me, and that was fine because every so often I felt his gaze on me. I kept mine on the TV, but my heart pumped a little harder when I knew he was looking at me.

After the movie, he took me back to my dorm and walked me to the door.

"Thanks for giving me a redo," he said.

I nodded, scraping my teeth over my bottom lip as my nerves hijacked the rest of my body, causing me to shiver like it was twenty below zero instead of sixty degrees.

Then it happened. He bent down to kiss me. It was my time to shine. But his aim was off. His lips touched my cheek, and I turned my head so our lips touched. I waited for him to cradle my face in his hands and move his lips in sync with mine like I did with Ben.

Instead, he stiffened. His aim wasn't off. He meant to kiss me on the cheek, and I turned it into something else. Or maybe he meant to whisper goodnight in my ear. *Gah!* What did I do?

"I'm sorry," I said, taking a quick step backward. "Uh, I didn't mean to ... I mean, I thought you were ... oh my gosh. I'm an idiot. Sorry. I just messed up the do-over." Tucking my chin, I covered my face with my hands. "Jeez, I'm so embarrassed."

"Gabby, don't be. Please."

I dropped my hands and lifted my head. Over his shoulder, a figure headed toward us. I narrowed my eyes until Ben came into view.

"Gabbs," Ben said, before licking his ice cream cone. He was a mint chip guy.

Matt turned. "Hey! Ben, right?"

Ben smiled. It was obnoxious and fake. "The one and only."

I held back an eye roll, but mumbled, "There are a billion people named Ben."

Both men ignored me.

"It's been a while. Nice to see you again." Matt was cordial and genuine.

Ben could have learned a few lessons from him. "Yeah, and yet it seems like yesterday because I hear your name so often."

My friendship with Ben was over, and he would find that out as soon as Matt went home. How dare him call me out like that.

"Is that so?" Matt smirked at me as I ignited into an inferno of embarrassment right there on the sidewalk.

"Well, I suppose not so much anymore since I'm no longer in Devil's Head, but yeah, you were a legend. The best pitcher our high school had ever seen. So everyone talked about you after you graduated."

Matt's back straightened as Ben pumped him full of lies. Sure, kids who played baseball after Matt graduated probably mentioned his name a few times. After all, it wasn't every day athletes from small-town Missouri got full ride scholarships to big colleges. But Matt wasn't the talk of the town unless Gabbyville was that town.

"Wow. I had no idea." Even Matt knew it was highly suspicious.

Ben licked his ice cream and shrugged. "How could you since you moved away and your family did too?"

"Well, I'll let you get to bed, Gabby. I had fun. See ya around, Ben."

Ben gave him a little chin lift.

"Goodnight," I said, feeling conflicted about Ben's timing.

Did he show up to save me from myself or to prolong further discussion of why I kissed Matt on the lips?

"Did I interrupt?" Ben offered me a lick of his ice cream cone.

I shook my head. "I had rainbow sherbet."

His eyes widened. "Rainbow sherbet? Whoa. Someone's trying to get to second base with you again."

"Shut up." I dug my key out of my bag while Ben opened the door for me.

I couldn't help but murmur a soft "thank-you" because even when I was mad at him, I wasn't really *mad* at him.

As we headed up the stairs, I waited for him to ask me about my date, an "Oh my gosh, tell me everything!" But Ben wasn't that kind of best friend.

"How was my night? Oh, thanks for asking. It was nice. I discovered I have no exceptional talents, I'm the only one who finds a good book utterly intriguing, and latch hook and macramé aren't as attractive as one might have thought."

"*One* might have thought?" He stopped at the door to my floor. "So you're implying there is at least one person who thought that? Is her name Gabriella Jacobson? And was that your go-to for getting Matt to want to kiss you? Latch hook and macramé?"

"Har, har. Of course not."

"Oh, thank god." He pressed his free hand to his chest.

"You're such a dork." I grabbed his wrist and shoved his ice cream into his face.

There wasn't much left, but it was enough to smear it all over his chin, lips, and the tip of his nose. Despite intending to do just that, I was surprised that it worked. I covered my mouth with my hand for a second, eyes wide, as I suppressed a giggle.

Ben narrowed his eyes, and I dropped my hand from my mouth. "Sorry," I squeaked.

He intentionally let go of the rest of the ice cream cone. *Splat!*

I stared at it on the ground for a second. Why did he do that? As I lifted my gaze, he grabbed my face and held it hostage while he smeared the ice cream from his face all over mine.

"Ben!" I grabbed his wrists. "Stop!" I giggled.

He smeared it along my cheeks and mouth, up my nose to my forehead.

"Ben!"

Then he licked it off my face. I couldn't stop giggling until his tongue swiped along my lips once, twice ... and then he kissed me. And I don't know why, but I kissed him back.

No thoughts.

No reason.

It just felt good.

The ice cream was no longer cold; it was warm, sweet, and sticky between our lips. And he didn't let go of my face. He gripped it while backing me into the door. I don't remember when my eyes closed, they just did. Nor do I recall when my lips parted to let the tip of his tongue touch mine. But it happened.

We cleaned every ounce of peanut butter from the proverbial spoon, and I didn't want it to end. I wanted a second helping.

I wanted the whole jar.

Ben pulled away, leaving me in a puddle just like the ice cream on the floor. For a few seconds, our labored breaths were the only sound in the stairwell as we eyed each other with what felt like confusion and disbelief.

I opened my mouth to speak first, to fill the painfully awkward silence, but someone pushed open the door behind me, giving me a nudge.

"Oh, sorry," the girl from my floor said, giving us a quick inspection and grinning before jogging down the stairs.

What had we done, and what did it mean?

I caved first, tearing my gaze away from his and making a beeline for my dorm room.

"Gabby," he called, but didn't chase me.

I was grateful for that because my brain was ready to explode from the lack of mental capacity to deal with kissing my best friend like that. Before I unlocked the door, I rested my forehead against it and fought back the tears.

I kissed my best friend for real, not for practice, and I liked it so much I could hardly breathe. Ben was my anchor, my protector, and my common sense when I went out of my mind. We couldn't cross that line and put our friendship in jeopardy.

What did we do?

My heart ached.

That kiss ripped open something inside of me, and it felt like I was bleeding feelings for Ben that I buried years earlier after he rejected me and went on to sleep with random girls.

That kiss knocked the wind out of me and left me gasping like waking from a dream so real, it felt like reality.

Was Matt nothing more than a dream?

"Hey! How was your date? Oh, my gosh. What happened to you?" Olivia sat up on her bed and set her book aside when I opened the door.

I touched my fingertips to my lips. Were they swollen? They felt like it. That was the kiss of all kisses.

"Did Matt come on your face?"

"What?" I wrinkled my nose.

"What are those dark spots?"

I looked in the mirror. There were tiny pieces of chocolate on my face. As I picked them off, I opened my mouth to tell her that Ben smeared his ice cream on my face, but that would have only been a half truth. The whole truth was, I didn't want to say his name in front of her or tell anyone what happened.

Except Ben.

I wanted to tell my best friend that a guy kissed me, and it was everything and a million times more than what I ever imagined a kiss could be. That kiss reached far beyond my lips. I felt it everywhere.

"We got into an ice cream fight," I murmured.

"Oh my god! That sounds sexy."

"Yeah," I whispered to myself. "It was."

Chapter Eleven

Tom Petty, "Free Falling"

Gabby

THE ELEPHANT WASN'T in the corner of the room; the elephant was the entire room. In fact, there wasn't even a room. Just a big, fat elephant.

As soon as Olivia left for breakfast Sunday morning, I hopped down from my bunk bed and called my sister, Sarah. We weren't Catholic, so confession wasn't our thing. Baptism and daily prayer sufficed for our religion. But after the events of the previous two days, I needed to clear my conscience.

"Hello?" Isaac answered.

"I need to talk to Sarah," I said, while nibbling on my thumbnail and pacing the room as far as the telephone cord would allow.

He chuckled. "Good morning to you, too, Gabby. Just a sec. She's a little indisposed."

"Indispo—" I cringed.

They were having sex.

Sarah giggled. "Hey, Gabbs. What's up?"

"Sorry to interrupt."

"You're fine. What's up?"

I tried to organize my thoughts into a coherent story with the events in order, proper punctuation, and delineated dialogue, but it came out as one big word vomit. "Matt had a party and removed my shirt. Then I worried a kiss might be next. So Ben showed me how to kiss on the mouth, which was really nice of him, but then after discovering I'm the most boring person on the planet and *Die Hard* has a lot of swear words, Matt leaned forward, and I thought he was going to kiss me, so I turned and pressed my lips to his. But that was all wrong because I don't think he was planning on that. Then Ben showed up and the next thing I knew he was smearing ice cream on my face with his, and then he licked it off and then we kissed. Like we totally really kissed like licking peanut butter from a spoon. Then the door opened and I ran to my room. But I can't tell Olivia because she likes Ben. And I like Matt, and I'm sorry if that upsets you, but he was always too good for you anyway, and I'm not trying to be mean. It's just a fact. At least I thought it was factual, now I don't know anything because stupid Ben kissed me. And now I don't know what to say to him because he's my best friend, but I can't tell my best friend that I kissed my best friend, and so you need to tell me what to do."

Silence—*such* a long pause.

"Sarah?"

She cleared her throat. "Uh, yeah. Sorry. I'm still here. I'm just processing all of that because it was a lot of information."

"Sorry." I turned in several circles to unwrap the phone cord from my body.

"Matt as in Isaac's brother?"

"Duh. Yes."

"Okay. Wow! Well, this is unexpected. And frankly, I'm not happy to hear that he removed your shirt."

"If I wanted a lecture, I'd call Mom. You're not allowed to judge me. It's in the Bible, and *you* are far from innocent. Besides, it wasn't how it sounds. I had beer on my shirt."

"You're drinking too?"

"No. It wasn't my beer," I said with frustration wrapped around each word.

"How did you and Matt even start hanging out?"

"Stop! This isn't about Matt. Well, it's a little about him, but mostly it's about Ben."

She chuckled. "Gabby, everyone knew you'd end up with Ben."

"What?" I pulled the phone away from my ear and stared at it for a few seconds.

"Gabby, Ben looks at you like you're the second coming of Christ."

"You haven't seen Ben in forever."

"Not true. I saw him at your graduation, and I talked to him at your graduation party. I write songs about guys who look at girls like he looks at you."

"You have no idea how he looks at me."

"I do because as we speak, a certain guy is giving me the same look."

They were totally having sex.

"I like Matt. I like him more than you ever did. And I like him more than his ex-girlfriend," I said like any of that mattered, like it had something to do with Ben. And I knew

Sarah wouldn't argue with me about Matt while Isaac was in the same room.

"Maybe you like him the same. I liked him, too, but fell in love with his brother. You supposedly like him, but kissed Ben. Perhaps there's something about Matt that's not quite the right fit for any Jacobson girl."

"Or I'm just confused because I've been saving myself for him, and in the process I missed out on kissing and hand-holding, and all the stuff everyone else does in high school. So I'm making up for lost time, and right now, Ben's the only one who's willing to kiss me."

"Babe, go make coffee," Sarah said to Isaac.

Then I heard a smack like they were kissing.

"You're going to fuck this up," Sarah said.

I bristled at her profanity.

"Excuse my language, but I don't know how else to say this to you. Ben's the one."

"The fact that you think you have to tell me this just proves he's not the one. Nobody had to tell you that Isaac was the one."

"Isaac did. He relentlessly told me in a million subtle and a few not-so-subtle ways. But I had it in my head that Matt was the one for me. The whole town thought he was the one for me. But Isaac really saw me. He brought passion to my life. Despite my resistance. Despite my brain telling me he wasn't the one. He. Was. It."

I sat in my desk chair on a big sigh. "Well, I'm not you."

"Then why are you calling me? Are you looking for my blessing to be with Matt? You've got it. Good luck with that."

"I just want someone to be happy for me. I've liked Matt for so long. And now, I actually have a chance with him. And Ben's messing with my head. And you're on Ben's side. I need someone to be on my side. Ugh! I should have called Eve."

Sarah blew out a long breath. "You're right. I'm sorry. You like Matt. I get it. He's a nice guy. Smart. Talented. And his brother's good in bed. There's really no reason you shouldn't like him."

"Stop," I said, trying not to giggle. "Why must you make everything about you? Everyone knows Isaac is good in bed." I blushed just talking about sex. "I've heard you two when you come home for the holidays."

"Yeah, well, take notes. If you can't stop thinking about him, then he might be the one. But if he makes you scream, toes curling, body shaking, mind-blowing ecstasy, then he's definitely the one. As long as he looks at you like you're the only girl in the world. Understood?"

"Understood," I grumbled.

"And just for the record, he wasn't too good for me. You can like Matt. You may even decide you love him. But he doesn't belong on a pedestal. He's not the god you need to worship. And you are *not* the most boring person on the planet. Now, I gotta go. Don't you have church?"

I looked at the time. "I suppose."

"I won that bet," she said.

"What bet?"

"Isaac said there was no way you were at a public college and still going to church on Sunday since Mom and Dad wouldn't know if you didn't go. But I said you were absolutely still going to church."

"Well, I might not go today because Ben usually goes with me, but now I don't know if he'll want to go with me after what happened last night."

Sarah laughed. "Yes, Gabby, I bet after kissing the girl

he's loved for approximately *eternity*, he won't be in the mood to go to church with you."

It was too confusing to think about Ben loving me like that because I risked a lot to follow the man of my dreams to college, having no idea if he could ever feel the same about me. And Ben was supposed to be my friend, supporting me, not loving me like that or kissing me like he did.

"Thanks for no help."

"Gabby." Sarah sighed. "I love you. And I'll support you no matter what. Just be yourself, and everything will work out how it's supposed to."

"And who am I?" It sounded like a dumb question, but after that kiss, I wasn't sure.

"You're kind. Everyone knows it. If you're kind, then you and everyone else will be fine."

I wasn't so sure.

"Okay," I said.

"See you at Thanksgiving. I'm here if you need anything."

"Thanks. Bye."

"Bye, Gabbs."

I hung up the phone, grabbed my toiletry bag, and opened the door to head to the bathroom.

"Oh!" I jumped, not expecting Ben to be on the other side.

"We should talk."

Pressing my lips together, I nodded several times. "I don't know why that happened. And I don't want things to be weird. Do they have to be weird?"

"What do you mean you don't know why?" He squinted.

"I mean, I know we're just friends, so maybe it's because

I pushed you to show me how to kiss, or maybe we're both adjusting to being away from home. So that's what I mean."

He studied me for a few seconds. I did not know what I meant because his proximity made me nervous and warm. *That kiss* ruined us. How would I ever look at him the same way again?

"I need to use the bathroom, wash my face, and get ready for church. Are you going?"

"So that's it? It happened. It's no big deal? Unknown cause?"

"Yep," I murmured.

"Because you like Matt."

I nodded. "And you like Olivia."

Ben stared over my head with a faraway gaze toward the window in my dorm room. "Fine," he whispered.

"Give me fifteen minutes. Have you had breakfast?"

He slowly brought his attention back to me. "Yeah, but I'll eat again with you."

I smiled. "Thanks." On instinct, I reached for his chest to rest my palm on it like I had done so many times before, but it suddenly felt too personal, so I just as quickly returned my hand to my side and brushed past him to the bathroom.

That day, something died between us.

Chapter Twelve

Martika, "Toy Soldiers"

Ben

GABBY KEPT her distance after the kiss in the stairwell. We walked to our only class together, and she jumped if my hand or arm accidentally brushed hers. At Sunday church service, she set her purse on the pew between us, where she used to set it on the floor at her feet. She couldn't look at me for more than a few seconds without averting her gaze. And she talked about the weather.

The. Fucking. Weather.

Olivia told me when Gabby went bowling with Matt, and he helped her with homework. To Olivia's knowledge, they were just friends, which made me feel like Matt had replaced me.

To make matters worse, I was sick with a sore throat and no energy.

"You should go to the doctor," Jason suggested as I

remained in bed for the sixth day in a row after spending days prior to that trying to attend classes while feeling like death.

"It's just a sore throat," I mumbled, turning onto my side and pulling the covers over my head.

"Are you taking any of the stuff in this sack?" he asked.

Gabby picked me up a bunch of over-the-counter-medicines after Olivia told her I was sick, but nothing worked beyond helping me sleep.

"Yes," I grumbled, feeling like absolute shit. I wasn't one to get homesick or miss my mom, but I was on the verge of breaking down and begging her to come take care of me. I didn't, though, because who called their mommy to bring them chicken noodle soup in college?

"Well, I'm heading out. Don't die."

I didn't have the energy to answer him. Eventually, I fell asleep.

WHEN I AWOKE, it was dark. How did I sleep the whole day away? How did I not hear Jason come back from his classes?

As I sat up, feeling unstable, I needed to pee, so I stood. It felt like I was on a boat, and I quickly lost my balance and fell. I pushed myself to sitting and cupped a hand over my ear. Something was off. There was a ringing in my ears.

I jumped when Jason touched my arm. Then he turned on the light.

I squinted against the light. His lips moved, but his words were distant and muffled.

"W-what?" I shook my head, tugging and rubbing my ears.

Again, Jason's lips moved, but the words were nothing more than faint, undecipherable noise.

"I can't hear," I said.

He squatted in front of me. I caught remnants of letter sounds, but not full words, and I felt nauseous.

"I can't hear." I plugged my nose and blew, like popping my ears at a high elevation, but it didn't work. Again, I stood and wobbled a little.

He grabbed my arm, and his lips moved.

"What?"

He pressed a finger to his lips. Was I being loud?

Panic set in. What was happening to me?

"Something's wrong. It's... I'm..."

Jason helped me sit back on my bed. Then he left the room. A few minutes later, he returned with Chris, our resident assistant.

Chris bent down so our faces were close. He spoke, and maybe he said hospital. I couldn't tell.

"Hospital. Yes. Get Gabby," I said. "Get Gabby!" I repeated because I didn't know if they heard me.

Jason nodded, pulling on a pair of jeans.

My heart pounded. Something was wrong, and I didn't know if it was my illness, my balance issues, or the panic, but I knew I was on the verge of vomiting, so I dropped to my knees and crawled to the wastepaper basket, expelling what little was in my stomach as a cold sweat covered my brow.

Chris helped me get dressed and looped my arm over his shoulder to assist me to the elevator. By the time we reached the main floor, Gabby and Olivia were waiting by the door with Jason.

Olivia ran up to me, but I pushed past her, reaching for Gabby.

"I can't hear. I can't hear. I can't hear." I broke down crying in a panic.

Gabby wrapped her arms around me, somehow holding me up with her tiny body. They helped me to Chris's car, and Gabby sat in the back with me while Olivia jumped into the front passenger seat.

I leaned toward the middle, and Gabby guided my head to her lap, running her fingers through my hair in slow, comforting strokes. Several tears escaped, running along the side of my face to her jean-clad leg.

What the hell was happening?

Chapter Thirteen

Kate Bush, "This Woman's Work"

Gabby

As soon as Ben was admitted to the hospital, I called his parents. It was a little after two in the morning, and they were both on the line and panicked that I had no more information other than he'd been sick for a week with a sore throat and fever, and he suddenly couldn't hear.

"Are they on their way?" Olivia asked after I hung up the phone in the waiting room.

"Yeah." I ran my fingers through my hair with a long sigh. "This is my fault. I should have made him go to the doctor, but ..."

"Stop blaming yourself. I checked on him every day. If anyone is to blame, it's me."

I appreciated her trying to make me feel less responsible, but Ben was my best friend. And if I hadn't been so busy trying to avoid him, I would have known just how bad he'd gotten.

"Are you ready to tell me why you two have been avoiding each other?"

I sat in a chair and shook my head. How could I tell Olivia that I kissed the guy she liked?

It didn't matter. All I cared about was Ben getting better.

"Why do you think he can't hear?" she asked.

I had no clue. As a child, I had a lot of sore throats. Eventually, I had my tonsils removed. Ear and sinus infections. I'd had about everything, but never had I experienced hearing loss.

An hour later, a doctor came into the waiting room to talk to us.

"Are you family?" he asked.

I shook my head. "I'm his best friend, but I called his parents. They live in Missouri, and they're going to get a flight here as soon as possible. But they're a ways from an airport."

He nodded. "We're waiting to hear back from the lab. From his clinical exam, I believe it might be meningitis which can cause hearing loss and other symptoms that's he's experiencing. We've started him on antibiotics."

"But he'll get his hearing back. Right?" Olivia asked.

"We don't know yet. In the meantime, he was distressed, so we gave him something to help him sleep. There's really nothing to do. I suggest you get some rest and come back during visiting hours. You're more than welcome to leave a number where you can be reached if anything changes."

"I'm not leaving," I said.

"Gabby—" Olivia squeezed my hand.

I kept my gaze focused on the doctor. "I'm not leaving."

He returned a sad smile and nodded. "I understand. There are vending machines down the hallway and the cafeteria is on the main level."

"Thank you," Olivia said.

The doctor turned and disappeared behind the double doors.

"I'll stay too."

I shook my head. "You don't have to. I just can't leave, not until his parents get here."

"I have an algebra exam at eight that I shouldn't miss, so ..."

"No. Don't worry about me. You grab a cab and go back to campus."

"What about you? Can you afford to miss your classes?"

"I can't think about that."

Olivia frowned as if my reply was a judgment on her needing to make it for her algebra exam.

"He's my family. I've known him a long time."

She studied me with indecision in her eyes before relinquishing a tiny nod. "Okay. But call me if anything changes."

"I will." I hugged her.

When she started to release me, I tightened my grip, trying to control my emotions before they broke free.

"He's going to be okay," she whispered.

I wanted to believe that. But if we were wrong, I would never forgive myself. When our parents drove Ben and me from Devil's Head to Ann Arbor before the first day of school, their parting words were for us to take care of each other.

I woke with a tap on my arm.

A nurse with a blond pixie cut smiled. "Are you Gabby?"

I nodded, sitting up in the chair while stretching and rubbing my eyes.

"Ben asked for you."

"He did?" I hopped up.

If he asked for me, it means he was well enough to make requests.

"Can he hear?" I asked, following her through the doors.

"Not very well. But I have a pad of paper and pen for you to communicate so you don't have to yell."

"But he'll get his hearing back, right?" I jogged to catch up to her.

She was shorter than me, but her legs were quick. "I can't say yet. Here. We recommend you wear a mask since he's been on antibiotics for less than twenty-four hours."

I stared at the mask a second before taking it from her. After looping it around my ears, I stepped into his room.

Ben's face and lips were so pale. Eyes tired. And I was glad to have a mask covering most of my face to hide my true worry because I couldn't bring myself to smile even though I tried when he glanced up at me.

I squeezed his hand and fought my tears. "Your parents are on their way."

He didn't react, not a single blink.

Stupid.

He couldn't hear, and to add to the confusion, a mask covered my face, so he couldn't see my lips to know I was trying to say something. I took the pen and pad from the table next to him.

Your parents are on their way.

His gaze rested on the paper for several heavy blinks, then lifted to mine, and he nodded.

My brave face slipped, and tears filled my eyes, so I looked down at the paper again.

I should have taken you to the doctor. I'm sorry.

When he read it, lines formed along his forehead, and he rolled his head from side to side. "No," he whispered.

I swallowed past the lump in my throat.

He stuck his fingers in his ears like they just needed to be cleaned out. "I can't hear."

They think you have meningitis.

Ben nodded.

I underlined my first line and added exclamation points.

<u>I should have taken you to the doctor. I'm sorry!!!!!</u>

He grabbed my hand and rested it on his chest as I lifted my other arm to wipe my tears on my sleeve before writing more.

How do you feel?

"Like shit. I may never hear again. Did they tell you that? This could be permanent."

I wiped more tears and looked away.

"It's not your fault."

Tears burned my eyes.

He squeezed my hand and pointed at his eyes. "Not your fault," he said. "You should get to class."

I shook my head, and Ben frowned while mumbling, "I'm tired."

I'll go to the cafeteria and be back in less than ten minutes.

He gave me a slight headshake.

"Be right back," I said, even though he couldn't hear me.

I didn't need anything from the cafeteria. I needed to call my parents. After accepting the collect call, Mom's concerned voice made the lump in my throat swell.

"Gabby, is everything okay?"

I pressed a hand to my mouth to hold back my sob.

"Gabriella?"

I cleared my throat. "Ben is in the hospital. They think he has meningitis." I swallowed another sob.

"Oh dear. Do his parents know?"

"They're on their way."

"We'll pray for him. God will take care of him."

"Mom"—my voice cracked—"he c-can't h-hear."

"What do you mean?"

"I mean he can't hear." I choked.

"Oh, Gabby. I'm sure it will be fine. What have the doctors said?"

I sniffled. "They said they don't know if his hearing loss is permanent."

"Well, one step at a time. Okay?"

"What if he's not fine?"

"Where is your faith?"

My faith had cracked and continued to chip away with each passing minute that Ben couldn't hear.

"I'll pray," I whispered.

"Good. Let him know the whole church will pray for him. And if either one of you need anything, just call. Also, I want updates as soon as anything changes or the doctors give you more information."

"I will."

"Sweetheart, I love you. It's going to be okay. I promise."

How could she be so certain?

"Bye." I hung up the phone.

Everything was the opposite of okay, but I sat in the waiting room before going back to Ben's room, and I prayed anyway, holding back nothing. I asked God to heal his body, let him hear again, and make his pain go away.

By the time I returned to Ben's room, he was asleep. So I sat in the chair next to his bed and watched him breathe until my eyes succumbed to sleep, too.

An hour later, his doctor, along with a group of students, came into the room. One student presented his case. She listed the antibiotics he was getting along with steroids for his loss of hearing. A few of the other students took turns listing potential outcomes and other therapies. Then the doctor asked me if I had questions.

"He can barely keep his eyes open. Is that normal?"

"Yes. When the tissue around the brain swells, it can affect the alertness of the brain, which makes it difficult for him to stay awake for long periods."

I nodded. "His parents are on their way. Will you come back and explain all of this to them when they get here? I'm afraid I'll forget some of it."

She smiled. "Of course. And if I'm not here, Dr. Stenson, a fourth-year resident, will update them and answer questions."

"Thanks. Oh! How long will he be in the hospital?"

"It's too early to say. A week, maybe two. It depends on how his body responds to the antibiotics and steroids and if there are any other complications. Sometimes full recovery from bacterial meningitis can take several months, but most of that time will hopefully not be in the hospital. One day at a time."

I returned a slight smile and a tiny nod.

Months.

What would happen with his classes? His scholarship? And how would he understand the lectures if he couldn't hear?

How will he be a conductor if he can't hear?

I didn't want to leave his side. I never knew my happiness was tied so tightly to his, but it was. If he couldn't be a conductor, I didn't want to be a psychologist. If he couldn't listen to music, I never wanted to hear it again. Friends shared good times and bad. I wanted to trade places with him.

Chapter Fourteen

Poison, *"Every Rose Has Its Thorn"*

Gabby

"GABBY?"

I opened my eyes. Ben's mom Carmen touched my shoulder.

"Hi. I'm so sorry," I said as we hugged.

"Don't apologize, dear." She released me to hold Ben's hand. "It's not your fault."

That was debatable.

Alan, his dad, stood on the opposite side of the bed, holding his other hand. They were in masks, too.

"He's been sleeping a lot."

"Yes. We talked to the doctor in the hallway," Carmen said. "How long has he been sick?"

My heart sank. "About a week."

"He should have called me. Why didn't he go to the doctor? Did he fight you on it?"

I couldn't look at her, so I bowed my head. "I didn't know how bad he was. I bought some over-the-counter meds for his sore throat and to help him sleep. My roommate gave them to him. I didn't see him enough to know things were so bad. I had class, and studying, and ..." I closed my eyes and shook my head. "I should have known."

"Why did your roommate take them to him?"

"They're, uh, kind of dating."

Her blue eyes widened. "Oh? He didn't mention he was dating anyone."

"It's not serious. I don't think. I don't know." I shook my head again. "Jeez, I should know," I murmured as the guilt suffocated me.

"Have you been here the whole time?" Alan asked.

I nodded.

"Take a break. Your parents wouldn't want you missing classes. Get something to eat. Go back to your dorm and focus on not getting behind. The doctor said he'll be here a while. We'll get a hotel nearby and take turns staying the night with him. Of course, you can visit when you have time, but there's nothing you can do, so take care of yourself. That's what Ben would want you to do."

I didn't want to leave him. But I also felt guiltier by the second, watching them stare at their sick child who might never hear again.

"Okay," I nodded. "Here's the pad and pen I've been using to communicate with him. And here's my number." I wrote my phone number on it. "Call me if you find out more from the doctor or if anything changes. Or if he wants to see me."

"Thanks. We'll do," Carmen said.

I stepped next to Ben's head and ran my fingers through

his hair. Then I pressed my palm to his cheek and his beard that had grown out since getting sick. "I'm sorry," I whispered so softly, I knew nobody could hear me.

OVER THE FOLLOWING WEEK, I stopped by the hospital every day after class. On the weekend, I spent most of the days there, studying at his bedside while his parents grabbed food and showered at their hotel.

It was, in fact, bacterial meningitis. And while he was feeling much better, his hearing was not any better. The doctors said it was rare to have profound hearing loss from meningitis, but not impossible.

You get to check out tomorrow. Are you excited?

He stared at the paper. Then he took a deep breath, closed his eyes, and leaned his head back while exhaling. Every day was a struggle to stay focused on the positive things. Plenty of people died of meningitis. Despite the late diagnosis and treatment, Ben was alive. Still, I felt like a fraud for trying to sell the "at least you're alive" angle.

I can't imagine what you're going through. How you must feel. I'm here for you.

I tapped his hand, and he opened his eyes to read my words. A few seconds later, his gaze slid to mine as if he was trying to gauge my sincerity. I lowered the rail to his hospital bed and crawled in beside him, resting my hand over his heart.

Maybe he couldn't hear me.

Maybe he doubted my words on a piece of paper.

But maybe he could feel me.

And maybe he could think of all the times I found solace in his arms, and how my hand always navigated to a spot over his heart because Ben had the biggest heart of anyone I had ever known.

After I counted his chest rise and fall ten times, he rested his hand over mine. I closed my eyes and prayed for him to hear again, and I prayed for him to forgive me if he didn't.

Ben was a lot of amazing things, but he was still human. Not super human. If he never regained his hearing, he would think of me and how my fear of facing him after what we did led me to avoid him. I abandoned him when he needed me the most.

After a few minutes, I sat up. Ben rewarded me with a sad smile, but it was a smile. I took whatever he would give me. I grabbed the pad of paper and pen.

I know I'm not as smart as you, but I will help you catch up on all of your homework. I'll even write your short story for creative writing class. I got an A on mine.

He offered a repeat of his sad smile and said, "I'm going home."

"What do you mean?"

He held a hand to his ear. So I wrote it down.

What do you mean?

"I'm deaf. There's nothing for me here."

I hated the word deaf. It sounded so permanent. I preferred to think he couldn't hear at the moment, that it was temporary. Tears stung my eyes because *I* was here. Was I "nothing?"

"I'll see a specialist closer to home."

I grabbed the pen.

There are students here who are hearing impaired.

Ben shrugged.

You can't leave me.

"What am I supposed to study?" he asked, and it was loud. Was it on purpose or was he having trouble finding an appropriate volume like the doctor said might happen?

Ben scrubbed his hands over his face, and I didn't know if his frustration was over me not wanting him to leave or if he was upset that he couldn't regulate the volume of his voice.

"Hey, how's it going?" Carmen asked.

I turned and stood as she and Alan came into the room. "Ben just told me he's dropping out and going home. But that's ridiculous. Right?"

They looked at Ben and then back to me.

"Given his circumstances, we think it's best for him to return home. Maybe he can re-enroll next semester or next year. But right now, we need to find out if or when he'll be able to hear again. Or if he's going to need hearing aids or surgery. There's a lot to figure out. And right now, we don't know how he'll learn if he can't attend classes and he doesn't know sign language." Alan offered me a similar smile, dripping with empathy because I was too stupid to see that school was no longer his biggest concern.

"What about his scholarship?" I asked.

"We'll apply for a deferral," Carmen said.

All three of us startled when Ben threw the pad of paper at us, hitting my arm.

"I can't hear you." Again, his volume was too high. "Stop talking about me when I can't hear you."

Pain wrinkled Carmen's brow, and she plucked the paper from the floor and wrote:

I'm sorry. We were just telling Gabby that you're going home and we're looking into having your scholarship deferred.

Ben read it then looked at me.

I didn't know what he expected me to say or write or feel for that matter. So I shrugged and shook my head. "I have homework to do." I held up my hand in a stiff wave.

Ben narrowed his eyes, not understanding what I said, but it didn't matter.

"We'll see you tomorrow after he's discharged," Carmen added.

"Sure," I mumbled on my way out of the room.

Chapter Fifteen

INXS, "Need You Tonight"

Gabby

"Did he ask about me?" Olivia questioned as we ate chicken sandwiches and fries at the dining hall.

"He doesn't talk much," I mumbled, squeezing ketchup onto my plate.

"I'll take that as a no. Does he know I've been there twice while he was sleeping? That I met his parents?"

"I don't know. I haven't been there the whole time. So maybe his parents said something or maybe they didn't. You said you didn't want a serious relationship. Just ninety-six."

Olivia snorted. "Sixty-nine. But we never got that far."

I was relieved. It bothered me to think that my mouth had touched Ben's mouth if his mouth had been between Olivia's legs.

"I can't believe he's going home." I released a heavy sigh.

"Gabby, what do you expect him to do? If he can't hear,

and he doesn't know sign language, and he's a *music major,* how is he supposed to learn?"

"Beethoven was deaf."

"I don't know if I'd throw that in Ben's face right now."

"I won't. I'm just really going to miss him. And if he can't hear, I can't even talk to him on the phone."

"Write him letters."

I stared at my plate, replaying the kiss between us. Then my thoughts jumped to the panic in his eyes the night I rode with him to the hospital. His head in my lap. The tears that he quickly wiped away when we got to the hospital. The agony on his face when he spoke too loudly because he couldn't hear himself.

"I'm not hungry." I stood. "So I'm going back to the room."

"Gabby ..."

I tossed my dinner and walked back to the dorm. When I got there, Matt was sitting on the floor outside of my room.

"Hey," I said, mustering as much enthusiasm as possible, which wasn't a lot.

"Hi. I heard about Ben. Your mom talked to mine." He stood. "Gabby, I'm so sorry. How's he doing?"

"He's deaf, and he's dropping out of school." I unlocked my door.

Matt, the boy of my dreams, the reason I was attending the University of Michigan, was at my door, ready to console me. But I didn't want him there because I couldn't fake a smile, flirt, or be the least bit attractive.

I stepped inside my room, and Matt followed me. "Oh, I forgot to mention that we weren't on the best terms when he got sick, so I didn't check on him like I should have. So it's most likely my fault that he's deaf because he waited so long to get treatment. And let's not forget that he's a music major —*was* a music major—so hearing is kind of important."

"Gabby, you can't blame yourself for what is obviously not your fault. Who would have ever imagined that he didn't just have the flu? And that it would be meningitis, and that he would lose his ability to hear? He has a roommate. Why didn't his roommate say something?"

"I don't know." I ran my fingers through my hair and sighed while sitting on Olivia's bed.

Matt pulled the desk chair close to me and sat down, taking my hands in his. "I know this isn't comforting to him or you or anyone else, but the truth is, it could have been worse. He could have died. But he didn't. And now he's going home. That's a good thing because he's not going home to be buried in the ground. But, yeah, it's also sad. You're going to miss him. You're going to feel abandoned. Then you're going to beat yourself up for having any feelings about yourself, like all of your thoughts should revolve around him and what he's going through."

I pulled my hands from his to wipe my tears. "Is that how you feel about Julianne?"

Matt returned a sad smile. "Yeah." He sat up, scratching the back of his neck. "She's choosing to be there for her mom. What an awful person, huh?"

I didn't want to laugh at his sarcasm, but I couldn't help but smile. "Ben's going home because he can't hear, and that's probably really scary and confusing. How dare he?"

Matt chuckled. "That's the spirit. They're both awful. Why aren't they thinking of us and our needs? Who are we supposed to hang out with on the weekends? Have they even thought about it for a second? Inconsiderate assholes."

I covered my mouth to hide my giggle. It felt wrong to

laugh while Ben was dealing with his world being turned upside down.

Matt returned a smirk.

My smile faded. "You love her."

Lines formed along his forehead, but after a few seconds, he nodded. "Yeah."

My heart didn't know how to reconcile my feelings for Matt, his feelings for Julianne, and my kiss with Ben. Part of me wanted to just come out and ask Matt what the chances were of us ever being more than friends. I didn't like not knowing things. I needed something to go right in my life, a spark of hope.

Maybe it was the emotional exhaustion of Ben's illness or the glimpse of Matt's vulnerability and true feelings for Julianne, but for whatever reason, I decided to share my secret. "I've had a crush on you since before you and Sarah were dating."

Matt grinned like he wasn't the least bit surprised by my confession. "I'm flattered."

Flattered? I wasn't trying to flatter him. His response made me feel like a child. How cute or sweet it was for me to have a crush on him?

"Well, that's good. That's what I was going for."

Matt's eyebrows lifted a fraction. I wasn't as well-versed in sarcasm. That was my sister Eve's area of expertise. But it just came out.

"You're Sarah's sister. It's a little weird."

"Sarah's with your brother. *That's* what's weird."

Matt pressed his lips together and nodded slowly.

"Ugh!" I covered my face, rubbing my forehead with the pads of my fingers. "I'm stressed. And confused. And tired. Please forget I said anything. I sound desperate. I'm not desperate. I mean, clearly I'm a little desperate, but—gah! Shut up, Gabriella!" I jumped up, hitting my head on the wood rail of the top bunk. "Ouch!" I seethed.

"Oh, shit!" Matt stood. "Are you okay?" He moved my hand out of the way to look at my head. "Luckily it's not bleeding, but you're going to have a nice goose egg." He kissed my head.

"I'm a mess, embarrassed, sad, tired, and all around miserable. You should go. Run. Don't turn back."

"Well, I'm sad, angry, unfocused, making poor decisions, and all around miserable too."

I looked up at him.

Matt smiled, brushing my hair away from my face. "Sarah's with my brother," he whispered as if he were thinking out loud instead of speaking to me. "So what if I kiss her sister, right?" The pad of his thumb brushed along my cheek. "So what if we make poor decisions together?"

I swallowed hard. "Such as?"

His gaze homed in on my mouth, and he wet his lips. "Such as doing something that feels really good so we can have a break from feeling so bad." He lowered his head just enough to brush his lips along mine.

"Yeah," I whispered.

Teasing turned into kissing. It was nice, better than the time I thought he was going to kiss me so I turned my head, but not as good as it felt when Ben kissed me. But I just hit my head, and I was sad about Ben, so could I expect it to be a mind-blowing kiss with so much on my mind?

Still, it was nice. Matt was far better than the back of my hand. Yet, I couldn't stop wondering what Ben was doing? Was he feeling better? I couldn't imagine him going and me staying in Michigan.

Matt dropped his hands from my face to my waist and kissed me deeper. It was still nice, but not Ben. So I continued to think of Ben because it helped my lips move in sync with Matt's.

Then his hands slid between us, and he unbuttoned my jeans.

I went into full panic mode, my body going rigid.

Matt paused. "Is this okay?" He kissed along my cheek to my neck.

I gripped his shirt, heart thrashing against my chest.

"Please say it's okay. I want to just fucking forget the world. Don't you?" He unzipped my jeans.

What was happening? Weren't we supposed to make out? Kissing and maybe a subtle graze of his hand along my breast on the outside of my shirt? Then I would giggle and playfully scold him because I wasn't having sex before marriage.

"Are you wet for me, Gabby?" His fingers teased the waistband of my underwear.

I grabbed his wrist to stop him, and he pulled back an inch, squinting.

I returned a nervous smile. "Um ..."

"You're not a virgin, right? You had a condom in your bra at my party."

"Yeah," I chirped quickly. "I mean, I uh, I did have one. My roommate gave it to me."

He continued to study me, then he stepped backward. "Gabby," he exhaled, running his fingers through his hair and shaking his head. "If you're a virgin, I can't—"

"No!" I shook my head so many times I was a little dizzy. "I'm not, I just ... uh, my roommate will be back any minute."

I was not a liar before college. In a matter of months, lying became my new pastime.

"I cannot take Sarah's virginity *and* yours. No way in hell." He mirrored my headshaking.

"I'm. Not."

I'm going to Hell.

Then the door opened behind him, and Olivia stepped inside, saving me. I quickly zipped and buttoned my jeans, and that's what she focused on before giving me wide eyes and then shifting her attention to Matt.

"Hey, uh, this is Matt. I don't think the two of you met at his party. Matt, this is my roommate, Olivia."

"Nice to meet you." He shook her hand.

Olivia's smile swelled, gaze ping-ponging between us. "You too. I've heard so much about you."

"Oh yeah?" Matt smirked, tossing me a look over his shoulder.

I returned a tight grin while feeling the bump on my head.

"Listen, I didn't mean to interrupt. I'm just going to go hang out with some other friends for a while." She walked backwards toward the door.

"Matt was just leaving," I blurted.

"Yeah. I should bounce. Again, it was nice meeting you, Olivia." He turned toward me. "Get some ice for your head."

I nodded.

"I'll call you."

Again, I nodded because I didn't know what to say.

"Night." He left the room.

As soon as the door shut, Olivia's jaw dropped. "Gabriella, you little hussy. Here I thought you were upset about Ben, but you skipped dinner for a booty call."

"A what? No. I totally did not. I didn't know he'd be waiting outside our door. And I was, I *am*, upset about Ben. It's not what you think."

She crossed her arms over her chest. "What I think is Matt was trying to get into your panties."

I pressed my lips together for a beat. "Okay, I guess it is what you think. Sort of. But I stopped him before you came through the door because I'm ..." I couldn't tell her I was saving myself for marriage.

Why was I embarrassed? That's not how my parents raised me. Why was I pretending not to be a virgin? Or was I discovering a new version of myself?

"Because you what? Have an aversion to incredibly sexy men? Oh my god, Gabby! He's so hot. How do you know all the hot guys? Ben *and* Matt?"

Ben ...

I continued to feel the bump on my head. "I knew you were on your way back."

"What happened to your head?"

"I hit it on the top bunk."

Her nose wrinkled as she sat at her desk and turned on the light. "Ouch."

"Yeah. Totally ouch."

"So were you going to have sex or was he just going to finger you? Oral? Sixty-nine?" She giggled.

I tipped my head to try to see the bump in the mirror. "I don't know. He didn't say what his plans were."

"What were you wanting him to do?"

"I don't know. I hadn't thought about it."

"Liar. Of course you've thought about it. You've been drooling over this guy since you got here. Don't tell me you haven't thought about it. And if you say something about spooning, I'm going to tell everyone on our floor that you're still a virgin."

"Why would you say that?" I eyed her reflection in the mirror.

She slid a tape into her Walkman. "Ben told me."

"He told you I'm a virgin?"

"Mm hmm. It's fine. I think it's kind of sweet. And a little weird, but to each their own."

"Why do you say it's weird?" I pulled my chair away from the bed where Matt had moved it.

Olivia glanced at me, pushing her glasses up her nose. "Because your first time is totally not cool. It hurts, and you just lie there praying for it to end, especially if you're not really turned on, if you know what I mean."

I nodded slowly.

She rolled her eyes. "You don't know what I mean, do you?"

I shook my head.

She leaned back in her chair, propping her socked feet onto her desk as she continued to fiddle with her Walkman. "If you're not really turned on, then you might not be wet enough, and there is nothing worse than dry sex your first time, or any time, but definitely not your first time."

"Are you wet for me, Gabby?"

I was embarrassingly naïve and inexperienced. Until Olivia mentioned being wet, I wasn't sure what Matt meant. Apparently, I wasn't that wet, or surely I would have felt it between my legs, like starting my period.

"Hypothetically, how wet is wet?" I asked.

She snorted. "I don't know. If your underwear is a little wet, then you're definitely good to go. Like, you know when you touch yourself and your fingers get really coated? That's where you want to be."

I blinked one too many times, which caused Olivia to gape at me in shock again.

"Stop! You're totally joking, right? Gabby, you've masturbated, haven't you?"

I swallowed hard.

She cupped a hand over her mouth and mumbled, "Oh, my god."

I blushed, biting my lips together.

"No wonder you're still a virgin. You have no idea how *amazing* it feels to orgasm. Gabriella! Ahh!"

I cringed, pressing my finger to my lips so she didn't alert the entire floor.

Olivia hopped out of her chair and grabbed my shoulders, shaking me. "You have to touch yourself! You are totally missing out on *the best feeling in the world!*"

She released me and hugged her body in an oddly seductive way. "Gabby, why do you think people have so much sex? It's not to make babies. I mean, sure, that can happen too. But there are over five billion people in the world because sex is that good, not because everyone is dying to change dirty diapers. And the songs ... all the good songs are about sex. Books. Paintings. Sculptures."

I thought about Ben telling me he'd had sex over thirty times. Then I thought about my sisters talking about it like a drug they couldn't quit.

"But you said the first time is the worst."

She collapsed into her chair again. "Well, yes. It's not great. Definitely try to orgasm before he penetrates you. It's still going to hurt, but each time it gets better until you crave it, and it's all you can think about."

That was a lot to consider on top of my guilt and the ache in my chest from Ben.

Chapter Sixteen

Guns N' Roses, "Patience"

Ben

IT FELT like someone had the TV set to the lowest volume. I could hear sound, but I couldn't make out what was being said. And when someone yelled at me, I could sometimes decipher a word or two beyond the ringing, but that was it. And even then, it felt like a guess.

After I was discharged from the hospital, my parents drove me in a rental car to my dorm. Their mouths moved, and I heard faint muffled sounds, but I couldn't make out a single word. Mom would occasionally glance back at me and smile.

"Turn on the radio," I said.

Dad eyed me in the rearview mirror as Mom leaned forward and turned on the radio.

"Turn it up."

She looked back at me as she turned the volume knob.

Their faces tightened, and I could tell they thought it was loud.

The rhythmic beat and vibration of the back speakers felt good, and I wanted to hold on to that feeling like an anchor because my world was drifting into the unknown. Then mom shook her head and twisted the knob. The vibration and the beat disappeared.

"Turn it back on."

She said something.

I narrowed my eyes. She grabbed the pad of paper and wrote on it.

It is on and it's loud. If I turn it any louder it will hurt our ears.

I stared at the paper, then leaned my head back and closed my eyes.

When we got to the dorms, I led them to the stairs, but Mom nodded toward the elevator.

I shook my head and took the stairs, but I only made it up one flight before I felt dizzy and on the verge of collapsing, so I sat down.

Dad helped me up and through the door to the elevators on the second floor. Just as the door dinged, mom touched my arm and pointed to my left at Gabby coming out of her dorm room with her backpack on over her red wool jacket.

She stared at me for a few seconds, redness filling her eyes. Then her ChapStick glossed lips pulled into a tiny grin as she walked toward me, lifting onto her toes to hug me. She smelled like flowers and vanilla. No sooner did her arms wrap around me, she let go and mouthed something to my parents.

Did they tell her I was weak?

My dad held open the doors to the elevator as Gabby and my mom had an exchange. Then Gabby waved at me before heading to the stairs.

"Where are you going?" I called, feeling desperate. We were there to pack up my things and drive back to Missouri. Was that our goodbye?

Mom pressed a finger to her lips. I was tired of people either holding their hands at their ears because I wasn't talking loud enough or shushing me for being too loud.

Gabby's gaze flitted between the three of us, but my parents pulled me into the elevator.

"Gabby!" I called.

Mom rubbed my arm.

After we reached my floor, my dad unlocked my room with the key Jason dropped off at the hospital, along with clothes a few days earlier.

There was a tap on my shoulder. I turned and smiled at Gabby. She handed me a piece of lined paper.

I have class. I'll be back as soon as it's over.
Your parents said they'd wait to leave. XO

XO. I liked XO.

She turned to head back toward the door, and I grabbed her arm to bring her back so I could hug her again. Was I weak? Hell yeah. I was dying to sit down. But I only had a little time left with my best friend.

After a second of hesitation, she wrapped her arms around my torso and rested her cheek on my chest. It wasn't how things were supposed to go. I kissed her in the stairwell, and she kissed me back.

Not a practice kiss. A real kiss.

I thought she'd take some time to see that the man who loved her the most had been right in front of her all along. But I no longer felt like that person or a man at all. I felt like a boy going home with his parents, no hearing, no future, and no best friend.

Matt would step in and sweep her off her feet.

Gabby released me, but I didn't want to let her go. Her hands slid up to my scruffy face, and she framed it, giving me her beautiful smile. Then she lifted onto her toes and kissed my cheek, letting her lips linger for more than a second. I grabbed her wrists to keep her there just a little longer. Then I let her go.

That was our painful destiny. Me letting her go.

AFTER MY PARENTS loaded my stuff, I told them I was waiting for not only Gabby but Jason, too. I didn't want to leave without thanking him for being there for me. So while I sat on the empty mattress staring at the door, my parents walked around the campus to take in the fall foliage. October in Michigan was a sight to see.

Way over two hours after Gabby headed to class, the door opened and I perked up only to deflate with disappointment when Jason dropped his bag onto the floor. But then Gabby walked in behind him.

I stood and smiled while handing Jason the note I wrote him. "I wasn't sure I'd get to see you before leaving, so I wrote you a note."

He nodded and read it.

> **HI. I GUESS I'M DEAF FOR NOW, SO AS YOU KNOW I'M GOING BACK TO MISSOURI. THANKS FOR BEING AN AWESOME ROOMMATE AND NOT LETTING ME DIE.**

Jason grinned. He turned the paper over and wrote a note back to me.

> **THANKS FOR NOT DYING. THAT WOULD HAVE LOOKED BAD ON A JOB RESUME. I HOPE YOU GET YOUR HEARING BACK AND RETURN NEXT SEMESTER.**

I nodded.

He patted me on the shoulder and said something to Gabby. She grinned and said something back. I hated not being able to make out actual words or read their lips. After stuffing a few books into his backpack, he slung it over one shoulder and gave me a hug before leaving.

Gabby grabbed my notebook and sat down on the mattress. I sat next to her as she wrote:

> *I was waiting outside of your room for 45 minutes after knocking until my knuckles bruised. I guess you forgot you can't hear and your door was locked.*

Shit.

I cringed. "Sorry. I heard something, but I thought it was the guys next door playing loud music."

Gabby's nose wrinkled before she nodded and scribbled on the paper.

Where's my note?

"You don't get one. Am I talking too loud or too soft?"
She shook her head.
"Will you do me a favor?"
She nodded.
"Let me braid your hair?"
Tears filled her eyes like they did earlier, but she held them in and sat on the floor in front of me. I braided her hair, loosely ran my fingers through it to undo the braid, and did it again. I repeated this, relishing the way she melted into my touch, missing the sound of her humming like a cat purring. Occasionally, she'd touch her face, and I knew she was wiping tears.

Finally, she turned toward me on her knees with puffy eyes and a somber expression.
"Why the tears?" I asked.
She shook her head.
I framed her face with my hands. "Why the tears, Gabriella?"
Again, she shook her head.
I ducked my head, stopping a breath from her lips; she didn't move away, so I kissed her. In the next breath, she jumped up and turned away from me.
My parents were back.
I stood, ignoring my mom's scrutinizing gaze. Yes, I kissed Pastor Jacobson's daughter. Yes, I kissed my best friend. Yes, I was miserable that everything that mattered to me was gone or about to be hundreds of miles away from me.

I was weak, deaf, and futureless.

Mom wrote **Ready?** on a sheet of paper.

Ready wasn't the right word for what I was feeling. I nodded anyway.

Gabby held out her hand, and I took it as we followed my parents to the elevator. When we reached the parking lot, words I couldn't hear were exchanged between Gabby and my parents. After they slid into the car, she hugged me again. I kissed the top of her head over and over.

She leaned back to see my face and mouthed a clear, "I'm sorry."

I shook my head.

She rested her hands on my chest and her two index fingers came together to draw a heart. I wanted to say "I love you," but why? I had nothing to offer her. I took her hands and pressed them to my cheeks one last time, closing my eyes and turning right, then left, to kiss her palms. Then, after one last hug, I opened the door and slid into the back seat.

Gabby put her hand on the outside of the window, and I pressed mine to the inside.

Panic raced through my body—panic over forgetting the sound of her voice, her giggles, and the way she called me by my full name when she was feeling goofy. She said the first part really slowly. "Buh-innn"—followed by a quick—"jamin." I berated myself for wishing she'd shut up about Matt. If only I would have known how much I needed to cherish every word that left her beautiful mouth.

Chapter Seventeen

Aerosmith, "Going Down / Love in an Elevator"

Gabby

"Everything okay?" Matt asked over dinner at his favorite Chinese restaurant.

It was a cheer-Gabby-up dinner, and I wondered if my mom put him up to it.

Our food was about gone, and I hadn't said more than a few sentences, mostly about the recent snow. However, it wasn't just me. Matt seemed off too.

"I'm fine," I said. "You?"

He poked around at the rest of his rice and beef. "Yeah." In the next breath, he said, "No." With a deep sigh he set his fork on his plate and sat back in his chair. "Julianne finally called me. I hadn't seen her since she stormed out of the party. She wanted to have dinner. So we did. And after dinner, she invited me up to her apartment to talk, but talking turned into more. But I stopped it immediately." He eyed me, studying my reaction.

I didn't have one.

"I told her I kissed you. She asked if it was just physical or if I had feelings for you. And I didn't know what to say." He drummed his fingers on the table.

I sipped my water. Was he waiting for me to say something? There wasn't a question in anything he said.

Still, where were my emotions? How could I be with the man of my dreams, talking about him kissing me, and not feel complete euphoria?

"It's okay if you have thoughts or feelings about this," he laughed a little.

"Um ..." I cleared my throat.

"After what happened with Sarah," he shook his head, "I don't know how to be anything but honest in a relationship. I don't want to lie to you or to Julianne."

"I kissed Ben." I twisted my lips for a second. "Actually, he kissed me. But I kissed him back. I don't know what it meant."

Matt paused his drumming fingers. "I'm not surprised."

"What?" I couldn't hide my shock.

"He clearly has a thing for you."

"Why do you say that?"

Matt shrugged. "It's how he looks at you with a permanent smile. I can't explain it, but it's obvious."

"Is that how you look at Julianne?"

Matt's gaze wandered around the restaurant before returning to me with a tiny nod. "I suppose."

"So you really like Julianne and Ben likes me. But she's moving, and I'm ..."

I'm in love with you?

I no longer knew how I felt about Matt. When Ben kissed me, up was down, in felt like out, and right versus wrong no longer made sense.

He grunted a laugh. "Ben and I sound lovesick and pathetic."

Ben was dealing with something much bigger than having a crush on a girl.

"Maybe we can scratch each other's itch. The loneliness itch."

Scratching itches didn't sound like a reliable road to matrimony. I didn't want to be anyone's back scratcher or calamine lotion. Where was the romance in that? I preferred the drunk version of Matt, the one who said I was prettier than my sisters and noticed the color of my eyes and the moles on my face. Was it time to abandon my dreams? Did I come this far to give up on Matt? Or did I need to adjust my idea of falling in love? Perhaps Matt wasn't the kind to fall. Maybe he moseyed into it without a big splash. Then one day, without realizing the exact moment it happened, he'd think, *"Wow! I love Gabriella. She's been everything I've ever needed and wanted. How could I be so blind? How did I mistake true love for a bottle of pink lotion?"*

"Gabby?"

I glanced up from my plate.

Matt smiled. "Penny for your thoughts?"

"It's nothing." I slid my plate aside. "I'm done. Are you?"

"Yeah. Let's get out of here."

After he paid for dinner, I popped three mint Tic Tacs into my mouth on the way to his car.

"Do you want to come to my place or should I take you back to your dorm?"

A flood of nerves ravaged me, so I slid my hands under my legs so he wouldn't see them shaking.

We were a long way from marriage. How was I supposed to get there without having sex with him? Tell him I was waiting for marriage? He already thought I was no longer a virgin.

I messed up and dug a hole too deep, and there was no good way out of it.

I needed to come clean or sacrifice my morals. But were they morals or just guilt? Did I genuinely not want to have sex until my wedding night, or was I afraid of the guilt from God? Maybe if my heart was pure, if I only had sex with the person who I intended to marry, God would show me mercy.

"Your place," I whispered.

WHEN MY SISTERS and I were younger, Mom and Dad promised to take us to Disneyland. The buildup to our trip was the most exciting and unforgettable time in my life. But then our car broke down, and not only could our parents not afford to pay for us to fly to California, they couldn't afford the park tickets after paying for the car to get fixed. So we went to Six Flags, and Mom bought us Mickey Mouse T-shirts to wear. We had to lower our expectations, but we still had a good time.

I wasn't going to have sex with Matt for the first time on our wedding night. Instead, I'd lose my virginity on a random Saturday night after Chinese food.

"Brett, this is Gabby," Matt introduced me to one of his roommates, while taking my hand to lead me up the stairs.

"Hey," Brett said without taking his eyes off the television.

"Do you think this is a good idea with one of your roommates here?" I whispered as we reached the top of the stairs.

Matt chuckled. "He doesn't care. Trust me, he doesn't think I'm bringing you up here to study."

Matt was steady and cool while my bones rattled, and my hands felt clammy. He closed the bedroom door behind us, and I turned in a slow circle. There were baseball posters on the walls, a cluttered desk in the corner, a dresser covered with trophies and dust, and a bed with messy sheets.

He drew the window shades, then turned toward me, toeing off his tennis shoes. "I love it when you blush."

I pressed a shaky hand to my cheek. Calling it a blush was like calling a volcano a bonfire.

"I know you might have imagined this, but I never did." He slid his hand into my hair and ducked his head to kiss my neck. "Such an unexpected surprise," he whispered between kisses.

My breaths quickened.

His hands and mouth felt good, but the guilt felt bad.

I closed my eyes and tried to think only about the good, but every time his hands moved to a part of my body that no man had ever touched, shame overshadowed everything.

He kissed my mouth and guided my hand to his jeans, rubbing it along his erection. I kept my fingers straight and stiff. Did he want me to massage it?

Why was it so difficult? Was I overthinking it like the time I asked Ben to show me how to kiss? My mind skipped to the second time Ben kissed me. I didn't overthink that. In fact, I didn't think at all. I just kissed him.

I felt desired and safe, and that made me feel like a real woman.

Kissing Matt deeper, I wrapped my arms around his neck. He grabbed my butt, squeezing it like he was teetering on the edge of control. Nerves of anticipation mixed with the euphoria of physical desire were a heady combination.

He dragged his lips from my mouth to my neck again while sliding his hand up my shirt.

"Gabby," he mumbled.

"Ben," I said in a breathy voice.

He froze.

I opened my eyes. Why was he stopping?

With a soft chuckle, he stepped backward and rested one hand on his hip while his other hand pinched the bridge of his nose.

"What's wrong?" I curled my hair behind my ears.

Again, he released a little laugh while shaking his head. "You said Ben."

"What? When?"

He dropped his hand and looked at me. "I said your name, and you replied with Ben's name."

"No, I didn't."

He nodded slowly. "You did. And that's okay. I'm not upset. It's just sex. You haven't hurt my delicate feelings or anything like that. But given our family history, I feel a little more responsible for you than if you were just some other girl. And if you're with me but saying some other guy's name, I think there's a high probability that you'll regret this. We're friends. I don't want to be that asshole friend."

I was usually a good listener. Even when I wrote poems about Matt in the margins of my Bible, I still listened to my dad's sermons at the same time. But after Matt told me I said Ben's name, I didn't register another word he said.

It made no sense. If anything, when Ben kissed me, I should have said Matt's name because he was my dream.

"I'm ..." I shook my head. "I'm so sorry. I didn't mean—"

"Gabby," Matt pulled me into his arms while mine remained limp at my sides, "don't apologize. I'm not mad."

Well, I was mad. Mad at myself for letting Ben kiss me and get into my head. Mad at Ben for not writing me back since he went home. Mad at Matt for being too nice.

Yes. I was mad at him for *being too nice*.

I laughed out loud at that thought. Then I laughed some more.

Matt released me, squinting. "What's so funny?"

I covered my mouth to muffle my amusement. An unexpected hysteria robbed my composure. Matt returned a hesitant grin, like he wanted to laugh with me, but he didn't know what was so funny.

"I'm here *for you*," I said between giggles. "I could have gotten a psychology degree anywhere, like in Missouri. But no. I had to chase you. So I took out a big loan to come here *for you*." I weaved my fingers through my hair and turned my back to him. "I thought Sarah was so stupid for not choosing you, yet I was relieved, because my crush on you was larger than life. Do you have any idea how many poems I've written about you? I dreamed of this moment for so long. Of course, it was our wedding night, but still, *you* have been my dream forever."

With tears in my eyes, I slowly turned to face him again. He bled remorse and sympathy. I hated the pain on his face. As if his girlfriend leaving him wasn't enough, I just dumped my emotional baggage onto him. I gave him the exact measurements of the gigantic pedestal on which I'd placed him atop.

It wasn't his fault that I felt humiliated, foolish, and lost. Love was the most vulnerable emotion. It exposed the heart.

It stole breaths.

Made sane people crazy.

And in its unrequited form, love was so humbling.

"Gabby—"

"No." I held up my hand. "Please don't say anything." I tipped my head back, gazing at the ceiling while taking a long breath. "And please don't tell anyone."

When I looked at him again, he returned a sad smile. "Ben's a lucky guy."

I laughed. "He's deaf. I don't think he would agree with you."

"Ben's a lucky guy," Matt repeated, matter-of-factly.

I bowed my head and stared at my fingers, picking at my nails. "I just really thought it would be you."

Matt sat on the end of his bed. "Come here." He held out his hand.

After a few seconds of hesitation, I stepped toward him, giving him my hand.

He pulled me to stand between his spread legs. "I'm still trying to figure out my life. But I can tell you from my experience of loving and losing people that timing is everything. When I told Julianne about Sarah, she said it was timing. But not like it wasn't our time. It was our time, but our time ended. As someone who was raised to believe that we're meant to find 'the one,' marry them, and spend eternity with them, that was hard for me to understand. But if Sarah hadn't left me, I wouldn't have met Julianne. And if Julianne weren't moving to California, I wouldn't have made a complete ass of myself in the bathroom with you."

I laughed, and in the next blink, tears escaped.

He wiped them from my cheeks. "And had I not done that, we might not be here now. And maybe our time is short, or maybe our time is yet to come. But no one has ever made me feel as special as you just did. I wish I could say I think I deserve it." He tucked his chin, resting his hands on my hips. "But I don't. Not now."

Maybe our time is yet to come.

His words swirled in my mind, kicking up possibilities like dust that would settle in time.

I wiped my eyes as he lifted his gaze to mine. "I picked the right guy to have a crush on."

He grinned. "I'm honored."

"Had this gone further, do you think you might have called me Julianne?"

Matt laughed. "Perhaps. Does that make you feel better?"

I nodded. "Are you lying?"

He rolled his lips between his teeth to hide his grin.

I stepped back, shaking my head. "Of course you wouldn't say the wrong name. Duh. Of course, I'm the only stupid one."

"Come on," he stood. "I'll drive you home, *Jules*." He shoved his feet into his tennis shoes.

I smirked.

"Oops. I mean Jenny. Wait. No. What's your name again?"

I shoved him playfully as he passed me to open the bedroom door.

Had someone told me that before the end of my first

semester of college, I would almost have sex with Matt Cory, kiss my best friend, and watch him get in a car to go home because he lost his hearing to meningitis, I would have laughed at an idea so preposterous.

As Matt drove me home, I mourned the loss of dreams and reluctantly welcomed the beginning of what my sisters promised would happen at some point: questioning my faith in God.

.

Chapter Eighteen

Janet Jackson, "Miss You Much"

Gabby

"How's Ben?" I asked my mom while Olivia painted her toenails red. Snow swirled with the wind outside our dorm room window. It was one week until Thanksgiving.

"Gabriella, I appreciate the daily calls as opposed to weekly check-ins, but you can't expect me to have new updates about Ben *every day*."

It had been seven weeks since he left.

Seven weeks without talking to him.

Seven weeks of sending him letters without a response back.

Seven weeks of feeling lost.

It was also the first time I'd gone more than a week without seeing or talking to him.

"Did you tell Carmen to tell him to write me back?"

"Yes, dear, but she said he's been shutting everyone out.

Your dad suggested we give him space, keep him in our prayers, and in time, God will speak to him. We just have to be patient."

"Is he learning sign language?"

"No. He has no interest in learning it right now. And until his parents learn it too, it won't do much to help him."

"Did you tell her you've been learning it?" Olivia mumbled.

I shook my head at her. It was my goal to surprise Ben at Thanksgiving. I was taking it three nights a week through Ann Arbor's community education courses. But it would not be a pleasant surprise if I was the only one who knew how to sign anything.

"How's he going to come back to school if he doesn't get his hearing back, and he doesn't learn sign language?"

"He was a music major. Carmen said he's going to need time to think about a new direction."

Ben loved music. He couldn't give up on his dream. "It's like everyone is praying for him, but nobody really believes in miracles which kinda feels like you don't believe in God."

I was one to talk.

"Gabby, you know that's not true. Enough about Ben. We can't do anything more than we're already doing. How are you? Are you getting good grades?"

"Yeah, I'm doing fine."

"Well, we love you. And we can't wait to see you in a few days."

"You too. I'll call you tomorrow."

She laughed. "I'm sure you will. Bye, hun."

I hung up the phone.

"No change?" Olivia asked.

"No." I untangled myself from the cord. "I need to get

home. Everyone else is praying for him while he hides in his room. What if prayer has nothing to do with God answering our requests or taking a bow every time we thank him for something? What if he made humans the most advanced species so we can figure things out on our own?"

Olivia glanced up at me, glasses low on her nose while she capped her nail polish. "I'm not as religious as you, so I haven't given it that much thought. But yeah, I feel like prayer is a little lazy if there's something you can do yourself."

"I hate that I can't talk to him."

"Yeah." She fanned a folder over her wet toenails. "It would be better if he were blind instead of deaf."

I didn't want to laugh, but I couldn't help but snort. "Stop. That's terrible."

"How's Matt?" She had a way of shifting every subject to Matt. "Have you two done the deed yet? You haven't mentioned him in a long time. Is he back with his girlfriend?"

I couldn't look at her because I had the worst poker face.

"Gabby, what aren't you telling me?"

"What do you mean?" I sorted through my clothes to figure out what I was taking home for break and leaving at the dorm.

"What do you mean, what do I mean? You know what I mean. And you won't look at me which means you're not telling me something."

I spared a quick glance at her and a dismissive "pfft."

"I can read people. That's why I'll be an excellent lawyer. And you're hiding something. Just tell me."

"Did you totally, honestly, for real not have sex with Ben?"

She set her nail polish bottle in a plastic basket filled with other bottles of polish. "No. We had sex, but it was fake sex, not *for real* sex, so I didn't tell you. Yes!" She rolled her eyes. "We didn't have sex. We barely messed around. Why?"

"Because he kissed me." I held my breath, waiting for her to fly at me, screaming profanities about betrayal. "Twice." I shook my head. Technically, it was three times, but I didn't count the day he left because his parents interrupted us. But my need to tell the truth turned into diarrhea of the mouth. "But the first time was just practice. Not practice for us, practice for Matt and me."

"Gabby?"

"But the second wasn't practice. It was more. I kissed him back, like totally kissed him back."

"Gabby?"

"But I don't know why. Why did I kiss him back like that? I've ruined everything."

"Gabby!"

I jumped. "Yes?" I whispered.

"Chill."

I nodded in the most unchill way.

"You're the only one who refuses to see it."

"See what?" I questioned.

"That you have a thing for Ben, and he has a thing for you."

I shook my head.

She propped her bare feet onto her desk and folded her hands behind her head. "I've never had a 'friend' tickle me until I almost peed my pants. I've never had a friend open doors for me, kiss me, or look at me with a million stars in their eyes."

"You think Ben looks at me with stars in his eyes?"

"Duh. And that's how you look at him. You not realizing it just blows my mind. You totally love him."

"He's my friend."

"There's nothing better than falling in love with your best friend."

I felt like everyone thought they knew us, but they didn't. I loved Ben, but not like that. I refused to love him like that. And if he loved me as more than a friend, why did he sleep with so many other girls knowing that I believed in waiting until marriage?

It was too late. After she tried calling me out over supposedly loving Ben more than a friend, I couldn't tell her about nearly having sex with Matt and saying Ben's name.

"Just so you know, Matt and I are staying friends."

"Because you love Ben?" Olivia smirked.

I threw one of my shirts at her. "Shut up." I laughed. "It's just not the right time." That was the truth.

Chapter Nineteen

Fine Young Cannibals, "She Drives Me Crazy"

Gabby

My parents picked me up at the airport and played twenty questions about school on the way back to Devil's Head.

Yes, I was passing my classes.

Yes, I liked my roommate.

Yes, I was making friends.

Yes, I was going to church every (most) Sundays.

Yes, I'd seen Matt on multiple occasions.

No, I wasn't drinking.

No, I wasn't doing drugs.

No, I wasn't tempted to have sex.

That last one was more complicated, but accurate enough.

"I want to see Ben," I said, staring out the window as we passed fields of browns and gold.

"Your sisters want to see you," Mom said.

"They can see me after I see Ben."

"I have some things to do this afternoon, Gabby. As much as I'd like to visit with Ben and his family, I need to get home." Dad gave me a quick glance in the rearview mirror.

I shrugged. "Just drop me off. I'll call when I need a ride home. Sarah or Eve will come get me."

My parents exchanged a look.

"What?" I asked.

Mom cleared her throat. "Ben's still having a rough time."

"He's still sick?"

"No. He's having a rough time dealing with his hearing loss."

"So." I shrugged. "I'll talk with him."

"That's just it. I talked with Carmen yesterday morning, and she said he's not up for company."

"Well, they don't usually have family in town for Thanksgiving anyway."

Again, my parents exchanged a look.

"Jeez, what? Just tell me."

"Ben doesn't want *any* visitors, including you. I'm sorry, honey. Carmen said you shouldn't take it personally."

Visitors? I wasn't a visitor. I was his best friend. And there was no way I would not take it personally. There was also no way I wasn't going to see him. "I will not let him sit in his room and rot. Just like I didn't let those stray animals die when Dad used to tell me to let them perish the way nature intended. So take me to his house."

Again, Dad looked in the rearview mirror.

I returned a toothy grin. "Please."

"You're acting like your sisters now. I knew public college was a bad idea," he said.

"I'm acting like an adult caring about people. How is that acting like my sisters? And I said please. Did they say please?"

"Fine, we'll stop by his house. But your mom and I will wait in the car while you run up to the door, and when Ben's parents politely tell you Ben doesn't want to see you or anyone else right now, you can turn around and get back in the car," Dad said.

"We won't even say 'I told you so.'" My mom shot me a grin that was just as toothy and sarcastic as the one I gave my dad.

"Fine. But when I disappear into the house, go home. I'll be a while because I'm not taking no for an answer."

As we pulled down Ben's gravel drive, I unbuckled and hopped out the second the car came to a stop. Carmen opened the door after I rang the doorbell twice.

"Gabriella." She gave me a smile, but it was more reserved than the one I was used to getting from her.

"Hi." I stepped inside before she could say anything. "Is Ben upstairs?" I headed for the stairs.

"Gabby?"

I stopped halfway up and took a deep breath while glancing back at her. "Yeah?" I smiled.

"I'm sorry. He's not in the mood for visitors."

"Well, I'm here. So maybe I can put him in a better mood."

"Gabby," she shook her head. "His door is locked. He won't hear you knock, and even if he could, he wouldn't open it. I'm sorry, sweetie."

My smile faded, but I continued up the stairs. His bedroom was the first on the right. I knocked several times.

No answer.

"Ben," I said as if he could hear me. I tried the handle. Yup, it was locked. I pounded my fist against the door again.

The door behind me opened, and his sister Tillie stepped into the hallway.

"Hi," I said with a pained smile.

"Hey, Gabby." She held up a straightened paperclip. "He's being an asshole. Excuse my language." She shrugged. "You just have to go inside. My dad drags him out twice a week and makes him shower, but he won't let anyone mess with his face, so he looks like Teen Wolf. And he'll probably yell at you."

I nodded slowly, taking the paperclip from her. The last time I saw him, he was sad, but he hugged me. He even tried to kiss me. And he braided my hair. What changed?

After unlocking the door, I slowly opened it and poked my head inside. He looked up from the floor where he sat in the middle of a pile of Legos.

No smile.

No words.

Just a brief glance before adding a new Lego to whatever he was building. Tillie was right; he had a beard that was longer than I had ever seen it. Ben looked thirty, not nineteen.

A pile of broken instruments cluttered the floor next to his open, bifold mirrored closet doors. A splintered guitar and cello. Something resembling a saxophone that looked more like a car after a head-on collision. My heart felt equally destroyed. What happened to my friend?

I closed the door behind me.

"Leave," he said without looking at me.

I grabbed a notebook and pen from his messy desk.

I'm sorry this happened to you. But you can't shut me out.

I set the piece of paper on the Legos in front of him. Without reading it, he ripped it into pieces and continued his building.

Why didn't you write back?

Again, he ripped the paper before reading it.

I cleared an area on the floor and kneeled a few feet in front of him.

"Look at me," I said, ducking my head to try to put my face in his line of sight.

He ignored me.

I reached for his hand, and he smacked mine. My heart ached, but I took a breath and pushed through my pain because I knew it wasn't about me. When I leaned forward to press my hands to his cheeks, he shoved me.

"Ouch!" I seethed, falling backward. The unforgiving edges of Legos dug into my hands. Tears filled my eyes for many reasons, but Ben didn't give me a single glance. He kept building like he didn't just shove me, like I wasn't in physical and emotional pain, like I didn't exist.

With a ragged breath and tears streaming down my face, I grabbed two fists full of Legos and threw them at him.

He flinched, gaze shooting to me with pure anger in his eyes. I threw more Legos at him. "You're so selfish! You could be dead, but you're alive! Stop acting like your world ended!" He batted away the Legos and stood, hooking his arm around my waist and tossing me out of his room, slamming and locking the door.

His parents rushed up the stairs as Tillie came out from her room.

"Oh my gosh! Are you okay?" Carmen asked.

"Open this door right now!" Alan banged on the door. "Where's a paperclip?" he asked Tillie, face red, and fists clenched.

"No," I said, fixing my hair. "I'm fine." I wiped the tears from my face and tried to find a smile to convey that I was okay, even though I was far from it. "I shouldn't have gone in there. It was my fault." My voice shook. "Please, just let him be like I should have done."

Alan's rigid posture relaxed a fraction. "He has no business treating you that way. I don't care what happened to him."

I shook my head. "It's my fault. I got frustrated and threw Legos at him. But I'm just going to go home now." I scurried down the stairs before my next round of tears released. I didn't know if my parents were outside, but I needed to get out of the house.

"Gabby?" Carmen called, but I didn't stop.

As soon as I opened the door, I felt relief that my parents had waited for me even though I told them not to. I ran toward the car.

Mom stepped out and hugged me as I broke down.

"It's m-my fault, and h-he h-hates me ..."

"No, baby. That's not true."

I didn't argue with her. She was my mom, and moms were hardwired to be cheerleaders for their kids. But I knew the truth; I was the worst thing that ever happened to Benjamin Ashford.

Chapter Twenty

Roxette, "Listen to Your Heart"

Gabby

When we arrived home, I headed straight to my room with my bag, but before I could get my door shut, my sisters filed inside.

"What happened? Did you get into a fight with Mom and Dad?" Sarah asked.

"No," I murmured. "I'm not like you two."

"Ouch," Eve said, sitting on my bed, but she knew exactly why I said that.

"Is it about Matt?" Sarah asked.

I looked at Eve, and her face confirmed Sarah had told her.

"No." I stared out the window.

"Ben?" Eve asked.

I didn't answer.

"Want to talk?" Sarah wrapped her arms around me, resting her chin on my shoulder.

As much as my sisters and I fought over the years, when one of us struggled, we all banded together to help. But there wasn't anything they could do.

"Ben is so angry," I whispered.

"You can't blame him. He needs time," Sarah parroted what everyone else said.

After being so violently rejected, I understood why they said that, but I didn't understand how time would matter unless it gave him his hearing back.

"Let's talk about Matt," Eve said.

Sarah released me as I turned. The sour expression on her face said she wasn't as enthusiastic to talk about Matt. Eve gave me a sly grin. Despite all that she'd gone through to find love, she still enjoyed stirring up trouble.

"Did you sleep with him?" Eve waggled her eyebrows.

"Stop," Sarah warned her. "Of course she didn't sleep with him." She eyed me. "Right?"

"Is it a problem if I did?"

"Oh man." Eve covered her mouth and snorted.

Sarah's lips pressed into a hard line as she shrugged. "No. Why? Did you?"

"Yes. And FYI, he had no problem putting on a condom. And he's *huge*. And I had seven orgasms."

Eve and Sarah looked at each other as if deciding which one would break the news that no one had seven orgasms. And I knew that, but I just wanted to say something to shut them up.

"I don't want to talk about Matt or Ben. I don't want to talk about school. Can't you two talk about yourselves, your perfect boyfriends, and your perfect lives?"

"I'll go first." Eve raised her hand.

Sarah scowled at Eve. "Gabby, I know you don't want to talk about Ben, but Mom said you've called her every day to do just that." At nearly twenty-three, Sarah already sounded like a mother, self-burdened with a need to fix everything and everyone around her.

I wasn't broken, but Ben was. However, after seeing him, I wasn't sure he could ever be fixed.

"What if he never hears again?" I exhaled. "What if he spends the rest of his life on the floor in his bedroom, playing with Legos in a deafening silence? What if he hates his family, friends, God, and life in general? How can anyone make him feel anything but sorry for himself?"

"Gabbs," Eve said, shifting her demeanor to a more serious sentiment, "speaking from my own experience, it's probably not going to be his family or friends who help him see light and feel hope again. It will be someone he probably hasn't met yet. Or it will be another life-changing event that wakes him up, and gives him a different outlook on life. And I know that sucks because you and everyone else want to fix him."

"Duh, I know I can't fix him. He's deaf. If they can't do surgery and hearing aids won't work, he'll never be fixed."

"What Eve means is everyone wants him to accept what has happened. They want him to embrace his new life, adapt to his disability, and move in a new direction. And maybe (we all hope) that he will. But he's doing it on his own time. You can't rush him. This isn't a nightmare that he needs to wake up from. This is his life, his new reality. Grieving the loss of someone, or in his case, something, is a lifelong process. You're never really 'fine.' You just figure out a way to move past the part where you hate God and everyone who tells you it's going to be okay. Acceptance becomes your new world, and each day you find yourself clawing another inch out of a dark hole in search of light—in search of hope."

"No one died," I murmured.

Sarah squeezed my hand. "If I could never sing, play, or hear music again, it would feel like the most irreplaceable loss."

"More than if you lost Isaac?"

She shrugged one shoulder. "Isaac is a man. And I love him so much. And if you tell him this, I will kill you." She pointed a finger in warning at both Eve and me. "But there are other men in the world. It would feel impossible at first, but I could love again. But if I lost music, there's nothing that would ever feel like a second chance. There's not another music. It would feel like a death."

I stared out the window again, willing my next round of tears to go away.

"But seriously, Kyle hooks both of my legs over his shoulders and does this thing with his tongue ..." Eve's comment was insensitive, ill-timed, and exactly what I needed.

I turned. Sarah looked horrified, as if she was afraid to breathe. Eve bit her lips together, her wide eyes unblinking. And just like that, those tears vanished.

That's what we did; that was our thing. We took really awful situations and worked through them together until we were a pile of flailing arms, kicking feet, and laughter on the bed.

Chapter Twenty-one

Bon Jovi, "Bad Medicine"

Ben

Cochlear damage.

Fibrosis and ossification.

Cochlear spiral ganglion.

Sensorineural damage.

There were too many scribbled words for me to comprehend. The good news? I was alive. The bad news? Hearing aids wouldn't work for my kind of hearing loss, and I wasn't the best candidate for cochlear implants, not to mention they were expensive and not covered by insurance.

I could technically hear, but nothing was distinguishable. It was like I was in an apartment and the people in the apartment below me were speaking. I could hear faint sounds but not words.

Even in a roomful of people, I felt lost and lonely. Seeing everyone's lips move and gazes flitting to and from me only made me feel paranoid that they were talking about me. Occasionally, I tried to laugh when other people would laugh or smile on cue. I felt like a mirror, reflecting everything around me.

It was easier to be in my room, but every day spent in isolation brought its own side effects, feeding my anger at everything and everyone. And I didn't know how to make it stop. So it grew and grew until it became my whole existence.

People are assholes

I ripped up every piece of paper anyone shoved in my face or slid under my door, except the lined pink paper. Those were from Tillie, my fifteen-year-old sister who was in a serious Madonna phase with short, edgy blond hair, heavy eye makeup, ripped denim, and high-top sneakers. She also pierced her own ears, which resulted in a nasty infection that lasted several weeks.

Her notes didn't make me smile, but they came close. I felt like there was still happiness somewhere inside of me, but I couldn't find it. Every day, anger won. I responded.

AM I "PEOPLE"?

A few seconds later, she slid the paper back under my door.

No. I'm talking about that jerk who threw Gabby into the hallway. HE'S a real asshole. My brother would never do that.

I read her words twice. Seeing Gabby hurt the most because I loved her the most. But she didn't love me the same way. Still, I'd thought I could prove that I was better than the baseball player turned lawyer. I was going to be a famous conductor who would write entire symphonies for her.

Overnight, I turned into her disabled friend with no future. I wanted all of her except her pity, but that's all she'd ever be able to give me. And suddenly, I didn't know how to be her friend with no hope of anything more.

Did that make me an asshole? Absolutely.

YOUR BROTHER WAS AWESOME. TOO BAD HE DIED.

I returned the paper. In the next breath, the door vibrated against my back. She was banging on it.

I stood and opened it a fraction. Tillie shoved her whole body into it until I took a step back to let her inside. She grabbed my shirt with both hands and tried to shake me; her lips moving while her eyes reddened with angry emotion.

Shaking my head, I narrowed my eyes. She slapped the piece of paper onto my desk and scribbled another note on the back of our original messages. Then she shoved the paper into my chest like she was punching me.

You don't get to leave this world! Do you understand? If you kill yourself, I will kill myself too!

I studied her for a few seconds before looking at the

paper again. Then I flipped it over to reread our previous notes.

TOO BAD HE DIED.

I shook my head a half dozen times. "That's not what I meant," I said.

Tillie looked deep into my eyes for a few seconds.

"That's not what I meant," I said, hugging her.

She pulled away, giving me a look that she learned from our mom. It was the silent scolding. After glancing around my room, Tillie eyed a framed picture face down on my nightstand. She set it upright. It was a picture of me giving Gabby a piggyback ride through our yard after a rare, record-breaking January snowstorm. She wore a big smile while trying to catch snow on her tongue. My mom took it from the living room window.

Tillie pointed to the picture and shook her head, more silent scolding. There was so much she didn't know and couldn't understand. To my family, it looked like Gabby was trying to be there for me, writing me letters and visiting me over Thanksgiving break. But they didn't know about the kiss. They didn't know how much I ached to mean as much to her as she meant to me.

I wasn't proud of my selfish heart wanting everything from her, nor was I in control of it. Feelings weren't a choice; they were a reaction to the mind rejecting logic. I was certain of it. After all, who would willingly choose to fall in love with someone who was in love with another?

Chapter Twenty-Two

Def Leppard, "Love Bites"

Gabby

I SMILED ON CUE, nodded, and answered "fine" to everything I was asked on Thanksgiving.

How's school? Fine.

How's your roommate? Fine.

Do you like the campus? It's fine.

Then Grandma Bonnie asked me another question. "How's Ben's hearing?" she asked.

I stared at my plate, absentmindedly rearranging my turkey and mashed potatoes. "He's deaf, but shit happens." My knee-jerk response silenced everyone at the dinner table, but it took me several seconds to register the words that fell from my lips.

Swearing wasn't my thing, and definitely not in front of my parents in the middle of Thanksgiving dinner. And the insensitive tone wasn't me either. There must have been a low level of anger that I was suppressing, then boom! It came out at the worst time.

As I glanced up, everyone gawked at me, except Eve. She grinned like a proud older sister.

"Well," Grandma Bonnie cleared her throat. "It's too bad that *stuff* happened to him. He's so young with his whole life ahead of him. I can only imagine how devastated he must feel."

"That's," I tried to recover with something between a sincere grin and regretful cringe, "what I meant. Devastated."

And cruel.

Mean.

Unrecognizable.

"Ben doesn't want to see anyone right now," Mom said. "So Gabby's a little sad that her best friend won't let her be there for him. We just have to keep him in our prayers."

I kept him in my prayers. I prayed for him to get food poisoning this Thanksgiving, and to fall on his pile of Legos and end up with a few lodged into his dumb, stubborn ass.

And when I wasn't praying for him, I was praying for myself—asking God to forgive me for thinking such awful things. I didn't really hate him; I hated how he shut me out of his life.

After dinner, my sisters and I helped clean the kitchen, then I escaped to my room, thinking about calling Ben's sister to get an update. Was he eating Thanksgiving dinner with them? Or was he still hiding in his room? Had he shown any remorse for how he treated me?

"Take off your clothes."

I turned toward Eve after staring at my phone for more than a minute.

"Why?" I glanced down at my shirt. There was nothing on it.

"You love Ben. Take off your clothes for him. No guy can stay mad at a naked woman."

I scoffed. "Then what? Dance?"

"No." Eve snorted. "Well, maybe. That would be quite the picture. It might brighten his day. But I was thinking you could then take off his clothes."

"Sex? You think the solution to him losing his hearing is sex?"

"No, Gabby. I don't think you have a magical vagina. I'm just saying it could break the ice between you two."

"Sex isn't an icebreaker."

"How do you know until you try?"

"I'm not you, Eve. I don't just ride a guy for the heck of it."

She chuckled, gathering her long brown hair over her shoulder while sitting next to me. "Maybe you should."

"You're going to Hell, and there's nothing anyone can do to save you at this point."

"Duh. I know that. So does the rest of the world." She nudged my shoulder with hers.

I didn't want to laugh. Damnation was no joke.

"Can you even imagine what it must be like to not hear?"

I slowly shook my head.

"Well, I don't know how he feels, but I can imagine just from my own experience with shitty tragedies that he's feeling scared and lonely. Lost and confused. He may never hear anyone speak to him again. Sure, he'll read words on a paper. He might even learn sign language. But he'll never hear his favorite song or the whisper of a lover in his ear while making love. However, he can still see the beauty of a woman's body. And he can feel her fingernails digging into his back and her breath on his cheek. He can see stars behind his eyes, and waves of pleasure as an orgasm rips through his body. And for a moment, he might even forget that he can't hear."

Fire ignited in my cheeks and down my neck. Eve talked about sex with the ease of reading off a grocery list.

I cleared my throat. "Just because you slept with my math teacher doesn't mean I'm going to take advice from you."

She giggled. "Your math teacher was so hot. I wonder what happened to him?"

I smirked. "I heard he got ran out of town after a sex scandal."

Eve stood and held out her hand. "Come eat pie. You don't have to choose between Heaven and Hell right now."

On Friday, I shopped with my mom and sisters.

On Saturday, I returned to Ben's house to see him one last time before going back to school.

"He ate Thanksgiving dinner with us, but since then, he's been locked in his room again," Carmen said as I slid off my wool jacket and hung it on the hook. "Did you and your family have a nice Thanksgiving?"

I smiled. "Yes. Thanks for asking." I stepped toward the stairs with a lot more hesitation than I had the day he tossed me out of his room.

"Tillie is in her room. She'll get him to open his door."

I nodded nervously while mumbling a soft, "Okay."

Madonna blared from Tillie's room, and it broke my

heart to think that Ben couldn't hear it and yell at his sister to turn down her "stupid music," because he wasn't a Madonna fan. Ben preferred more sophisticated music.

I came prepared, pulling a paperclip out of my pocket and straightening it to open Ben's door. There didn't seem to be any point in knocking first. In hindsight, I should have announced my arrival with a note under his door. Ben's back was to me, hair wet, green towel around his waist, and rivulets of water running down his back. He dropped his towel, and I slapped my hand over my mouth to muffle my gasp, realizing in the next second that he couldn't hear me.

Having never seen a naked man, I had no comparison, but my best friend was hot. Broad shoulders, trim waist, tight butt, and defined muscles. He pulled on a pair of white briefs and turned. His eyebrows shot up his forehead as water dripped from his shaggy, wet bangs.

I jumped back into the hallway and closed his door. A few seconds later, Tillie emerged from her room.

"Oh, hey Gabby." She grinned. "Just a second," she said, stepping back into her messy bedroom then returning with a paperclip.

Before I could say anything, she jabbed it into the round hole, stabbing it in different directions. "Hmm ..." she turned the knob. "Oh. Wow. He didn't have it locked." She pushed open the door.

Ben eyed both of us with a cautious expression. He had on gray sweatpants and a white T-shirt. Tillie waved at him and mouthed, "Be nice."

Was he reading lips?

I was on the fence between stepping back into his room and running away. Ben broke eye contact first, sitting on his bed to put on his white tube socks. On a deep breath, I stepped into his room and closed his door behind me. There was no hiding the residual embarrassment that lingered like a warm washcloth over my face.

I navigated the minefield of Legos to get to his desk where I picked up a pen to write something. But what? Suddenly, I'd forgotten why I was there or what I wanted to say. Seeing my best friend naked messed with my train of thought. Was I there to apologize? It's not like I did anything wrong. He's the one who kicked me out of his room. Maybe I was there to tell him goodbye and good luck for ... being deaf? Closing my eyes, I shook my head at that stupid thought.

Was I there to take off my clothes? If so, he beat me to it. My stripping would have felt like a copycat.

I started to write on the notebook paper.

I'm

That's it. That was as much as I could think of. I was what? Never had I felt such a loss for words around Ben. Just the opposite. He was used to enduring my long spiels about everything from my sisters to how lucky he was to be a boy and therefore had no menstrual cycles. Everything came easily with Ben. He'd been an extension of myself. We had no secrets. No lines. In fact, nothing in life felt real until I told Ben, and I had always thought he felt the same.

But writing the words was different, and I don't know why it felt so hard. Writing was easy for me. I wrote all my feelings in the margins of books or the blank pages of journals. My every emotion and entire existence had been recorded in ink.

I X'd out the word and set the pen on the notebook.

Then I noticed the pile of unopened letters I sent him. He was completely shutting me out, so I made my way to him, finding a few open spaces to step. He looked so sad with his forlorn eyes, downturned lips, and curled shoulders.

I wedged my way between his legs to stand as close to him as possible, simultaneously bracing for him to physically kick me out of his room. When he didn't move, I pressed my palms to his cheeks, the softness of his beard teased my skin. When he closed his eyes and leaned into my touch, it made my chest ache. To distract myself from the tears burning my eyes, I leaned in and kissed him. It was slow and easy, unlike our previous kisses. A leisurely stroll in the park on a sunny afternoon. At first, I couldn't tell if he was kissing me back, but then his hands slid up the back of my legs and he leaned into the kiss.

Those tears burned hotter instead of going away. I'd missed him so much. The longing and loneliness mixed with the guilt and uncertainty had left me feeling broken and lost. My nerves were replaced with need.

I needed Ben to hold me, piece me back together like one of his Lego creations. As I threaded my fingers through his damp hair, he guided my legs, one at a time, to straddle his lap without breaking our kiss. He made a noise that sounded like a drawn-out groan, and I wondered if he could hear himself. As he flicked my tongue with the tip of his, he hugged me to him, laying me on his bed with his pelvis cradled between my legs.

We kissed for what felt like forever, yet I never wanted it to end. I liked kissing my best friend, and I wanted to tell him as much, but he couldn't hear me. That brought more tears to my eyes, so I turned my head to catch a shaky breath while Ben kissed along my jaw to my ear and down my neck.

JEWEL E. ANN

When his mouth returned to my face, he opened his eyes, seeing the first few tears escape.

His brow tightened, and his lips moved, saying something, but his attempted whisper wasn't audible, but it looked like, "Are you okay?"

I quickly nodded and lifted my head to kiss him again. He rested his elbows on either side of my head and brushed his thumbs along my wet cheeks while we kissed. A soft hum unexpectedly escaped my chest, and he must have felt it because, in the next breath, he rocked his pelvis. His erection pressed firmly against me.

It made my heart skip a beat before sprinting out of the gate. What were we doing?

Ben lifted his head, his lips hovering over mine as he gazed into my eyes and thrust his hips again. My breath caught. It felt foreign and forbidden, but it also felt good.

He whispered, "Is this okay?"

I nodded a half dozen times before kissing him and closing my eyes. I couldn't look at him because I was too afraid he'd see my vulnerability. Everything was novel and unexpected. I didn't know where it was going, but as a flood of new feelings hijacked my body, I didn't want him to mistake my nerves for fear and then decide to stop.

For the record, I wasn't stupid despite the sixty-nine misunderstanding. I knew why it felt good. I'd passed my anatomy class. But it was the firsthand experience that was new to me. The fullness in my breasts. The pressure building between my legs. The euphoric jolt I experienced every time the bulge behind his sweatpants rubbed just the right spot between my legs.

We kissed for a while, but then he broke the kiss to catch his breath, eyelids heavy as he worked his erection against

208

me harder. I curled my fingers, digging my nails into his back. My thoughts jumbled between wondering what was happening and berating myself for thinking it ... because I knew. And I had no idea where it fell on the spectrum of sins. We were fully clothed. It wasn't sex. But it was ... something.

It was *something* the way I dug my heels into the mattress and lifted my body toward his.

It was *something* the way he kissed me so hard I felt like we would be melded together forever.

It was *something* the way he grabbed a fistful of sheets above my head while every muscle in his body went rigid.

But the biggest *something* of all was the explosion of sensations that ricocheted through my body in wave after wave as my heart throbbed in my chest.

Ben rested his forehead on mine as we exchanged breaths in our little cocoon. Then he slowly deposited kisses over all of my face, even my eyelids as they drifted shut. Without a word, because there were no words, he rolled onto his side and pulled me into his embrace. I nuzzled my face into his neck, and we took a long Saturday afternoon nap.

Chapter Twenty-Three

INXS, "Never Tear Us Apart"

Ben

It was a pity dry hump.

And I knew it, but I still allowed it to happen.

Did she orgasm? Undoubtedly.

Was it her first? I didn't know.

But I couldn't stop wondering if I was the schmuck grinding into her, fully clothed, after Mr. Baseball Star Future Attorney had already taken her virginity. I wasn't stupid. He was a guy with needs, and Gabby was the girl who had fawned over him for years.

I knew she would save herself for marriage, not letting any guy past first base, or she would lose every inhibition and prove her dad right: College was a sinner's haven.

Either way, she would go back to her dream man while I stayed in my parents' house, putting together Legos in the silence of a living nightmare.

Gabby stirred, moving her hands between us and drawing a heart on my chest. God, I wanted it to be real. I wanted a lot of things, but it didn't mean I could have any of them. She sat up, letting her legs hang off the side of the bed while twisting her body toward me. Had I not been deaf and a pain in everyone's side, no one would have allowed us to be in my bedroom alone with the door closed.

She gave me a shy smile. I took a mental picture, knowing that I'd take a lot more of them since the soundtrack to my life was over.

Gabby stood, grabbing the paper and pen before sitting on the edge of my bed again.

I'm going to miss you, but I'll be back in a few weeks for Christmas break.

I read it and nodded my response.

Why were you so mad?

"Because I hate my fucking life," I said.

Gabby flinched. After chewing on the corner of her bottom lip, she started doing weird things with her hands.

"I don't know what you're doing," I said.

She stopped and scribbled more words on the paper.

You'd know if you'd learn sign language.

"You learned it?"

She nodded with a big smile, then her nose crinkled while she held up her thumb and forefinger an inch apart.

A little.

"Well, go find some other deaf person who gives a shit."

She shoved my chest, her lips moving a mile a minute, face red. Then she wrote another message.

I've been taking ASL three nights a week JUST to talk to you. Why are you being such a jerk?

Because you deserve better than me.

But I couldn't tell her that. She wouldn't see it or understand.

"Good job making it about you, Gabbs," I said, staring at the ceiling. "Everyone makes it about them. How they feel. All the things they've done. How their life has changed. Unless you can give me my hearing back, then leave me the hell alone."

You blame me.

She shoved the paper in my face.

No. I could never blame her, but maybe she'd run and save herself if I didn't deny it.

I laughed. "Still about you."

What am I supposed to say?

"What are you supposed to say? Again ... still about you."

I hate that this happened to you!

"You. You. You. It's always about you. You're in love with Matt. You follow him to college. You can't stop talking about him. You don't know how to kiss. You need other people to take you to a party. You feel bad for kissing me when you're supposed to kiss him. You avoid me because you're uncomfortable. You don't understand why I've dropped out of school. The whole fucking world doesn't revolve around you."

Except it did. My world revolved around her, but I couldn't tell her because I was scared it would burden her to be the center of my world.

My. Shitty. Awful. World.

So it was easier, maybe even necessary, to push her away.

Gabby stood with a blank expression, then she lifted her arm, making a fist before slowly raising her middle finger.

It took everything I had left, which wasn't much, to keep from grinning. I didn't recognize the girl flipping me off. Did I create her? Mold her from my miserable existence? Did I sharpen her with each lash of my tongue?

Her lips moved into a slow and undeniable "fuck you." For that one moment, I liked not hearing her. It had a grander effect to think she was mouthing the words, craftily clinging to a piece of her Biblical innocence by choosing a muted gesture.

"Did you learn that in ASL?" I smirked.

Keeping her chin high, she pivoted, took all the unopened letters she sent me, and exited my bedroom.

I was the world's biggest asshole, by plan, of course. I loved her too much to accept her pity. I loved her too much to let her be with anyone but Matthew Fucking Cory.

I loved her too much.

I loved her more than she loved me.

Chapter Twenty-Four

Tears For Fears, "Head Over Heels"

Gabby

"Was your break better than mine?" Olivia asked as we unpacked our bags Sunday night. "My parents spent the whole time fighting. I couldn't wait to leave."

"It was fine," I said, returning to my favorite word.

"Did you see Ben?"

"Yeah."

"How's he doing?"

I grunted. "He's taking self-pity to a new level. I bet he could get into the *Guinness Book of Records* with his level of pity."

"Seriously? That doesn't seem like Ben. I thought he was more confident and positive than that."

"Well, Olivia, it's not about you and what you think."

"What?" She laughed. "I didn't mean—"

I shook my head. "I'm kidding. That's just what Ben

kept throwing at me. I couldn't say anything that involved the word I or me. I can't believe he treated me that way after ..."

"After what? Everything you've been through?"

"Yeah. That too."

"You're acting weird. I told you, I'm not crushing on him or anything like that. You can totally tell me everything."

I twisted my lips, considering what good could come from telling her. Probably nothing. But I needed to vent. "We did something, and afterward, he was so mean that I didn't recognize him. Then I did something I've never done, and it felt really good in the moment, but now I regret it. I don't like when someone brings out the worst in me, and that's what he did."

She shook her head. "You lost me. What did you do?"

I wrinkled my nose. "I gave him the middle finger."

"Oh. Wow. You?" Again, she shook her head. "But no. I don't mean that. You said 'we did something.' What did you and Ben do?"

I bit my thumbnail.

Olivia's eyes widened. "Oh my god. Did you have sex?"

"No. Well, kind of, but not really."

"What does that mean? Oral sex?"

I shook my head.

"He fingered you?"

Another headshake.

"Anal?"

My eyes bulged. "No!"

"Then what?"

I folded and refolded the same pair of jeans.

"I'm your friend." Olivia laughed. "You can tell me."

"Our clothes stayed on the whole time, but we kissed

and he was on top of me, and we sort of ..." I tugged at my sweatshirt's neck, feeling really warm.

"Like he ..." she stood and thrust her hips, which only doubled my embarrassment.

"Stop!" I covered my face. "Yes. That."

"You dry humped. Just say it."

I dropped my hands. "What?"

Olivia giggled. "Have you never heard of dry humping?"

I didn't respond.

"It's rubbing your genitals together with your clothes on. No bodily fluid is exchanged, so it's, you know ... dry." Olivia was a sex encyclopedia.

I nodded several times.

"Did you orgasm? I'm sure he did. Men will hump anything."

I winced.

"Oh. No!" She shook her head. "I didn't mean it that way, like you're not special, like him dry humping you is equivalent to a dog humping someone's leg."

"Wow. Thanks."

Olivia's giggles intensified. "I just meant that a guy always orgasms, well maybe not *always*, but most of the time."

I tucked my chin and unzipped my toiletry bag. College was a painful experience for the inexperienced.

"Hey, there's nothing wrong with a good dry hump. It's a useful tool for getting off in public situations. I once dry humped with a guy during a football game. I was sitting on his lap, and we had a blanket over us. It was probably the best one I've ever experienced because we had to go so slowly that by the time I came, I was dying."

Olivia having a ranking of her best to worst dry humping

experiences didn't help me feel better. It made me regret not having sex with Matt. My virginity no longer felt like a trophy or even a gift to be given to my future husband. It made me feel like Linus Van Pelt sucking my thumb while hugging a security blanket.

"I did," I said with as much confidence as possible.

"Did what?"

I cleared my throat. "Um ... orgasmed," I mumbled without going into detail about it being my first one.

"Did you both do it at the same time? That's the best! Or did you go first and have to wait for him to finish grinding it out?"

Grinding was never a word I equated with any part of sex. I was more of a making-love girl. A synchronized rhythmic dance. A well-choreographed ballet with a symphony and Ben as the conductor.

"Together," I said. Gosh, it was so hot in the room.

"That's good because if he comes first, you're on your own to finish later. Men are too lazy. They don't know how to fake it like women. They just blow their wad and quit. So we're like, 'Oh, you're done? Yeah, me too. Oh, God! Yes. Yes. YES! It was so good.' But not guys. If you come first, they don't care, they just keep on riding along, taking their sweet time. I don't know why we feel like it's okay to not only let them be quitters, but to stroke their ego at the same time. Our moms warned us about guys like that, but sometimes you don't know what you're getting until it's too late."

First, my mom never warned me about guys who failed to keep going until I orgasmed. My mom never said the word orgasm. Second, I was in *way* over my head. Olivia did proverbial back handsprings off a balance beam while I did one somersault on a crash pad. The most embarrassing part was I felt so proud of myself, like such a woman. There was even a moment afterward that I prayed I wasn't pregnant.

Two DAYS later I mailed Ben a letter.

Dear Ben,

Sorry I gave you the finger. You were a jerk, but I forgive you. Also, sorry I've used the word "I" three times. Let's try this instead. Gabby misses you already. Olivia says hi and so does Jason. Can you believe there's six inches of snow here and it's not even Christmas yet? Remember how excited we used to get when it snowed in Devil's Head?

Gabby has a test in social science tomorrow that she's not ready for. She's envious that you got straight A's. Are you excited for your birthday? Gabby wishes she could be with you that day. She'll bring your present when she's there for Christmas? Speaking of Christmas, have you thought about what you want? Gabby wants mittens. Her gloves are not that warm. She needs to keep her fingers together.

Gabby hopes you don't regret what happened, except the part where you were a jerk. Gabby thinks you're a phenomenal kisser. Gabby hopes you don't let anyone else read this letter. Mostly Gabby hopes you write her back.

Love,
Gabby

Ben didn't reply.

The following week, I sent Ben a birthday card. Again, no reply.

Then the week before heading home for Christmas break, Olivia had news.

"I hope you don't hate me," she said, two seconds after getting back to the dorm room after her last class.

I looked up from my text book. "I don't like where this is going."

"Cassidy and Becky are moving to an apartment and they asked me if I wanted to move in with them. It's three bedrooms, and they need one more person. I talked to my parents, and they're fine with it." She wrinkled her nose. "So I'm moving out at the end of the semester."

I didn't have a good response, but as soon as I opened my mouth to ask her a question, she added, "If they don't need to move someone in with you, you'll have this whole room to yourself. That's pretty awesome, right?"

"Sure. I suppose." I shrugged.

"Are you mad that I'm leaving you? I know it's been hard since Ben left, but I really want to live off campus."

"It's fine." I returned my attention to my text book, rereading the same sentence because nothing was sticking in my brain.

Ben consumed a majority of my thoughts, but Matt still occupied space along with the pressure of finals. I wasn't sure I had the mental capacity to think about Olivia moving out. It wasn't like we were best buddies. We were roommates who occasionally ate together and talked about sex, but she spent most of her evenings and weekends with Becky and Cassidy or on a date. Moving to the bottom bunk was a big bonus.

"Are you sure?" She hugged me from behind. "I'll still come visit you."

I laughed. "It's fine."

"If Ben comes to visit, you two can get it on without worrying about me interrupting."

I couldn't imagine a world where Ben would visit me, so I just replied with a tight-lipped smile.

A week later, with no word from Ben, I headed home for Christmas.

Chapter Twenty-Five

Richard Marx, "Right Here Waiting"

Ben

EVEN I WAS sick of myself. The monotony of each day mixed with a lack of direction and a nonexistent level of motivation was not only exhausting, it was annoying. But what was the alternative? How was I supposed to get motivated? That wasn't something I could pull out of thin air.

I never took the time to formulate a Plan B. Music was my first love. The possibility of going deaf never entered my conscience. Blind, sure. I had a BB gun, and my sister liked to use it and was a terrible shot. Even losing a hand while working in the meat department of the grocery store or becoming a paraplegic from a car accident would not have shocked me.

Perhaps, aside from death, going deaf was the most unimaginable thing for someone like me. Therefore, I just ... never imagined it.

However, after dry humping my best friend, which was better than any actual sex I had ever had because it was Gabby, I scrounged enough joy to leave my room for a birthday dinner and to help decorate the house for Christmas.

Did I open the letter Gabby sent? No.

The card? Nope.

Why? Well, that was a good question. The answer wasn't so simple. It laid between a lack of self-esteem and the fear that, without music, I'd try to make her my whole world. Being someone's everything sounded romantic, but it was a lot of pressure. To love her the way she deserved, I had to want her more than I needed her.

Without the ability to hear, I felt pretty fucking needy.

Tillie poked her head into my bedroom and pointed to her watch. I nodded, adjusting my red tie in the mirror. I was going to church for the first time since losing my hearing. It was for my mom. She wanted the whole family there since it was the Sunday before Christmas.

I dragged my feet on the way to the car. "I need to pee once more," I said.

Mom frowned and her lips moved before I moseyed back into the house, wasting more time. My goal was to get to the service no more than a minute or two before it started, so I didn't have to endure watching everyone smile and try to communicate with me. Also, Gabby was home from school, and I hadn't seen her yet. I needed a little more time to figure out what to say or how to act. Since I wouldn't hear the sermon, I could watch her the whole time and gauge her demeanor and mood.

After pissing a full ounce, checking my tie again, and grabbing gum from my desk drawer, I returned to the car.

Mom continued to scowl at me while Dad rolled his eyes and Tillie smirked. I shrugged like I'd done nothing wrong.

As planned, we arrived just as Gabby's dad, Pastor Jacobson, walked to the lectern. He smiled and said something, then the congregation bowed their heads in prayer. Our family squeezed into a small space in the last row of pews. I followed the lead a minute later when everyone sat down.

Hearing virtually nothing in my bedroom or among my immediate family was weird. Hearing faint sounds as the choir stood to lead everyone in song was jarring. I felt like an outsider looking in, removed from reality—a ghost.

As I surveyed the packed sanctuary, my gaze snagged on Gabby, glancing over her shoulder at me from the front row, standing next to her mom. She didn't smile, nor did she give me the middle finger, and after a few seconds, she returned her attention to the front of the church. For the following forty-five minutes, Gabby shot me an occasional quick glance and my mom elbowed me, pointing to her Bible as if I needed to follow along with the scripture even though I couldn't hear the sermon.

After church, the congregation spilled out of the front doors, some people heading straight to their cars, others huddling in small groups to talk despite the cold. My head swiveled when someone kicked the back of my shoe. Gabby sauntered to the side of the church. I waited a few seconds to slide away from my family who were chatting with our neighbors, then I meandered in the direction of the parking lot before redirecting to the side of the church.

Gabby wasn't there, so I continued to the back of building. There she stood with her hands in the pockets of her red wool coat, shoulders by her ears, and cheeks pink from the nippy air. I stopped several feet from her, and she stepped closer. No smile. No movement of her lips. Her right hand slid out of her pocket, and she held up her palm where she'd written words in blue ink.

You're a jerk.

I read it before looking at her face, and I replied with a slow nod.

She frowned as if my acceptance of her assessment somehow angered her more. Then she removed her other hand, balled into a fist, and opened it to reveal more words on that palm.

Kiss me anyway.

I read it several times before my gaze moved to hers. The corner of her mouth curled into a faint smile. That's when I should have turned and walked away. I couldn't kiss my best friend *and* push her away. It wasn't fair to give her mixed signals. It also wasn't fair that she looked so pretty in her white and green dress with a red ribbon around her waist. It wasn't fair that her lips were freshly glossed with her signature cherry ChapStick. Keeping my hands in my pockets, to keep things from getting out of hand, I bent down and kissed her.

Again, she didn't play fairly. As I started to pull away, her cold hands touched my cheeks, and she lifted onto her toes, pressing her chest into mine. I told my hands to stay put. No touching. Just wait it out and she'd release me. But she didn't. Gabby's tongue teased my upper lip. It was cruel.

What happened to the good girl who never would have

made out with a guy in her Sunday best behind her father's church? I wanted to say that I missed that girl, but it was hard with her lips on me.

The kiss ended when said lips lifted into a beaming smile. I wanted nothing more than to feel her warmth forever. She signed something with her hands.

I shook my head. "I told you I don't know sign language."

She shrugged before sauntering back toward the front of the church, tossing me a flirty grin over her shoulder at the last second.

I was terminally lovesick.

Chapter Twenty-Six

Thurl Ravenscroft, "You're a Mean One, Mr. Grinch"

Gabby

I CAVED.

Armed with the best intentions of giving Ben the cold shoulder, I tried not to look back at him during the service. After all, he didn't deserve anything from me after how he treated me over Thanksgiving and not responding to any of my letters. Then I made the mistake of taking a peek at him, and he looked so handsome in his suit. He also looked sad and lost.

Why did his parents make him attend church when he couldn't hear the music or the sermon? As soon as the question popped into my head, I let it spark a little hope that maybe he was there to see me. By the time I sneaked a half dozen unnecessary glances in his direction, my need to hug and kiss him was unbearable, so I wrote two messages on the palms of my hands.

His kiss didn't disappoint. Ben was either a spectacular kisser (even better than Matt) or I was biased.

"It was nice seeing Ben at church," Mom said as we ate Sunday dinner with Grandma Bonnie.

I wrinkled my nose at Mom's oyster soup. Was I being punished? She knew I hated it. "Yeah. I'm sure he enjoyed sitting in silence for forty-five minutes, watching Dad's lips move and his hands make a bunch of gestures. I mean, Dad..." I grinned "...if you're going to use your hands so much when you talk, then you should learn sign language."

Dad wiped his mouth. "Does Ben know sign language? The last time I talked with Alan, he said Ben wasn't interested in learning it."

I fished all the oysters out of my soup. "Well, I've been learning it, so I'm going to teach him."

Everyone at the table returned skeptical expressions.

"Since when?" Mom asked.

"Since Ben dropped out of school. It's a community education class I found in Ann Arbor. It's three nights a week."

"Why didn't you tell us?" Mom narrowed her eyes.

"I wanted it to be a surprise, mostly for Ben. But that's when I thought he would learn it. So when I was home over Thanksgiving and I found out he was not surprised or impressed that I'd been learning it, I lost my enthusiasm over telling anyone else. I didn't want anyone feeling sorry for me that I wasted time and money on it. But now since ..."

Since all I can think about is kissing Ben until he makes me orgasm.

I cleared my throat. No one needed to know my true motivation. "Since Ben seems to be less aggressive toward everyone, I'm going to convince him to let me teach him sign language. And I hope he then learns more on his own. He's pretty competitive, so maybe I can spark his interest."

"How are you going to convince him to let you teach him?" Grandma Bonnie asked.

I tucked my chin to hide my grin and focused on dumping a bunch of oyster crackers into the broth. It was the only way I could get it down. "I don't know yet, but I'll figure something out."

A lie.

I knew exactly how I was going to convince him—by taking Eve's advice.

On Monday, with two days until Christmas, I needed to finish up my Christmas shopping. So on my way to the mall, I stopped by Ben's house.

"Gabby, what a nice surprise," Carmen said, opening the front door and gesturing for me to come inside.

"Hi. I have some Christmas shopping to do. I thought Ben could come with me."

"Oh," she gave me a nervous smile, "I'm not sure he's out of bed yet."

I pushed up my jacket sleeve to look at my watch. It was a quarter to noon.

Carmen shook her head. "I know. He should be up by now. I never know what his mood will be, so I usually just let him get up on his own. When I wake him, he tends to be extra grumpy."

"Well, good thing I'm the one waking him today." I shrugged off my jacket, hung it on the hook, and headed up the stairs.

"Good luck," she said with a chuckle.

When I reached the top, I peeked into Tillie's room, but she wasn't there. I had my paperclip in my pocket, but when I tried the door handle, it was unlocked. The room was dim from the drawn shades, sans the light from his alarm clock. I softly closed the door behind me, and tiptoed toward his bed, praying I didn't step on any Legos.

I slid into bed with him, and he jumped.

"It's me," I said, but he continued to back away. "It's Gab —" I was an idiot. Why was it so easy to forget he couldn't hear?

I guided his hand to my face and my hair, and he relaxed.

"What are you doing?" His voice was faint and raspy.

I rubbed my nose along his neck before kissing it.

"What are you doing?" he repeated.

I grinned against his skin then kissed along his jaw toward his lips.

"Gabbs, we can't do this." He grabbed my wrists and climbed over me to get out of bed. After plucking things from his dresser drawers, he left the room.

I threw an arm over my face and breathed slowly. What was I doing? Before the rational part of my brain could answer, Ben returned and turned on the light. He wore jeans ripped above the knee and a gray T-shirt as wrinkled as his anguished face. It was the look my parents gave me any time I disappointed them.

On a slow deflate, I stood and grabbed paper and a pen from his desk.

I need to finish my Christmas shopping. Come with me.

He shook his head while balancing on one foot to pull on his socks.

You need to finish your Christmas shopping. I'll take you.

Ben stared at the paper with a dead expression.

It's not about ME. It's about YOU. Happy now?

His gaze lifted from the paper to my face, and I returned a toothy grin. As hard as he tried not to smile, the corner of his mouth twitched.

"I'm skipping Christmas," he said.

I tapped my temple and pulled my hand away with my thumb and pinkie finger pointed outward (the sign for "why") while saying it too.

As much as my signing seemed to irritate him, he couldn't pretend that he didn't understand what I asked. Once again, the unopened letter from me was on his desk. I made of show of ripping it into pieces before writing:

Why didn't you write me back?

After a brief glance at the paper, he sighed and ran his hands through his hair. I told myself I wouldn't be that person—the one who made everything about me. But what we did in his bed over Thanksgiving wasn't just about me; it was about us.

Do you regret it?

Tension pulled at his brow as he stared at the paper. "I don't know."

What was that supposed to mean? We didn't have sex. So why did he say that?

"We should just be friends." Every word he spoke dug into my heart, exposing its fragility.

Again, I signed, "Why?"

"Because our friendship should come first."

Ben always had a way of tripping up my thinking. I was a dreamer floating in the wind, and he was my gravity, my gentle anchor to reality. Of course, our friendship came first. Except, there was a "but" that came after that thought. I didn't know what came after the "but," *but* something did because we were friends.

Best friends.

But we were more.

"Don't overthink it," he said.

Reading each other's minds wasn't always a good thing. It made me feel so transparent in his eyes.

Why kiss me if we're just friends?

He shrugged and opened the blinds, letting the bright easterly sun hit me in the face. "You asked me to teach you. So I'm teaching you."

"Teaching me? Are you kidding me?" Anger bubbled up my chest and straight out of my mouth. I sighed and grumbled at the same time as he gave me his dead look because he couldn't hear me.

Just slow blinks.

Every time I spoke on instinct and he returned that expression, it felt like God was knocking the wind out of me. I turned and blinked back my stupid tears while scribbling something that was less about me.

Thank you for your help. I'm relieving you of your teaching duties. See you later.

Ben stared at the paper for longer than it took to read my words. "Thought you wanted to take me shopping," he murmured without lifting his gaze.

You said no.

He looked at me. "Now, I'm saying yes."

I wanted to give up and go home. Ben's awful attitude stole my Christmas cheer. But I had presents to buy, so I nodded before pivoting to head down the stairs. Ben followed me.

"You got him out of bed. That's a Christmas miracle," his mom said as we put on our coats and shoes by the front door.

I mustered the best smile I could despite my crestfallen heart. "Yeah. He's Scrooge for sure."

Ben stared at the floor when I looked at him. He had been so cruel to me; I shouldn't have felt sorry for him, but I did. It had to be awful knowing that people were talking around him, but he didn't know what was being said.

Then again, it was kind of his fault.

I tapped the bottom of his chin, making him look at me. Then I signed, "Learn ASL."

Of course, it only intensified said pouty face.

"Is that sign language?" Carmen asked.

I nodded, keeping my gaze locked with Ben's. "Yes. I'm taking a class three nights a week, but your stubborn son won't do the same. I don't know a lot. But I know some basics."

He narrowed his eyes at me, and I returned a tiny smirk.

"Wow, Gabby! This boy of mine doesn't know how lucky he is to have you in his life. I hope you can convince him to learn it, too, because Alan and I want to." She grabbed his arm to get his attention and slowly mouthed "be good" to him.

He frowned and nodded. "Yes, ma'am."

She hugged him while winking at me.

He could be the biggest jerk, but Ben loved his mom. And I loved that about him. If I ever had boys, I wanted them to respect me the same way.

After we pulled out of his long drive, I reached for the knob to turn on the radio but froze before turning my wrist. Then I slowly sat up and placed both hands on the steering wheel.

Ben didn't hesitate before turning it on ... all the way.

I flinched, fumbling with the knob to turn it off so it wouldn't blow out the speakers in my car. When I shot him a scowl, he turned away, focusing out his window. Again, tears burned my eyes.

It wasn't about me, and I resented my emotions for betraying my will to be strong. But witnessing the grief and the death of what felt like the essence of my best friend was too much for my immature heart to take.

Every time he rubbed or tugged at his ears, as if it were nothing more than water clogging them, a lump swelled in my throat. I would've given *anything* to take away his pain.

After finding a spot at the far end of the mall's parking

lot, I looped my arm around his and we headed inside. Ben's gaze ping-ponged in all directions. Music played and the Salvation Army bell ringer chimed behind us. With two days until Christmas, it was packed. Armed with a pen and small spiral notepad, I wrote:

Who do you need to shop for?

He shrugged.

Everyone?

He nodded.

We weaved in and out of stores. I managed to find clothes for my mom and sisters and two new ties for my dad. Whenever I held up something for one of Ben's parents or his sister, he just shrugged.

I frowned and made the executive decision on what to get.

After the presents were purchased, we grabbed lunch in the food court. No matter what I did or said, he looked miserable. As I sipped my drink, his gaze continued to survey our surroundings.

I thought I was a good kisser, but I think it's just you.

I tapped his arm with my pen, drawing his attention to my notepad.

He read it and eyed me.

I bit my lower lip to control my grin, but it still wasn't enough to get him to smile.

*What we did over Thanksgiving—I want to do it
again.*

I felt an unavoidable blush, but he still remained straight-faced except his lips parted and he wet them.

Without clothes.

I didn't care that everyone could see my red cheeks or that I needed to unbutton my jacket because just writing those words made me hot.

Ben narrowed his eyes a fraction and glanced over my shoulder returning a slight headshake.

I tried to hide my disappointment.

Did you not like it?

Again, he shrugged. I hated his stupid shrugs and dismissively quick glances.

Did he know how much I was putting myself out there for him? Exposing all my insecurities.

I have to use the restroom.

I scooted back in my chair, hiked my purse over my shoulder, and escaped before he could see my tears. After taking a few minutes in the stall to gain my composure, I washed my hands, and returned to the food court. But there was another couple at our table.

No Ben.

No bags.

I looked in both directions, but he was nowhere in sight.

I headed in one direction until I reached the far end of the mall, then I walked in the other direction, scanning everywhere to find him. Panic gripped me. He couldn't hear. Why did he leave me? Where did he go? How would he communicate with people if he needed to? I couldn't even go to the information desk to see if they would announce his name because he couldn't hear it.

People stared at me as I aimlessly darted in every direction wiping my tears. I had to call my mom or his mom. He was just gone.

As I waited in line for a payphone, wiping my tears, I looked out the glass entrance doors and there he was, leaned against the building with one leg propped up, the bags on the ground beside him, and his gaze pointed toward the parking lot.

"Why did you leave?" I yelled, on my way to him.

Ben startled when I grabbed his jacket and shook him. He narrowed his eyes.

"I was so scared. Why did you leave?"

He slowly shook his head, and I fumbled with my jacket to dig the pen and paper from my pocket.

Why did you leave? I was so scared!

He read my words then his gaze swept along my face before he wiped my tears.

"Sorry. A couple asked if they could have the table, so I figured you'd assume I was meeting you outside."

"Well, I didn't—" I sighed, stopping myself and writing it down.

Why would I assume that? Why not wait in the food court? I had no idea where you were!!!

Ben chuckled. I'd been trying all day to get him to smile, and my anguish is the thing that brought him joy?

I wiped my face with the back of my hands, grabbed all the bags, and stomped toward the parking lot, not giving a single glance behind me. If a car hit him, that was too bad. He caught up with me and tried to take the bags. I jerked away from him.

"Gabby?"

I picked up the pace and ignored him, giving him a taste of his own medicine.

"Gabby, I'm sorry."

When I got to the car, I tossed the bags in the back seat.

Ben opened my door, but I shoved him.

"I can open my own door." I no longer cared if he could hear me.

Chapter Twenty-Seven

Breathe, *"Hands to Heaven"*

Gabby

"Gabby, I'm sorry," Ben repeated multiple times on the way to his house, but I ignored him.

As soon as I shut off the engine, I retrieved his bags from the back, and carried them inside while he followed me. I looked around for his parents.

"They're gone. Tillie had an appointment, and they were going to lunch," he said.

I turned and relaxed my hands, letting the bags fall to the ground. Then I shrugged, just like he had done to me all day, and started to brush past him to go home.

Ben grabbed my wrist. "I should have broken up with Susie. In the eighth grade, when Michelle said you liked me as more than a friend, I should have broken up with Susie."

I closed my eyes.

"Maybe it would have changed the trajectory of my life.

I wouldn't have had to be your best friend while you fell for other guys. I missed my chance, and I was too scared to ask for a second one. So I stood in Matt's shadow. I watched you fall for everyone but me. And I told myself that someday, I would be everything you wanted and more." He laughed. "For every dream you've had about Matt Cory, I've had a million more about you. And now I'm nothing. Less than nothing. You deserve *something*."

Ben didn't play fairly. Why couldn't he let me stay mad at him? He didn't deserve my sympathy. I wasn't sure he even wanted it. My brain struggled to sync with my heart. One thought I should love Matt Cory, the other knew I loved Benjamin Ashford.

I pulled out the pad of paper and pen. Ben plucked them from my hands and tossed them aside. When I gave him a confused look, he shook his head.

"I don't want to talk."

I shifted my focus from the discarded notepad to his face. With anguish in his eyes, he tilted his head and lowered to kiss me. We were so good at kissing each other. *That* was my talent.

He dragged his lips toward my ear. "Let's go upstairs," he whispered.

I was too intoxicated from that one kiss to think of a reason not to go with him. He took my hand and gathered the bags with his other hand. Then he led the way, closing his bedroom door behind us. In the next breath, he kissed me again, holding my face and retreating toward his bed, kicking Legos out of our way.

He pulled me on top of him, as his back hit the mattress, and gripped my legs to straddle him as we kissed a little deeper.

"Can I remove your shirt?" he whispered.

My hair brushed his face as I hovered above him and nodded. He pulled it over my head and tossed it onto the floor. My breaths quickened as he teased his fingertips along my back. He started to unhook my bra, and I shook my head. So he kissed me instead while his hand cupped my breast over the bra.

It felt good. Too good.

He broke the kiss again and teased my earlobe with his teeth. "Can I take off your pants? We'll leave your underwear on."

I swallowed hard before trying to slide his shirt up his torso. He grabbed the hem and shrugged it off. I sat up and stared at his chest as he used both hands to cup my breasts, thumbs brushing along the soft material over my nipples. My heart raced, and my mind swam with confusion because I knew it was wrong, but it felt so good. His hands drifted to my hips, guiding me to rub myself against his erection. It was good, but I wanted a little more.

When we did it over Thanksgiving, he had on his gray sweatpants and I had on leggings. This time, we both had on jeans, so I climbed off him and started to remove mine while eyeing him and rubbing my shaky lips together. Ben scanned me from head to toe and relinquished a tiny grin.

Standing next to his bed, I nodded toward his jeans.

"You want them off?"

I nodded, feeling a full-body blush spread along my skin.

"Just my jeans?"

Again, I nodded.

Ben removed them, and I stared at his erection straining against his briefs. He guided me to straddle him again.

Oh my gosh ...

Two layers of cotton between us wasn't much. I could feel the heat between us as I leaned forward to kiss him. His hands tangled in my hair as our tongues shared space. I hummed and he lifted his hips. I wasn't sure if it was in response to feeling me hum, but when I did it again, he repeated his tiny thrust. It was better than Thanksgiving because I knew what to expect, and right or wrong, I couldn't wait to experience another orgasm. That's when I realized I was doing exactly what Olivia said. I was *grinding* against him.

With one hand on my butt and his other pressed to the mattress, he rolled us so I was on the bottom.

"Slide your hand down the back of my underwear," he whispered in my ear before kissing and sucking the sensitive skin along my neck. His beard kind of tickled.

I hesitated, resting my hand on his lower back for several seconds before slowly sliding it beneath his waistband. As I curled my fingers into his taut flesh, he groaned and squeezed his butt muscles on a hard thrust.

My eyes drifted shut because his erection rubbing against me felt so good. Ben rocked into me over and over before lifting his head and shoving my bra over my breasts.

I gasped, feeling exposed and insecure, but he quickly sucked one of my nipples into his mouth. There were no words to describe all the sensations firing along my skin and into the most intimate places.

Why did something that felt *so* good have to be a sin?

"You're beautiful and perfect, Gabriella," he murmured over my lips before kissing me. When he released my mouth, he continued, "Don't ever let any man make you think otherwise."

Other man?

I was nearly naked with the person who I trusted more than any other human. Why was he imagining me with anyone but him?

I clawed at his back, and when his hips shifted a fraction, I felt him—the head of his erection brushing the top of my inner thigh. It was no longer completely covered by his briefs.

Oh, God ...

Not only was he exposed, my panties were bunched up and only partially covering me.

And then it happened. I felt his warm, wet flesh touch mine. My breath caught and he groaned, stopping for a few breaths and lifting his head to look into my eyes. His lips parted, eyelids heavy with slow blinks, as he ever so slowly moved a fraction of an inch, touching me in the most arousing way. I thought I might die, feeling him *inside* the crotch of my panties. It was wrong—*so* wrong. But I felt certain damnation was worth it because nothing had ever felt so good.

Ben made tiny movements, stroking my bare flesh with his as we gazed into each other's eyes.

"Do you like that?" he whispered before softly kissing my lips.

I returned a tiny nod and felt him grin against my mouth.

"Do you want me to stop?"

I shook my head and accidentally moved my hips just enough that the head of his erection slid down instead of up.

He froze.

I froze.

It was there. Right. There.

"I can stop," he said with tension to his voice.

Stopping was the smart thing to do. But I was on holiday break and so was my common sense and fear of God.

When I didn't answer, Ben pushed down the front of his briefs, grabbed himself, and stroked me over and over until I was breathless, coming apart, and whispering "oh, oh, oh" over and over as I orgasmed. Then, just like he kissed me for the first time without warning, he pressed his erection inside of me.

I gasped, arching my back, as the waves of my orgasm started to subside.

"I'll stop if it hurts too much," he said then kissed my neck. "Okay?"

I nodded quickly and threaded my fingers through his hair. It didn't hurt yet. All I felt was a clash of nerves and excitement mixed with a little fear. Ben moved slowly, each time pushing into me a little deeper. It felt good at first, but then it started to hurt. And maybe it would have hurt more with anyone else, even Matt. But love won.

I loved my best friend, and there was no one else I wanted more than him. And even if it wasn't okay in God's eyes or anyone else's, feeling Ben inside of me, whispering such beautiful things in my ear, was by far the greatest moment of my life.

He made me feel beautiful.

Desired.

Cherished.

And I felt like a woman in every sense of the word.

"I love you," I said.

Even if he couldn't hear me, I hoped he felt my love. I closed my eyes and focused on that love more than the pain that came with a rite of passage.

He moved a little faster, and I bit my lip. It hurt, but it

wasn't awful. Nothing with Ben could ever be awful. He drew back, pulling out of me.

I looked at his tense face for a second before dropping my gaze to his hand as he stroked himself. What was happening?

Oh ... my gosh.

He orgasmed *on* my stomach. My mind reeled. Why did he do that?

Then on a long exhale, he collapsed beside me. I didn't move. How could I? His *stuff* was on me.

"Gabby ..." he mumbled. "God, that was good."

After a few breaths, he leaned over the edge of the bed and grabbed his T-shirt, then he used it to clean up the mess on me.

"I don't think we need a baby." He gave me a sheepish grin.

I pressed my lips together and nodded before rolling out of bed to retrieve my clothes from the floor. Then I peeked into the hallway. When I didn't see or hear anyone, I made a mad dash for the bathroom.

After cleaning up, dressing, and fixing my hair, I returned to his room. Ben was back in his jeans and a clean shirt, sitting on the edge of his bed. The anguish on his face pierced my heart.

I sat at his desk and wrote him a note.

> *That's not the look I expected. You sure know how to make a girl feel like a regret.*

Ben offered a barely believable smile. "I would never regret being with you."

Then what's wrong?

He furrowed his brow. "I'm not him."

"Who?" I signed with a shrug.

"Matt."

I frowned.

"Be honest." He eyed me. "Can you say he's no longer the man of your dreams?"

Matt and I are just friends.

"Yeah?" He laughed. "We were just friends too."

I set the pen and paper aside then straddled Ben's lap, wrapping my arms around his neck.

"I have nothing to offer you." He broke my heart with those six words.

Where was my confident friend?

I pecked at his lips, keeping my eyes open. Then I sucked on his bottom lip, teasing it with my teeth.

Ben pulled away, but not without relinquishing a grin. "Did it hurt?"

I twisted my lips and shrugged while holding my thumb and index finger an inch apart.

"I'm sorry."

I shook my head. Ben released a long sigh with worry lines on his forehead and indecision in his eyes. Why the agony? I took off my clothes. I did the thing. Eve would be proud. So why did Ben look tortured? What else could I have done, short of becoming Jesus and healing his body?

"I'm so confused, Gabby. I feel lost and angry. My mom calls it the stages of grief because a part of me feels lost forever. But *I'm* not dead, so why can't I see the light? Every tiny piece of joy or reprieve is temporary. It's like I'm falling and hitting branches of a tree that slow my descent, but only temporarily before I fall again. Rock bottom feels inevitable. The gravity of what has happened is stronger than anything or anyone. And I ..." He shook his head.

I opened my mouth to speak, but clamped it shut and slid off his lap to write him a message. Losing his hearing made me second-guess everything. There was no spontaneity, no saying the first thing that popped into my head. Every thought filtered through my mind, assaulted by doubt, a victim of overthinking.

I'm sorry you feel so lost. I can only imagine. What do you need?

Since he lost it with me over Thanksgiving, I tried to keep my concerns solely on him and not make anything seem like it was about me, even though I felt desperate for reassurance that we didn't just destroy our friendship by crossing a line.

Ben slowly shook his head. Of course, he didn't know what he needed. Had he known, he would have already been doing it.

"Go back to school and forget about me."

My head reared back. "What?"

I can't forget about you. We just had sex!

Ben read the note with no expression, no emotion. Maybe having sex over thirty times with multiple women made him calloused to it, like just another daily activity. Nothing special.

My heart deflated.

"Who wants to have sex with a deaf guy who plays with Legos all day?"

I pointed to myself like "Me. Duh!"

Ben's face screwed in disapproval. "Set your standards higher."

What if I'm pregnant?

Lines formed along his forehead. "Unlikely. I pulled out."

But not impossible.

Ben shook his head. "Take a test if you need peace of mind."

I didn't think I was pregnant, but I was upset that he wouldn't even consider it. Didn't he need peace of mind?

I signed, "I love you."

He eyed me so I wrote:

I love you.

Then I made the sign again with my thumb, index, and pinky finger out. Mr. Grumpy didn't make any effort to even try, so I grabbed his hand and bent his fingers to make the sign that was a combination of I, L, and Y.

Why say so many nice things to me when I let you touch my body, but afterward you act like a grump?

"Because you're a branch, slowing my fall. But then it's over, and gravity wins again. That's why I want you to go back to school and forget about me. Don't let me bring you down. Don't let me break you."

I heard a door shut downstairs.

Your parents are home. That was close. I should go. I need to wrap presents. Do you want me to take your gifts to my house and wrap them for you?

"Yes. Deaf people can't wrap presents."

I wadded up the paper and threw it at him, but not in a playful way. Then I stood and headed right to his door.

"Gabby!" He lunged for me, hooking his arm around my waist and pulling my back to his chest. "I'm sorry," he murmured in my ear. "I'm just ..." He sighed. "Sorry."

What was he sorry for? It felt as if he threw that word around like shoving all his Legos under the bed and calling his room clean. It wasn't clean. And a generic sorry didn't mean anything to me after what we did in his bed. Maybe sex wasn't a big deal to him, but it was to me. I peeled his hands from my waist and headed downstairs.

"Hey, Gabby!" Carmen chirped as she and Tillie carried grocery bags toward the kitchen. "Did you two get all of your shopping done?"

"I think so." I threaded my arms through my jacket.

She returned to the entry and untied her gray scarf. "Thanks for making him get out of the house. Did everything go okay at the mall?" She draped her scarf over a coat hook.

"Mm hmm." I smiled as if he didn't scare the life out of me.

"Well, we'll probably see you at the Christmas pageant. But if not, have a Merry Christmas."

"Thanks. I might come by on Christmas to give Ben his gift."

"Oh," she stepped closer and whispered, "what did you get him?"

"I bought him a journal and an old fountain pen. Since he won't write back to me, I thought he could write down his feelings in a journal."

"That would be nice. I'm sure he'll love it."

I was glad she felt so confident because I had no confidence since sex only kept his spirits up for ten seconds.

Chapter Twenty-Eight

Wham!, "Last Christmas"

Ben

What did you get Gabby for Christmas?

TILLIE SLID the small dry erase board to me in the back seat of the car on our way to church for a Christmas Eve pageant. Mom thought the dry erase board was a great idea. My dad suggested I get a rope and tie it around my neck, but I declined that suggestion.

"Nothing," I said.

Mom glanced back at me, eyes narrowed.

"Tillie asked what I got Gabby for Christmas."

Mom held out her hand for the board and marker. Tillie handed them to her while shooting me a tight-lipped grin and wide eyes as if I were in trouble.

Gabby got you something. It's not expensive. I just don't want you to be caught off guard when she gives it to you.

Fantastic.

"What did she get me?"

Mom grinned, making a lock and key gesture at her mouth.

"I can't hear you. And I suck at reading lips. So just say it. If I know what you're saying, we'll call it a Christmas miracle."

Dad's shoulders bounced with laughter.

Mom said something and glanced back at Tillie who smiled and eyed me.

"Jack-in-the-box?" I asked.

Mom laughed and shook her head.

"Hula hoop? Legos? Pine cones?"

Everyone laughed. I imagined it sounded nice.

"Hearing aids?"

The laughter died.

"Oh, come on. That was a good one," I said.

She got you Madonna's new album

Tillie smirked after writing her guess.

I rolled my eyes and grinned.

Mom read it and gave Tillie an uneasy look.

"It's funny," I said to my mom so she wouldn't be mad at Tillie.

A Walkman

Tillie covered her mouth to hide her grin after her second guess.

Mom faced forward, no longer caring to participate in our form of humor. Tillie took the board and angled away from me so I couldn't see what she was writing. She bit her lip as if she wasn't sure if she should do whatever she was doing.

I tried to peek, and she hugged it to her chest.

After a good minute or more, she handed the board to me, facing it away so Mom couldn't see it.

She's getting you more condoms because you had SEX! I took out the trash yesterday because you forgot to do it, and I saw the note in your waste bin.

I felt Tillie watching me as I read her message twice. Then I lifted my gaze to hers. She wasn't a tattletale like most younger siblings because she had too many secrets that I'd kept for her. So I shouldn't have needed to press my index finger to my lips, but I did anyway. She rolled lips between her teeth, and I took that as a sign that my secret was safe with her.

When we arrived at the church, Mom grabbed my hand and gave it a reassuring squeeze as we stepped through the doors. A young girl in a black and red dress handed us a program.

Tillie nudged me with her elbow and nodded to our right

where Gabby floated toward us in a green velvet dress, pantyhose and black shoes. She grinned at the last second before wrapping her arms around my neck. I stiffened.

It felt like everyone knew we had sex, but how would they have known? Gabby and I had been friends forever, and hugging was normal for us. But this hug was different, even if no one else noticed. It lasted a little longer, and she released me a little slower, purposefully brushing her lips along my ear and the angle of my jaw.

She smelled like cherry ChapStick and vanilla lotion. Sweet and sexy.

"You look nice," I said, sliding my hands into my front pockets as she took a step back. I wanted to say beautiful, but that might have turned a few heads.

Gabby blushed, knowing my "nice" meant more. She brought her fingers to her lips and extended her arm out and down while mouthing, "Thank you." Her signing didn't bother me that night because I knew she wasn't trying to teach me anything.

Mom tugged on my sleeve. I glanced behind me, and she nodded toward the sanctuary.

I followed her, weaving our way into the lineup of people filing down the aisle to find seats. A warm hand touched mine. I looked down as Gabby hooked her index finger around my pinky. She wore a conspiratorial grin.

"Are you sitting with me?"

She nodded.

The church was packed so we were crammed into the pew like sardines. I leaned forward to remove my leather jacket. My mom helped me get my arms out in the crammed quarters, and I rested it over my lap. Gabby slid it so that part of it rested on hers too. Then she and everyone else bowed their heads for prayer. Before I closed my eyes, I spied Matt Cory in the front row, sandwiched between his mom and older brother. Gabby didn't mention the Cory family spending Christmas with hers.

She slid her hand into mine under the jacket and laced her fingers with mine, so I closed my eyes.

After prayer, she stretched out her fingers to flatten my hand, palm up. Then she used her finger to draw on it. After a few seconds, I realized she was trying to draw letters. I closed my eyes to focus.

I L O V E Y O U

I curled my fingers through hers again and squeezed her hand, but I didn't open my eyes because my stupid emotions got the best of me. My mind scrambled to make plans. What could I do to be the man she deserved? If I wasn't going to be a conductor, maybe I could be an accountant and sit in an office by myself, feeding numbers into a calculator. It would be a soulless job, but if Gabby were mine, who cared? Of course, I'd have to go back to college, learn sign language, make sure everyone knew I was deaf. I wouldn't be able to talk to her on the phone. If she needed me, too bad. She'd have to come find me. Would I hear her knock on my door? Of course not. I'd be pretty useless at protecting her and being there for her.

However, there was a perfectly capable guy in the front of the church who could give her everything.

Gabby glanced at me when I released her hand and rubbed my face. Every time I tried to imagine a life without hearing, my heart raced, I became restless like I was crawling out of my skin, and I started to sweat.

We were too close. Everything was too close. Too packed in. Too suffocating.

I pulled at my ears and pursed my lips to slow my breathing, but nothing helped. I needed out. With a shaky hand, I grabbed the back of the pew in front of me and stood, wedging my way past legs and purses on the floor. Then I ran out of the church, gasping for air as I tipped my head back and fisted my shirt over my heart.

Warm arms wrapped around me from behind. I knew it was Gabby, but I didn't want her there, seeing me lose my shit.

"Just go, Gabby." I fought for my next breath. "I ... I can't do this. Go inside. Go b-back to school. Go be with Matt. I can't be what you need. Don't ask me to try. I can't. I'm ... I'm fucked-up. Just go."

She stepped around in front of me and reached for my face, but I batted her hands away.

"Go! No. I don't want this for you." I shook my head and stepped back to keep her from touching me.

She slid her hands along her sides, like she had pockets, but she didn't.

No pockets.

No notepad.

No pen.

"I know you love me." I swallowed hard because I didn't want to cry in front of her. My inability to hold myself together was emasculating enough. "I *know*. And I love you too. But it's not enough. I would hate myself for disappointing you."

She shook her head over and over, stepping toward me.

"No!" I held up my hands. "I'm sorry. I'm *so* very sorry. Life is unfair." I paced back and forth, trying to expend some energy from all the nerves in my body that felt like they were misfiring. "It's ... it's cruel. And love doesn't conquer everything. Not this. I'm sorry. I want it too. I do. But I also want to rewind my life so I can do something to not get sick. And I want to hear again. I want to feel normal. But I don't." I wiped my eyes, angry that my emotions were stronger than my will not to cry in front of her.

"I don't feel normal, Gabby. I will never feel that way again. I will never stop hating my life and hating myself for being so weak when other people who have been through far worse are brave and resilient. You deserve a strong person who will protect you, who you can call if you need them, who will hear you if you yell *fire* or *help* or *rape!* But that's not me. I'm too fucking weak!" I bent over, resting my hands on my legs, then I slowly dropped to my knees.

While I shook with emotion, I readied myself for Gabby's touch, and when I felt it, I dropped my hands and batted her away again, only it wasn't her. It was my mom, and Gabby was nowhere in sight.

"I don't want this life," I said, but I couldn't tell if she heard me because I didn't try to say it aloud.

As tears filled her eyes and spilled over with a single blink, I knew she heard me. I was twice as big as my mom, but the second she kneeled in front of me and wrapped her arms around my neck, I fell apart in her embrace.

Chapter Twenty-Nine

Eartha Kitt, "Santa Baby"

Gabby

Eve and Kyle spent Christmas with his family, so Matt's parents stayed in her bedroom. Matt slept in Sarah's room with Isaac, and Sarah slept with me because my parents wouldn't let Isaac and Sarah sleep in the same bed, even though they lived together.

"You were going to have sex with Matt? For real?" Sarah asked the second I turned off the light and slid into bed.

I didn't want to talk. After Ben ran out of the church and said what he did, I felt crushed. It took everything I had to keep it together, so no one suspected anything. With the Cory family staying and it being Christmas Eve, I didn't want to bleed out in front of everyone. But it was hard because I felt every beat of my heart, heaving and aching in my chest.

"What?" I bought myself time.

"Don't pretend you don't know what I'm talking about. Don't lie to me, young lady."

For the first time since Ben ran out of the church just hours earlier, I found a tiny smile. "You sound like Mom."

She nudged my leg with hers. "Just tell me."

"I didn't sleep with him." I nudged her back.

"But you were going to?"

"I'm not sure."

"Gabriella." Sarah rolled toward me, but I kept my gaze on the ceiling.

"Yes." I sighed. "I thought about it. Okay? I considered it. But I didn't, and I'm not going to, so it doesn't matter."

"Why? Why would you even consider it?"

"You're one to talk. You totally couldn't wait to get rid of your virginity."

"Yes, Gabby. But you always wanted to wait until marriage. Did Matt pressure you?"

"What?" I rolled my head toward her. "No! Of course not. What did he say?"

She tucked her hands under her cheek. "After the program tonight, people were chattering about Ben running out and you following him. Matt told Isaac that you liked Ben a lot. Isaac said you and Ben were best friends, and Matt mumbled you were more than friends. So Isaac pressed him as to why he thought that, and he said you two were messing around and you said Ben's name instead of Matt's."

I opened my mouth to tell her it meant nothing, but that was a lie. "Well, it doesn't matter if I like Ben because he wants nothing to do with me." I nearly choked on the last few words.

"What do you mean? Like he doesn't want to be friends or just more than friends?"

The pillow absorbed my first tear. "I don't know. He's just so miserable, and he doesn't want my help. His mom keeps telling me to give him time, but it's been months. I feel like he's stuck, but he doesn't want help. Like he had one dream, and anything else is equivalent to death."

"I can only imagine. It's going to take time, Gabby."

"Time? It's been months."

"Yeah, but he spent nearly nineteen years with the ability to hear, so accepting his new lot in life will take longer than a few months. He's grieving something really big. It has to suck."

"He won't let me grieve with him. He keeps pushing me away."

"Gabbs, grieving isn't a group sport. It's the most personal emotion a human is capable of feeling. If you dropped ten vases from the exact same distance onto the same floor, they would all break differently. One or two might not break at all or just have a chip out of them. But no two would have the same number of pieces. No two would be put back together in the same way. No one knows *exactly* what Ben is feeling or how long it will take for him to feel pieced back together. And you can't do it. Nobody can put Ben back together except Ben. You'll only get cut if you try to fix him."

After a few seconds of not knowing how to respond and letting her words play in my mind, I whispered, "I got cut tonight."

"I'm sorry." She rested a hand on the side of my head, her palm touching my cheek. "But don't sleep with Matt."

I knew she was trying to lighten the mood, but it only made me more emotional.

All the tears came at once, and a tiny sob broke free.

"Oh, Gabbs ..."

"I s-slept with Ben."

She hugged me.

"But d-don't t-tell anyone."

AFTER A RESTLESS NIGHT, I woke a little before five on Christmas morning. My eyes were still swollen from crying, and my mouth was dry. Sarah must not have slept well either because she wasn't in bed. I wrapped up in my terry-cloth robe and tiptoed down the stairs. The second I turned the corner, I covered my mouth to silence my gasp, then jumped back to hide. I should have turned around and bolted back up the stairs. It's what God wanted me to do. Even if I sometimes ignored my moral compass, I still had one. And it was Christmas, the celebration of the birth of Christ. All arrows pointed upstairs.

But that stupid little pitch-forked demon on my shoulder convinced me to slowly peek around the corner again. It was *so* wrong.

The family room was dim sans the soft glow of the Christmas tree lights. Dad unplugged them every night. Except on Christmas Eve, he left them on all night so we'd come downstairs to a lit-up room with presents under the tree. Sarah was on the sofa, partially reclined. Her night shirt was bunched up above her breasts, leaving the rest of her naked and exposed. Isaac had on a pair of gray sweatpants, no shirt, and he was kneeling on the floor, gripping her inner thighs while his head was between her spread legs.

She arched her back and pulled at his hair with one hand

while her other hand clawed at the couch cushion. "Oh my god, baby ... yesss," she softly moaned.

Something or someone (perhaps the Holy Spirit) screamed for me to go back upstairs. I had no business watching them, but I could not turn away.

Isaac kissed his way up her body, camping out at her breasts as he slid his sweats and briefs just past his butt. He had a nice butt, firm and defined like Ben's. Isaac kissed Sarah hard and they moaned together as he thrust into her. It wasn't like Ben slowly working into me a fraction at a time. No. Isaac showed my sister no mercy as he rammed into her over and over, but she seemed to like it. And I suddenly wanted nothing more than a do-over. I wanted to have Ben do to me exactly what Isaac was doing to Sarah.

My body heated and I swallowed hard. I was turned on. Ick ... why was I turned on by watching my sister have sex? That was so messed up, so I bolted upstairs as quickly and quietly as possible and jumped back into bed.

I considered everything and concluded that if Ben and I had that kind of sex, he would realize there was more to life than mourning the loss of his hearing. Right?

Less than ten minutes later, Sarah crept back into my bedroom and eased into bed. With my back to her and breath held, I remained completely still. I told myself to just relax and try to go back to sleep, but I was still thirsty, and there was no way I could sleep after watching them. So I rolled toward her.

I leaned closer to see her face in the dark room. She had her eyes closed and a content smile on her face.

"I know you're awake," I whispered.

Sarah opened one eye. "Sorry. I just had to use the bathroom. Go back to sleep."

"Liar. I was thirsty, so I went downstairs for a glass of water. Want to know what I saw?"

Sarah pulled the sheet over her head. "Gabriella, please don't say another word."

I tucked my pillow under my head so it was propped up a little. What did she think I was going to say? For a few seconds, I thought about it.

"If that's all he got you for Christmas, you need a better boyfriend."

Sarah snorted, kicking her feet to roll away from me. "Stop!" She giggled.

For a minute or more, I bit my tongue and held still. Sarah probably felt relieved that I stopped talking. She might have even asked God to make me go back to sleep.

"Oral sex must be pretty great, huh?"

"Gabby!" she hissed, rolling toward me and pressing her fingers to my lips. "Stop talking. We are never talking about this. It didn't happen. Okay?"

I pulled away and batted at her hand. "Eve would talk about it."

Sarah sighed. "What?" she asked in exasperation. "What do you want to know? I thought you had sex with Ben."

"I did, but not oral sex."

"Good. Don't. In fact, just stop having sex until you're married. And stop talking about it."

I bit my lip and nodded, but a few seconds later, I had more questions. "Which feels better? Oral or actual sex?"

"Ga-byyy!" She groaned, covering her face.

"Is it weird being kissed where you pee?"

"Stop!" She rolled partway on top of me and covered my mouth.

I pushed her off and we continued to giggle.

"What is going on?"

We jumped at Mom's voice.

"Gabby farted and it stinks. I'm going to shower." Sarah flew out of bed and straight into the bathroom.

"It's 5:30 in the morning," Mom said.

The bed dipped as she sat on the edge.

"I know. I didn't sleep well. And I wasn't farting."

Mom rubbed my leg. "Did you have trouble sleeping because of Ben?"

Every ounce of giddiness I felt from my sex talk with Sarah died when my mom mentioned Ben's name.

"I'm sure it wasn't fun watching the program last night when he couldn't hear it," she said.

I didn't know what triggered Ben's response, but I doubted the program caused it. Every time we were together, I felt a powerful push and pull from him, like he wanted me so much but also he didn't want me, or he thought he shouldn't want me.

"Ben thinks his life is over, and he doesn't want to be a burden on anyone." It wasn't until the words came out like a generic excuse that I realized there had to be a lot of truth to them. If I tried to put myself in his shoes, that's how I would have felt.

"Give it time," Mom said, lying next to me, stroking my hair.

I was going back to school in less than two weeks. I didn't have much time before I wouldn't see or hear from him until spring break.

Chapter Thirty

Cher, "If I Could Turn Back Time"

Gabby

"Hey! Merry Christmas," Matt said, coming out of the bathroom just as I opened my bedroom door.

"Why did you tell Isaac about that thing that happened between us?" I wasted no time with pleasantries.

Matt chuckled. "That thing?"

I rolled my eyes. "Don't play dumb."

"He'd been on my case about you, and no matter how hard I'd tried to convince him we're just friends, he didn't believe me. So when Ben's name came up, I thought mentioning *that thing* might get my brother to back off."

"Thanks." I crossed my arms over my chest. "It was nice of you to sacrifice me so that Isaac doesn't interrogate *you*. Now I'm the one getting grilled with questions from Sarah."

"What did you tell her? Did you deny it?"

"I told her we didn't sleep together, but then I told her I

275

slept with Ben." For some reason, I wanted no one to know about that because if my dad found out, he would be disappointed beyond words. On the other hand, I wanted to tell everyone because I felt different, like an adult who did adult things instead of a wannabe who didn't have enough experience to sit at the grown-up table.

Matt scratched the back of his head and offered a smile that looked almost bashful. "Wow. Okay. Thanks for sharing that."

Pressing my lips together, I pinched the bridge of my nose. Perhaps I wasn't correct about what it meant to sit with the grown-ups. Thinking back to Sarah's reaction to my questions, I backtracked and came to the brilliant conclusion that intimacy and privacy went hand in hand. My sister Eve was an outlier who loved talking openly about sex, but most normal people preferred to keep their intimacy private.

"Maybe forget I said that," I mumbled.

"I'll forget you said that if you forget about the bathroom incident the night Julianne and I broke up."

I glanced up, and Matt scrunched his nose. "Deal." I nodded.

"Thanks. And for what it's worth, I'm happy for you and Ben. But I'm sorry he's going through something so awful."

"There is no Ben and me *because* he's going through this, and he doesn't want me as his girlfriend or even his friend. I don't know." With a deep, shaky breath, I willed myself to keep from crying.

Matt gave me a sad smile. "Sorry, Gabby. It's his loss."

Since having sex with Ben, I didn't think Matt could make me blush. I thought the intimacy we shared erased the crush I had on Matt. But after Ben broke my heart less than twenty-four hours earlier, said heart clung to Matt's words like a lifeline.

"Thanks," I whispered.

I liked how Matt looked at me. It was honest and comforting, and I knew I would never regret crushing on him.

"If Ben's the one, fight for him."

"How do I know?" I averted my gaze. "I thought you were the one."

"Then you said Ben's name when *that thing* almost happened."

I rolled my eyes.

"Stop smiling at each other. Put your dick back in your pants," Isaac said, reaching the top of the stairs.

I blushed not only at his crude comment, but I couldn't help but wonder if Sarah told him I saw them.

"It won't fit. Some of us don't have little pecker syndrome." Matt smirked at Isaac.

"Uh ... I need to shower," I murmured, scurrying into the bathroom.

AFTER BREAKFAST and gift-opening where Isaac and Sarah watched Matt and me like we were going to strip and have sex right in front of everyone, I headed to Ben's house to give him the journal and antique fountain pen.

"Merry Christmas, Gabriella," Alan said, opening the door. "Come in."

"Thanks. Merry Christmas. Here," I handed him a plate of cookies, "my mom sent these."

"They look amazing. Tell her thank you. I think Carmen

has something for your family as well. So check with her before you leave. Tillie and Ben are in the back room playing darts."

"Thanks." I slipped off my shoes and hung up my coat before heading to the bonus family room at the back of the house that they added the winter before our graduation. There was a pool table, two leather sofas, and a big screen TV.

Tillie spied me first and smiled, but it wasn't her usual exuberant smile. "Hey, Merry Christmas," she said.

Ben threw a dart, then glanced over his shoulder. Tillie pinched his arm and pointed upstairs. Then she stopped on her way out of the room and handed me her darts. "You can finish for me."

I nodded, giving her a smile, but she only managed a weak one in return. After setting the darts on the edge of the pool table, I handed the present to Ben and signed, "Merry Christmas."

He stared at it. "I didn't get you a gift," he murmured without an ounce of regret to his words.

I shrugged, keeping my grin in place despite the uneasiness I felt from Tillie *and* him.

Ben tore open the paper and gave the journal and pen a brief inspection. "Thanks," he said with no emotion.

I looked around and found a notepad and pen on the sofa's arm.

I'm sorry I didn't know the right thing to say or do last night. Are you feeling better today?

He read it and grunted. "Better? How would I feel better? I'm still deaf."

Ben's moods gave me whiplash. I set the pen and paper next to the darts and wrapped my arms around his torso, resting my cheek on his chest. He didn't move. It was an awkward, one-sided hug. After squeezing him a little tighter, hoping for any sign of reciprocation, I sighed and released him. Emotion burned my eyes, but I kept it in check.

Please don't treat me like this after what happened.

Ben stared at the note for a long time before lifting his gaze to mine. "What happened? You mean between us or between you and Matt?"

I narrowed my eyes.

He shook his head. "Don't insult me by acting like you don't know what I'm talking about. You were going to fuck him."

I winced and shook my head again.

"Tillie overheard Matt and Isaac talking after the pageant. You were going to have sex with him, but he stopped it because you said my name. Which is unfortunate because now I'm sure he doesn't want you, and neither do I, now that I know you had sex with me only after he rejected you."

I swallowed hard.

"Cat got your tongue?" Ben wasn't the person he used to be. Losing his hearing turned him into a bitter and cruel human.

My heart ached for many reasons, least of all was his loss of hearing. It was everything he lost in the process: his sense of decency, his manners, and his way in life.

I couldn't save him, and that felt like its own death. My Ben was gone.

You've had sex over 30 times with multiple girls but I'm in the wrong for NOT having sex with the guy I've had a crush on for years because I said YOUR name? Please tell me you see the irony in this? THE HYPOCRISY!

Ben crumpled up the paper. I think he read it, but I wasn't sure.

"We kissed. I had to drop out of school. And I was here dealing with it, and you decided it was a good time to sleep with Matt Fucking Cory?"

I scribbled so hard on the notepad, the tip of the pen poked a hole through the paper.

You wouldn't write me back! I wrote you so many letters, but you sent me nothing!!!

"Sorry, I was a little busy dealing with my life being turned upside down. But it's nice to know that if I don't get back with you, you'll crawl in someone else's bed."

I shoved him. Then I scribbled more angry words.

I said your name! I was with him but wishing it was you! I gave you my virginity. I gave you everything. And I want to be with you but you're being a bully and a jerk and an ASSHOLE!

Ben eyed the note intently, jaw muscles twitching. "You're right. I'm an asshole. A deaf asshole. So why the hell would you want to be with me?"

Tears raced down my cheeks, and I made no attempt to wipe them away. "Because," I whispered and signed, "I love you."

His eyes reddened while he kept his teeth clenched. I knew he'd rather die than break down in front of me twice in less than twenty-four hours. "Well, don't waste your time loving me." He shrugged, gazing over my shoulder like he couldn't stand to look me in the eye anymore. "And if the day comes that I figure out how not to be such an asshole, maybe we can be friends again." He forced his attention back to me. "But for now, go. Go back to school. Have sex with Matt. Pursue your dreams. Waiting around for me is an insult to both of us."

My heart stopped. He stomped all over it, and I wasn't sure it would beat again.

"You're better than any dream I've ever had. And he was just a dream," I said.

He narrowed his eyes in confusion.

"And I'm sorry it took me so long to figure it out."

Ben shook his head. "I can't hear you."

"And I can't believe you think our friendship is so conditional and ... disposable." I finally wiped my face and sniffled. "So fuck you, Benjamin Ashford, for making me love you. You're the world's worst friend. And I will never forgive you for this." I turned.

He grabbed my arm. "What did you say?"

I pulled away from him, wiping my face.

"Gabriella," he said, dropping his gaze to the floor, "I love you *so* much, but I don't know how to be with you when I feel worthless. And I'd rather you hate me now than later." He lifted his gaze. "It's not about Matt. It's not about you. I'm a terrible person for pointing fingers and making excuses. It's me, Gabbs. Just ... let me go."

His words were too little and too late. I headed to the front door without saying goodbye to anyone or checking with his mom about the gift for our family. My courage was on its last breath, and I needed to get out of there.

Chapter Thirty-One

George Michael, "One More Try"

Gabby

MATT and his parents went back to Asheville the following day, and Sarah and Isaac went home too. I spent the rest of my break acting like everything was fine, putting together puzzles with my mom and playing Scrabble with my dad. Every few days, I took a drive to make my parents think I was visiting my best friend Ben.

I wasn't a fan of school and homework, but I couldn't wait to go back to Michigan. When I got there, Olivia was gone, and I had the dorm room to myself. Just me, my thoughts, blank journal pages, and a large supply of tissues.

The first of February, I wrote Ben a letter. In hindsight, I should have left my thoughts as a journal entry, but something inside of me needed to send those specific words to Ben, even if he never read them. He was going through the stages of grief after losing his hearing. I was going through the stages from losing him.

Dear Ben,

How's your room? Are you making fun Lego creations? I heard a song the other day and thought of you. I'd tell you the name of it, but what does it matter? You can't hear. That's your new job, right? Being deaf? Does that pay well? Or do you have a part-time job working for Hallmark? You really should since you have such a way with words. You could write breakup cards.

Did I tell you that Olivia moved out? I have the dorm room all to myself, so when I want to have sex with Matt, no one interrupts us. Speaking of sex, I've taken two pregnancy tests and they were negative. I bet that makes you happy.

I hope you're doing well. Say hi to Tillie and your parents.

Regards,
Gabby

I reread it at least ten times, and all ten times I contemplated wadding up the paper and tossing it into the trash. It was a cruel and hurtful letter that I would undoubtedly regret later. But he was cruel and hurtful. Did he take even two seconds to think before he said mean things to me? No. So I sealed the letter in an envelope, stamped it, and carried it to the nearest mailbox. After all, he wasn't going to read it.

When the letter dropped into the metal mail bin and there was no taking it back, I blew out a long breath that plumed in the cold air and smiled. It felt good to get that off my chest. Is that how he felt? Did saying mean things to me feel good?

I continued to write him letters with no response from him. And when I talked to my parents on Saturday mornings, they made no mention of the letters, so I assumed he either didn't read them, or if he did, he didn't share them with his mom.

Dear Ben,

What's the newest Lego design? Maybe you should build yourself a girlfriend since no woman will ever want to be with you because you're just mean. I thought by now I'd be better, less angry, but I'm not.

I saw a blind student on campus the other day, and I stopped them to ask why they were there. After all, they can't see. I told them they should go home and give up on their life. You would have been so proud of me. I mean, how dare they think they can pursue a college degree when they can't see. How dare they feel deserving of happiness. How dare they seek any sort of purpose in life. Right?

Did I mention I walked in on Sarah and Isaac having sex early Christmas morning? He was giving her oral sex. She really seemed to enjoy it, so that's what Matt does to me now and it's AMAZING!

I bet you're glad you had so much sex before you got meningitis because you'll probably never have it again. Who wants to have sex with a deaf person?

I hope your family is doing well. Say hi to Tillie and your parents.

Regards,
Gabby

Did it occur to me that I might go to Hell for writing such awful things even if they were written in jest? Yes. But it felt so good to jab him back. I really hoped he was reading them, even if he didn't indulge me with a reply. I thought if he could see how ridiculous he was being, he might reengage in his life again. But mainly, I was desperate—desperately missing my friend.

Dear Ben,

Did you have a good Valentine's Day?

Matt got me two dozen roses and he sprinkled the petals from another dozen all over my bed and we made love all night on the petals.

I set my pen down and ran my fingers through my hair as my eyes filled with tears. Everything was a lie. I hated the lies, the silence, the vast space in my aching heart where memories of Ben slowly died with each cruel intention. The ugly was winning so much it made me nauseous. I crumpled up the paper and threw it at the trash bin. Then I opened up my journal and started ripping out the pages of poems I'd written about Matt, giving up halfway through and slamming the whole journal into the trash even though there were other journals.

I kicked the bin, sending it across the room. Then I swiped my arms along my desk, sending everything crashing to the ground. Grabbing my pillow, I covered my mouth and screamed into it.

Memories of us in his bed flashed through my head. I felt his hands on my skin, his breath along my lips, and I couldn't get the look in his eyes out of my conscience. Our connection caused everything else to fade away. That's what I saw in his eyes. I was enough.

Ben made me feel like *we* were greater than anything that was lost, and he did it without saying a word. Everything beautiful about our friendship came together in what felt like the most pivotal moment of my life. I didn't think about Matt. He blurred into the background. There wasn't a moment of regret.

At least ... not in my mind or heart.

I wiped my face, picked everything off the floor and put it neatly back on the desk. Then I took a deep breath and started another letter.

Dear Ben,

Remember how you used to find a new song and listen to it over and over until you knew every word and beat? You said those songs kept you awake at night and popped into your head first thing in the morning. You called them inspiring, and one day you wanted to write something that consumed another just like that.

You are my song. I know every word and every beat. You keep me awake at night and pop into my head first thing in the morning. You inspire and consume me.

I'm sorry if I held on too tightly when you needed to be set free. I'm sorry if you felt like I was making everything about me. It's just that my love for you makes it hard to distinguish where you end and I begin. For as long as I can remember, it's been us—Gabby and Ben.

It's going to take time for me to see myself in this world without you by my side. And maybe it's just selfish of me to tell you all of this. It's not your fault. I should have been there for you. I'll spend eternity wondering what if. What if I would have swallowed my pride and been there for you when you were sick? What if I would have taken you to the doctor? So many what-ifs.

Maybe you love me too much to blame me, but what if you need someone to blame? What if letting go of your need to protect me is what will set you free? Free to move on. Free to dream of something new for your life? Free to love yourself and perhaps someone else again?

I'm truly sorry.
Gabby

NOT GETTING any replies from Ben sucked the life out of me. I lost focus on everything except my ASL classes. My grades plummeted. And I had no friends.

On top of all that, I had missed three days of school. By the fourth day, I went to the emergency room. Something was wrong, and I wasn't going to be like Ben and wait until something awful happened to me. I didn't have a roommate to save me.

"Hi, Gabby. I'm Dr. Leighton." The woman with a long, gray ponytail greeted me, pulling the curtain shut behind her. "Your labs are back. Everything looks good. Were you aware that you're pregnant?"

I squinted for several seconds before blinking. "Um, I took two pregnancy tests. They were negative."

"Perhaps it was too early to detect. It explains the fatigue and nausea. Do you know when you last started your menstrual cycle?"

"He pulled out," I said just above a whisper.

Dr. Leighton smiled. "The withdrawal method is about twenty percent less effective than condoms. And it doesn't protect you from STDs. Even with perfect timing, you can be exposed to pre-ejaculatory fluid which contains sperm."

I nodded as if I knew that, but I couldn't recall hearing the words "pre-ejaculatory fluid" in junior high health class.

"Do you have an OB-GYN you see? If not, I can give you a referral."

"I don't have one." I stared at my hands folded in my lap because I was too embarrassed to look at her.

Nothing had gone as planned. I was supposed to be in love with Matt. We were supposed to have sex on our wedding night, and a doctor was supposed to congratulate us on our pregnancy without using the words "pre-ejaculatory fluid."

"Just stay hydrated and have small snacks on hand like crackers. I can write you a prescription for prenatal vitamins if you're planning on keeping the baby."

Was I keeping the baby? Of course. My parents. God. My conscience. All would be in favor of keeping the baby.

My parents.

I was the good child. The only one to go to college. I was saving myself for marriage. The disappointment in their eyes would kill me.

"If you need time to think—"

I shook my head. "I'm keeping it."

"Very well. Before you leave, I'll get you a prescription and we can set up your first appointment with an OB. If you don't know the date of your last period, they'll take an ultrasound to determine how far along you are."

I heard nothing but the echoing of her voice.

Chapter Thirty-Two

Madonna, "Papa Don't Preach"

Gabby

I HAD NO ONE.

My best friend broke up with me in every sense of the word, and I couldn't talk to him on the phone. Olivia said she'd visit me, but I'd only seen her once since the start of the semester, and that was just because she was missing a shirt that she thought might have accidentally gotten put in my laundry hamper.

I hadn't heard a peep from Matt since Christmas.

And I'd been too busy mourning the loss of Ben in my life to carve out time for a social life.

No friends.

No degree.

No job.

No boyfriend.

No direction.

And I was barely passing my classes.

"I'm pregnant," I said, talking to God as if he didn't already know. "I'm sorry. I know this isn't how you wanted me to get pregnant. But I'm keeping the baby so that counts for something. Right?"

The thing with God was He didn't answer prayers directly. I had to look for clues. He wasn't the best verbal communicator.

"I suppose you think I should tell Ben," I said, staring at the empty bunk bed above mine in the dark. It was nearly midnight, but I couldn't sleep. "What do you want me to do when he rejects me again *and* his baby?"

I exhaled a deep sigh. "You can think on all of this and get back to me. But don't wait too long because I can't hide this baby forever."

The next morning, I heard someone yell "Ben!" And I jolted out of bed and opened my door. Some guy with red, curly hair hugged the girl two doors down from me. Then they kissed and disappeared into her room. I deflated and shut my door.

"Oh no," I whispered, reaching for the waste bin and retching twice before expelling the chicken sandwich I ate the previous night. Then I collapsed onto my desk chair.

"Is that a sign?" I whispered.

Whether it was a sign or coincidence, I uncapped my pen and wrote Ben a letter.

Dear Ben,

I know you're not reading my letters, or if you are, you're being a jerk and not responding. So I'll keep this short.
I'm pregnant.

Sincerely,
Gabby

Two WEEKS LATER, after no response, I sent another letter.

Dear Ben,

Here's a photo from the ultrasound. It's too early to determine the sex, but I said I didn't want to know anyway.

Sincerely,
Gabby

When I returned from mailing the letter early Saturday morning, Matt was waiting at my door with a bouquet.

"Hey," I said, trying to smile past the morning sickness that seemed more all day, not just morning.

"Happy birthday," he said.

My eyes widened. "How did you know?"

"Your mom mentioned it at Christmas, so I made a mental note."

I unlocked my door. "Thanks. You're the first one to wish

me a happy birthday. My parents will call around ten. They call me every Saturday morning." I tossed my purse and keys on my bed and took the vase of yellow roses from him.

"Listen, I haven't been ignoring you on purpose. I've just been really busy." He slid his fingers into his front pockets, giving me a sheepish grin that said he wasn't *that* busy.

I smiled with a nod, letting him off the hook. "Hey, I get it. I've been busy too, otherwise I would have called."

He mirrored my slow nod. Neither one of us had to say it. We knew the avoidance was mutual and intentional.

"Are you doing okay in your classes? If you ever need help, the offer still stands," Matt said.

"I'm good."

If C's and D's were good, then it wasn't a lie.

"Are *you* doing okay in your classes? If you ever need help"—I smirked—"don't ask me."

Matt barked a laugh. "Thanks. That's good to know." He sat on the edge of my bed. "Have you heard from Ben?"

"Nope. Have you heard from Julianne?"

"Actually, yes. She called to let me know she made it safely to California. And we've talked every week since. It's ..." He twisted his lips. "Nice."

Yes. I imagined it was nice to have the person you loved communicate with you.

"What are you doing for spring break?"

"Uh ..." I fiddled with my hoodie strings.

"Going home?"

My gaze caught on my pillow just inches from his hand. It was the ultrasound picture. I stared at it every day.

As if I wasn't already nauseous, the idea of Matt finding out made me feel faint as well. Before I could answer, his gaze followed mine. My jaw unhinged to speak, to distract him, anything to bring his attention back to me.

But it was too late.

He took the picture and stared at it through squinted eyes. "Who's pregnant?" he murmured.

It felt like an honest, innocent question, as if he assumed there was no way it could be me.

I had a tiny window to make up anything and deliver it with confidence.

Olivia's pregnant. Big surprise, huh?

I found it in the hallway. I don't know who it belongs to, but I'm going to ask around.

Eve's pregnant. She sent me a picture.

Sarah's pregnant, didn't you know?

But I waited too long. My silence screamed the answer. And when he glanced up at me, the tears filling my eyes confirmed it.

"Jesus, are you serious?"

I wiped my face and nodded.

"Is it—"

"It's yours," I said through a laugh and a sob.

Matt eyed me with a weird expression for a moment as if he questioned my sincerity, as if he needed to recall if he'd been drunk another night and accidentally had sex with me.

I grabbed a tissue from the box on my desk and wiped my eyes and nose. "Sorry. That was a bad joke."

"Does he know?"

I nodded, then I shook my head. "I wrote him a letter, but either he's not reading them or he doesn't care."

"Who else knows?"

I shrugged. "My doctor. And God. I told him first."

Indecision warred on Matt's face as if he wasn't sure if it was a laughing matter.

It wasn't, but what else was I supposed to do? Continue to cry my eyes out? Have an emotional breakdown because I was in way over my head without so much as a single trusted friend with whom to confide?

"What did God say?" Matt pressed his lips together to hide his grin.

"He said, 'Well, shit, Gabriella. You really fucked up.'"

Matt's eyebrows shot up his forehead as I slapped a hand over my mouth.

I didn't cuss. Well, I didn't do it unless someone (Ben) provoked me. And I definitely didn't do it and blame God. That felt like an exponentially worse sin than anything else. Would He allow me to give my baby up for adoption before sending me straight to Hell?

Matt fisted a hand at his mouth to hide his snickering. "He did, huh?"

I plopped into my desk chair and fished a handful of crackers from the box. "How does it feel to have four years of college under your belt and be on your way to becoming a successful lawyer?"

He dropped his fist and frowned. "Gabby ..."

I laughed. It sounded a little maniacal. "I'm serious. What if you would have followed Sarah to Nashville like a lovesick puppy? Not a penny to your name. No job. No skills. And just for fun, let's pretend you had a uterus, and some other person got you pregnant. Can you even imagine? Oh wait! Did I mention said person doesn't want to have anything to do with you? And said person lives with their parents and plays with Legos all day?"

Matt stood and took slow steps in my direction. Then he

squatted in front of me. I shoved the crackers into my mouth, very unladylike. I couldn't fully close my mouth while I chewed.

He took my hands. "No. I can't imagine. But I know how it feels to think your life, as you imagined it, is over. And so does Ben. But I moved on. So will you, and so will Ben. In ten years, when you have this child and maybe one or two more running around your house, you'll think back to this moment and laugh. You'll think of all the things that turned out to be so much bigger than this moment, and you'll laugh at the nineteen-year-old version of yourself who felt like the world was ending." He squeezed my hands. "But it's just beginning."

I slowly chewed the crackers, tiny pieces falling from lips onto my lap. "That was an excellent speech," I mumbled.

He wrinkled his nose as cracker crumbs shot in his direction.

"Tell me what you really think," I said.

He chuckled, releasing my hands and sitting back on his butt, hands flat on the floor behind him. "I think ... well shit, Gabriella. You really fucked up."

I loved Matthew Cory. Maybe not like I loved Ben, but Matt was a good guy. He didn't have to bring me flowers or give me a pep talk. No one expected him to keep an eye on me or even be my friend. He did it because it's just who he was. Ben was a good guy too. At least, the Ben I knew before he lost his hearing. I wasn't sure that Ben still existed, but I hoped so. That's the Ben who I wanted to be my child's father.

"What are you going to do, Gabby?" Matt asked with a more somber expression. "You have to tell your parents."

"I know," I whispered. "But I want to tell Ben first. He

deserves to know before anyone, but I can't exactly call his house and ask his mom to relay the message. And he won't respond to my letters. I don't think he's reading them, so I'm just going to wait."

"Wait? Wait for what?"

I shrugged. "Wait for him to open them."

"What if he doesn't?"

"He will. He has to."

"Just tell him when you go home for spring break."

I shook my head. "I'm not going home because my dad arranged for me to volunteer at a kids camp here at the church I've been attending. And I can't tell them over the phone."

"So when are you going to tell them? Or are you planning to go home after the semester nearly ... six months pregnant? And then be like *surprise!*"

"I don't know. I'll figure it out."

Matt twisted his lips and nodded slowly. I knew he was holding back his judgment.

"Thanks again for the flowers."

"You're welcome. When is your next appointment?"

"In two weeks."

"Want company?"

"You want to go to my OB appointment with me?" I squinted at him.

"I would. It has to suck going alone."

I leaned forward, resting my elbows on my knees. "Matthew..."

He grinned. "Gabriella..."

"You're pretty awesome."

He lifted his chin and puffed out his chest. "I know."

Chapter Thirty-Three

Phil Collins & Marilyn Martin, "Separate Lives"

Gabby

TWO WEEKS LATER, Matt took me to my OB appointment.

"This must be the lucky dad," the nurse said as Matt followed me from the waiting room to the exam room.

"You bet," he said.

I shot him a look over my shoulder as the nurse stopped at the scale. He winked.

"Turn around," I said.

"Huh?" He squinted.

"I don't want you to see my weight."

"Gabby—"

"Just do it."

He turned while giving me a heavy sigh. The nurse eyed me as I stepped onto the scale. It was a silent tsking, as if I had a terrible boyfriend who judged me for my weight. Matt was neither my boyfriend nor overly judgmental. And while

I was no longer actively pursuing him or trying to impress him, I didn't want him to know my weight.

"Okay, follow me," she said after jotting down my weight. "Your boyfriend can wait in this room," she pointed to the exam room on the right, "while you pee in this cup for me. The restroom is down the hall on the left."

I nodded as Matt sat in the chair next to the exam table.

After peeing in the cup, I returned.

"This is weird," I said, sitting on the exam table, legs dangling off the side. "What would Julianne think of you being here with me?"

He made duck lips for a few seconds. "Good question."

"Would she be mad?"

He shook his head, crossing his arms over his chest. "Would Ben be mad?"

"No. Well, maybe. Yes. He'd be mad because you've been his nemesis."

"Me? Why?"

"Because he had to endure my talking about you when he liked me. And he was mad when he found out that we almost had sex."

"Mad? You said his name."

"Exactly. Thank you. That's what I said."

"Good afternoon, Gabriella. How are you?" Dr. Murray came into the room.

"I'm good. This is my friend Matt."

She shook his hand. "Nice to meet you. The father?"

"Yup."

I rolled my eyes. "No. He's just a friend."

She smiled at him. "Well, you're a good friend."

Matt ate up her compliment, sitting up straighter in the chair.

"Your weight is good. How has your morning sickness been?"

"Better," I said.

"That's great. Can you lie back for me?"

I nodded, lying on the table with one hand propped behind my head while my other hand lifted my shirt.

She folded the waist of my sweatpants to expose more of my lower abdomen. I glanced at Matt to see if he was looking at me, and he was.

"Might feel a little cold," Dr. Murray said, squirting some lube onto my belly, then spreading it with the wand. The machine made a static noise as she moved it around, stopping occasionally to press a little harder. "There it is." She smiled when my baby's heartbeat pumped to a fast rhythm.

My grin doubled, and Matt's did too.

"Is it okay?" I asked.

She nodded, removing the wand and wiping my belly with a wad of tissues. "It's perfect." She proceeded to measure my belly.

"I just look chubby, not pregnant. What are you really measuring?"

Dr. Murray gave me a reassuring smile. "I'm measuring your uterus. And it's exactly where it should be for twelve weeks. You've made it to the end of your first trimester. Congratulations. Your baby is about the size of a lime."

Matt grabbed my hand and squeezed it. Who would have imagined that he would be with me while I was pregnant with another man's baby?

After my appointment, he took me to dinner and then back to my dorm.

"You don't have to walk me all the way to my room." I laughed.

"I do." He opened the front door for me and followed me up the stairs and down the hallway.

After I unlocked my door, he took a step backward. "Call me if you need anything. Okay? And I'll add your next appointment to my calendar."

"I shook my head. It won't be necessary. Ben will be here by then. But thank you so much."

Matt tried to smile, but it fell short of a real one. Instead, it was obvious he felt bad for me. Poor me ... thinking Ben was going to read my letters and immediately return to Ann Arbor to be with me and his baby. But I had hope, and that was enough.

Dear Ben,

The nausea has subsided. Hydrating works well along with a bottle of ginger ale mid-morning. I had a good birthday. Your card to me must have gotten lost in the mail, but thanks for thinking of me.

Our baby has a strong heartbeat. I think it's a boy. I don't know why, but I do. Have you thought about names?

I haven't told my parents because I want you to be the first to know. So I'm patiently waiting for your reply. However, when the semester is over, I'll have to move back home, and I suspect I'll have a noticeable bump by then. Right now, I just look full in the middle. Enough to make my jeans tight so I've been wearing elastic waist leggings and sweatpants.

How's it going with learning ASL? I'm getting so much better at it, but my instructor said it will take a year to learn enough signs to have extensive conversations, and another year or two after that before I'm good at it.

I love you. XO
Gabby

I wasn't happy that Ben refused to open my letters or reply, but I knew that eventually he would miss me so much that he would cave and read them. Hope was enough to keep me going, passing my classes (just barely), and eating healthy for our baby.

And nothing could have prepared me for the gut-wrenching feeling of losing that hope.

"How was the camp?" Mom asked when we talked on the phone the first Saturday morning in April.

"Uh, it was fine. How are you and Dad?" I quickly changed the subject.

"We're good. We miss you."

"Miss you too." I curled the phone cord around my finger. I hated lying (even if by omission) to my parents. "How's Ben? I haven't heard much"—*anything*—"from him recently."

Mom made a clicking sound with her tongue. "Oh, well, he's working now. He's back at the store in the meat department, but he doesn't have to tend to the counter or have interaction with customers. Carmen said when he's not working, he still spends hours in his room. But ..."

"But what?"

"Well, um ..."

"What?" I repeated.

"I guess I should just prepare you. He has a friend he's been doing things with occasionally."

"Oh, that's good. Right? Someone he works with?"

"No. It's someone who just moved to town. They met at church."

"Oh, even better. Is he our age?"

"*She's* actually twenty-three. And she's a substitute teacher at the school for now, but Agnes Kline is retiring at the end of the year, so Ben's new friend will teach the third grade full-time in the fall. Her name is Laurel, and her father is deaf. She knows ASL. Carmen hopes she'll convince Ben to learn it."

At some point, all the tears broke free. There were no sobs, not so much as a peep, but my eyes hemorrhaged emotions. Pain mixed with pregnancy hormones.

"Gabby?"

I swallowed hard and cradled the phone between my ear and shoulder to wipe my face. "Yeah?"

"Just making sure you're still on the line and we didn't get cut off. Carmen didn't know if I should tell you about Laurel since you and Ben had a rough moment over Christmas break. But I told her you'd be happy for him. We all just want him to get better and adjust to his new way of living without hearing. It's not like you wouldn't want him to make new friends."

Friends ...

Ben's history with female "friends" involved sex. I was

his only platonic female friend until he kissed me in the hallway.

I rested my hand on my stomach. "A friend," I murmured. "Good for him."

Benjamin Ashford was a cruel asshole, and had I not been pregnant with his baby, I would have vowed to never speak to him again.

But—and it was a big *but*—I was having his baby. It wasn't a secret I could keep forever. And I wanted nothing more than to sneak into his house and steal all the letters that I knew were unopened. Except the first few I sent him. He deserved every nasty word in those.

"Any boys we need to know about? Are you being good?"

I glanced at the ultrasound picture beside my bed. "Brushing and flossing every day."

She laughed. "You know that's not what I meant, but I'm glad to hear you're taking care of your teeth. We didn't spend all that money on braces for you not to take care of them."

I barely registered her words because my heart ached too much, and my mind was numb from the shock.

"Tell Dad I love him."

"I will, hun. Talk to you next week."

I nodded without so much as a mumbled "goodbye" before hanging up the phone.

Chapter Thirty-Four

Guns N' Roses, "Sweet Child O' Mine"

Ben

Laurel laughed at everything I said. I couldn't hear her, but I felt her. She was growing on me, not like Gabby, but enough to make me leave my room for a trip to McDonald's or the bowling alley. And my relationship with her seemed to pacify my parents and keep them off my back.

I had a job.

I had a friend.

No one seemed to care that I still didn't feel like I had much of a purpose in life.

If you weren't so young, I'd invite you to my apartment.

Laurel slid me the note after I finished wadding up my wrapper and stuffed it into the bag.

When I eyed her with a raised eyebrow, she returned a flirty grin while blushing. She was pretty enough. Curly, blond hair and blue eyes. She was shorter than me, maybe even shorter than Gabby, but she had huge breasts.

"You're twenty-three, not forty-three," I said, not because I wanted to go to her apartment. I was just stating a fact: She wasn't *that* much older than me.

She bit her lip and batted her long eyelashes.

Was she cute? Yes. Did I like her big boobs? Sure. Had I thought about having sex with her? Of course. Was I going to? Not likely.

She signed something and then wrote.

Come to my apartment.

If I went there, we were going to have sex. I wasn't stupid. And after the fact, I would hate myself because I took Gabby's virginity, and I had a stack of unopened letters from her in my room. I felt an odd responsibility to let Gabby know I was moving on before actually moving on. And I pitied whoever came after Gabby, who would always feel like the only girl for me.

Laurel wasn't really me "moving on," she was just a good time. I enjoyed hanging out with her. And if we had sex, I felt certain I wouldn't be taking her virginity, and she wouldn't expect it to mean anything.

"Maybe another time," I said.

Laurel nodded. She was cool like that.

We dumped our garbage on the way out, and she hugged

me before waving goodbye and getting into her beige Toyota Corolla.

As soon as I arrived home, I headed straight to my room —my spotless room. I inspected it for a few seconds, not sure how I felt about someone (probably my mom) invading my space. All of my Legos were in bins. My bed was made. The trash was empty instead of overflowing. And my desk was cleared, except for the journal and pen from Gabby.

My parents had been on my case to clean my room, clearly my mom was tired of waiting.

I turned when someone tapped my shoulder. Tillie scowled at me.

"What?"

She handed me a note. Whatever she had to say was premeditated and scripted before I got home.

I cleaned your room.

I nodded. "I didn't ask you to, so if you're waiting for a thank-you, you'll be waiting for a long time."

She handed me a second notecard.

I found a pile of letters from Gabby.

I shook my head and shrugged. "So?"

You never opened them.

Again, I shrugged.

Tillie averted her gaze for a few seconds while worry lines etched along her brow.

She handed me another notecard.

I read them.

I frowned. "Stay out of my stuff."

She nodded toward my nightstand, where the letters were neatly stacked.

You're an asshole.

I rolled my eyes. "Thanks. I'm aware. Stay out of my business."

Tillie smacked the notecard into my chest with a punch, and her lips moved. I didn't understand her words, but I read the anger in her expression, the emotions in her eyes. I didn't open Gabby's letters. So what? Tillie had no idea how much just receiving them hurt me. I didn't have the strength to read them. And Gabby deserved a man who wasn't weak like me.

Tillie had one notecard left, and I plucked it from her hand before she willingly gave it to me. Then, I shoved her out of my room and shut the door.

If you don't read them, I'm telling Mom what's inside.

Sex.

Gabby must have mentioned we had sex. Did I want my mom reading "how could you treat me that way after taking my virginity" letters? No. But Gabby was angry, and rightfully so. I stared at the letters. Her words would cut deeply because I loved her and hated myself.

I sat on the edge of my bed and picked up the first letter. Tillie had them in the order in which Gabby sent them.

Dear Ben,

How's your room? Are you making fun Lego creations? I heard a song the other day and thought of you. I'd tell you the name of it, but what does it matter? You can't hear. That's your new job, right? Being deaf? Does that pay well? Or do you have a part-time job working for Hallmark? You really should since you have such a way with words. You could write breakup cards.

Did I tell you that Olivia moved out? I have the dorm room all to myself, so when I want to have sex with Matt, no one interrupts us.

I hope you're doing well. Say hi to Tillie and your parents.

Regards,
Gabby

"Fuck you, Tillie," I said, tearing the letter into tiny pieces. I wasn't going to read another word. And if she thought she could blackmail me, she had another thing coming.

I took the next envelope and tore it up.

And the next.

And the next.

I would tell my mom that I had sex with Gabby and deal with her disappointment and the risk that she'd tell Gabby's parents. But I would not read a pile of letters about Gabby and Matt Fucking Cory.

By the fifth letter, I noticed something in the pile of torn pieces. It wasn't white paper with writing. There were fragments of dark paper. I fished a couple pieces from the pile, then a couple more. A few of them had white markings. Curiosity took over. I didn't want her venomous words, but I wanted to see what the black pieces were supposed to be. After I fished out all the dark pieces I could find, I deposited them onto my desk and pieced them together.

"What the fuck?" I stared at them. As panic set in, I grabbed all the torn up letters to put them back together, but it was useless, there were too many pieces.

My heart pounded, so I unfolded the next letter that I hadn't ripped up yet.

Dear Ben,

The nausea has subsided. Hydrating works well along with a bottle of ginger ale mid-morning. I had a good birthday. Your card to me must have gotten lost in the mail, but thanks for thinking of me.

Our baby has a strong heartbeat.

Our baby.

Our. Baby!

I felt ...

Before I could finish that thought, I ran to the bathroom and threw up the contents of my stomach.

Chapter Thirty-Five

Roxette, "Listen to Your Heart"

Gabby

I DIDN'T WANT to be a complete disappointment to my parents when I returned to Devil's Head for the summer, so I buckled down and focused on my classes. Straight A's were out of my reach, but I aimed to get all D's raised to C's and a few C's up to B's. It was easier to concentrate with the nausea gone. And aside from having to get a few more elastic waistband pants, and a couple of new bras for my bigger breasts, I felt good.

I felt beautiful.

Good and beautiful without Ben. Every morning, I started my day with the mantra "I don't need Ben." It was the only way to keep it together, to not spiral into a dark hole thinking about Ben and Laurel.

While studying for my developmental psychology test, my phone rang.

"Hello?"

"Hey, how's it going?" Matt asked.

"Good." I lied. "How are you?"

He chuckled. "Good. Nothing new. I've been busy, but since I had a minute, I wanted to check on you. Is there anything you need? Help studying? Pickles and ice cream? Want me to help you tell your parents?"

"I'm good," I giggled, and it felt good, like a real breath of air in my deflated lungs. "And I know you hate keeping this secret with me, but I appreciate it."

"I was hoping it would no longer be a secret, but I fear you'll be heading home for summer break with news that might give your dad a heart attack."

I hummed. "You may be right."

"Do you ever wonder if Ben read your letters, but just didn't respond? Didn't ..." Matt stopped short of saying the rest, but I knew what he meant.

Ben didn't care.

Of course, that thought went through my mind, but my heart wouldn't let the words escape. It wouldn't let me give them power. Maybe it was in self-preservation mode because the idea of Ben knowing but not caring was too unbearable.

It was too unforgivable.

The thought of him having a new "friend" while knowing I was pregnant with his baby threatened to crush my soul. So I didn't go there. I couldn't.

I cleared my throat. "Have you heard from Julianne?"

"Oh. Wow. So this is how you're playing it."

I grinned. "Or we can agree not to talk about Ben or Julianne."

"That's not really fair, Gabby. Julianne is not pregnant with my child."

"Are you sure?"

"Not funny."

I giggled. "It's totally funny. I appreciate you checking in on me. If I crave rainbow sherbet, I'll let you know."

"My mom once mentioned having pregnancy cravings for things she never liked before getting pregnant. Maybe what you need is a half gallon of rocky road."

I wrinkled my nose. "Nice try."

"Well, if you change your mind ..."

There was a knock at my door.

"I gotta go. And I won't change—" I opened the door.

"Gabby?" Matt said my name.

"I'll call you later," I murmured, releasing the phone.

Ben lunged to catch it and stepped past me to hang it up. I slowly turned, backing into the door to close it. He blurred behind the tears in my eyes.

"I'm pregnant," I whispered, and a sob immediately followed. I hadn't realized how strong I'd been, subconsciously holding myself together because no one else was going to do it. And him being there meant I could tell everyone else. The secret was killing me.

I didn't know if Ben understood what I said, but he nodded anyway and pulled me into his arms before my knees gave out.

He was there.

It didn't feel real. And I was scared to move or even breathe because I feared it was a dream.

After the initial shock wore off, and I felt certain it wasn't a dream, a pang of anger hit me, and I stiffened before extricating myself from his all-consuming embrace. His gaze dropped to my stomach, and I fought the urge to roll my eyes. I had a barely detectable bump that was impossible to see unless I had my stomach exposed, and even then, I just looked a little bloated.

"How's Laurel?"

I never hated that he was deaf. In fact, I bled with empathy for him. The tragedy of it lived deep in my heart, but I never resented or hated it. However, I did in that moment because I wanted him to hear my voice. I didn't want to write down my words and let him imagine that I wasn't livid.

I was.

I nudged him away from my desk and flipped my notebook to a blank page.

How's Laurel? Is she pretty? I hope you use a condom with her. I don't think you can afford two babies with your job in the meat department.

Ben's gaze returned to mine, and the corners of his eyes twitched with a slight flinch.

I channeled all of my anger to fight my tears, but I had too many hormones in my body to completely mask how badly he hurt me.

"She's just a friend."

"I was your—" I balled my fists. *Gah!* I needed to yell and scream at him.

I WAS YOUR FRIEND!!!!

Pain wrinkled his face as he read my words. Then he slowly nodded. "I'm sorry, Gabby. Had I known—"

I cut him off with a half dozen hard headshakes.

You knew I loved you. You knew we had sex
without a condom. You knew I wanted to be there
for you. YOU KNEW!

I stabbed the pen into the dot of the exclamation point instead of Ben's heart, which was where I wanted to shove it.

His shoulders sagged. "You're right."

I didn't know what I wanted from Ben. Well, that wasn't entirely true. I wanted the impossible. I wanted to erase the previous seven months. A do-over.

Did you sleep with her?

Ben shook his head, but I didn't believe him.

"I didn't," he said.

Did it matter? I was still pregnant with his baby, even if he did.

"We're having a baby, Gabby. I don't know how to do this. I—"

"No!" I shook my head.

You had your time. Everything was all about you
and you made sure everyone knew it. Then you made
me feel selfish for having feelings. You're a jerk. I'M
PREGNANT! Not you! It's about me now. I don't
care how you feel about this. I don't care if you want
this baby or me. You have been selfish! I don't know
if you can ever make this right.

I slapped the pen onto the pad and sat on the edge of my

bed. Ben read my note and faced me. It didn't matter that his expression was twisted with regret. He couldn't make things right. All I'd wanted was for him to read my letters and come back.

And there he was. I got what I wanted. But it wasn't good enough.

"What do you want from me?" he asked.

I stopped fighting my tears. The pregnancy hormones were too much. "I want you to hear me."

Ben squinted, shaking his head.

I laughed through my tears, wiping my face, so I signed the words instead.

He continued to shake his head. "Write it down."

I slowly lifted my chin and shook my head. "Read my lips."

"Gabby," he sighed. "Just write it down."

I pointed to the door.

He looked over his shoulder.

I flicked my palm away from my body. "Go away."

"Just write it down." He tried to hand me the pen and paper.

I brushed past him and opened the door.

"Where am I supposed to go?"

I offered no response, just a blank look. He needed to figure it out on his own. I had my hands full with passing my classes and growing a human being.

"Is this all about Laurel?"

"Nope. It's about me, so deal with it."

"I can't hear you!" He rubbed the back of his neck. "Please, just write it down."

Again, I signed, "Go away."

Ben hung his head and strode toward the stairs. I closed the door, resting my forehead against it. "Oh, baby, your dad's an ass." I pressed a hand to my belly.

Chapter Thirty-Six

Bad English, *"When I See You Smile"*

Gabby

THE NEXT MORNING, I opened my door to shower before my first class. On the floor in the hallway was a sack. I pulled out a cup of tea that smelled like ginger and honey, a banana, and a breakfast sandwich with eggs and sausage. There was a note folded inside as well.

DEAR GABBY,

    IF YOU NEED ME, I'M STAYING WITH JASON. MY BED WAS STILL AVAILABLE. I'M AN EXCELLENT STUDY PARTNER IF YOU NEED HELP. HOW ARE YOUR FEET? I GIVE GOOD FOOT RUBS, AND I CAN BRAID HAIR. SO IF WE HAVE A GIRL, YOU WON'T HAVE TO DO ALL THE BRAIDING.

Love,

Benjamin Ashford, baby daddy in training

I didn't want to smile. He had a long way to go before earning any part of my happiness.

After enjoying my breakfast, I showered and hurried to my first class. Instead of going back to my dorm room between classes, I grabbed lunch and hid in the library. I wasn't ready to risk seeing Ben.

Of course, I was mad about Laurel.

Of course, I questioned if he would have come had I not been pregnant.

Of course, I loved him.

But it really wasn't about him, and I needed to always remember that.

When I returned to the dorm after my last class, there was another sack with an orange, trail mix (my favorite kind with chocolate instead of raisins), and a baby name book. I tried not to think about Ben casting me aside for Laurel. It hurt to feel disposable and replaceable.

I was young and selfish, which meant I wanted to take an imperfect situation and paint it in gold and glitter. What if Ben had opened every letter the second they arrived, and without hesitation, he hastily wrote me back? A yearning to the urgency in which we communicated. What if he rushed back to Michigan the second he learned of my pregnancy? And when he arrived, I was blown away that he'd been learning to read lips and sign.

My imagination was as vast as the divide I felt between us. But no matter the distance, our baby tethered me to him. It felt inevitable that I would drown before we found common ground, an island to save us.

OVER THE FOLLOWING WEEK, Ben left meals and snacks along with the occasional note, always signed *Benjamin Ashford, baby daddy in training.*

He wanted to know the date and time of my next doctor visit, if my feet were swelling, how much water I was drinking, and if I'd felt the baby move. I resisted the temptation to answer him in any form. Ben's gestures, while sweet, were low-hanging fruit. I needed something more.

Friday after my last class, I took a nap, but before I reached the good kind of sleep where I drooled and had vivid dreams, someone knocked at my door. I yawned while opening it. Ben held a plant, not flowers or a box of candy, a green houseplant.

"Spider plants clean the air," he said, stepping inside uninvited. "How are you feeling today?" he asked, setting the plant on the floor by the window.

When he faced me, I said, "okay."

Tiny lines formed across his forehead and he scraped his teeth along his bottom lip. "I hope you said fine, great, fabulous, or something like that. I won't ask you to write it down, since that ended poorly for me last time." He scratched his scruffy jaw.

I tried not to grin at his goofy gesture.

"Can I see our baby?"

I rolled my eyes.

"You know what I mean. Your belly."

I frowned. There wasn't much to see, but I sat on my bed and leaned backward, legs dangling over the side. Then I lifted my shirt. Ben hesitated for a few seconds before sitting next to me. He rested his hand on my belly above my navel, too high to feel my bump. So I took his hand and slid it beneath the waist of my sweatpants, over my uterus.

He smiled, cheeks a little pink, eyes sparkling. But I kept a neutral face because I was still mad at him. My heart skipped when he ducked his head and pushed down the front of my sweats so he could press his lips to my tiny bump. "I love you," he whispered.

I wasn't sure if he was talking to our baby or me. Either way, he twisted my emotions. I refused to cave so easily. Still, I liked his lips on my belly, his whiskers tickling my skin. It wasn't planned or intentional, but my fingers found their way into his hair, and he kissed my belly again.

My heart stopped skipping and took off sprinting. A heavy feeling settling in my breasts. Ben lifted his head, and I curled my fingers, tugging at his hair.

He eyed me as I wet my lips and slowly blinked. I felt heady and ... aroused. And suddenly, all I could think about was Isaac and Sarah on the sofa on Christmas morning.

Keeping his unblinking gaze glued to mine, he kissed my belly again and again, working his way a little lower each time until his lips grazed the waistband of my white underwear.

I didn't let go of his hair.

He tested my response, tucking just his fingertips under the cotton-covered elastic band. My chest rose and fell a little harder, so he inched his fingers a little farther, pulling the front of my panties down another fraction, trailing his lips in the same direction.

When I didn't protest, he slid off the bed and kneeled on the floor, keeping a sharp eye on my reaction. The only thing I could do was repeatedly wet my lips.

Ben removed my sweatpants, and again, eyed me with

caution, looking for the slightest hesitation in my response. His gaze flickered lower, settling between my legs. He skated his hand up my inner thigh and his thumb brushed along the *wet* crotch of my underwear.

Every move was agonizingly slow, and even though I knew it was because he needed permission, it also drove me mad with need.

Ben trapped his lower lip between his teeth and peeled off my underwear. A full body blush heated my skin and intensified tenfold when he spread my legs and hooked one over his shoulder. He turned his head to the side and kissed his way up the inside of my leg.

I thought I might have a heart attack, and I knew he couldn't hear me, but I was panting hard.

Scared.

Excited.

Dizzy.

Aroused.

My legs tried to close as he reached the top.

Oh God ...

Again, I fisted his hair, unsure if I wanted to push him away or pull him closer. It was new and euphoric. Frightening and forbidden. When his warm tongue breached the space between my legs, I jumped, and my other hand gripped the sheet beneath me.

Ben gazed up at me for a second before closing his eyes. His tongue and lips moved in slow, languid strokes along my sensitive flesh. My legs relaxed, opening wider. It felt *so* incredibly good, unlike anything I had ever experienced. I knew why Sarah moaned the way she did because I was making the same noises.

I wiggled and twisted my body the closer I got to orgasming, and that drew a moan from Ben as he guided my other leg over his shoulder and moved his tongue faster and sucked harder.

"Bennn!" The explosive sensation and unrelenting waves of pleasure nearly blinded me as my body jerked in response.

Ben's lips teased my inner thighs again, and I felt him smile against my skin. It was good. Who was I kidding? It was the most spectacular feeling I had ever experienced.

However, when I came down from the extreme high, reality seeped back into my conscience. My burning need to orgasm got me into this situation. I couldn't let him manipulate me with his tongue.

But dear God, I wanted to.

I jackknifed to sitting, forcing him to sit back on his heels. Then I hopped off the bed and pulled on my underwear and sweats. In the next breath, I opened the door and signed, "Thank you. Go away."

Ben remained on his knees, eyeing me with a smirk. When I kept a straight face, he wiped the back of his hand over his mouth and stood. That made me blush again, but I didn't give away anything else. He stopped at the door, regarding me while I kept my gaze pointed at his chest.

"You're welcome," he said and sauntered down the hallway.

I shut the door before he had the chance to glance back at me.

Chapter Thirty-Seven

Chicago, "I Don't Want to Live Without Your Love"

Ben

BOTH JASON AND CHRIS, the resident assistant, were cool with me crashing in my old dorm room while I ironed things out with Gabby, which I thought I did when I made her orgasm. It wasn't my intention. I wanted to feel our baby. The last thing I thought would happen, well, it happened. It was like she knew what she wanted. I only reacted to her subtle gestures and nudges.

And just when I thought she couldn't surprise me more, she kicked me out.

However, that wasn't the most impressive part. In a matter of days, rule-follower Gabriella Jacobson, the pastor's favorite daughter, did it four more times. I delivered healthy snacks or a book on pregnancy every day, but on the days she was there, she reclined on her bed, lifting her shirt for me to feel her belly.

I kissed it and talked to our baby. Then it led to me on my knees, servicing her, followed by her booting me out. She wrote no notes. The only words spoken or written were mine. Except she did her usual sign language when opening the door for me to leave.

After a trip to the library to get as many books on ASL as I could find, I learned those signs: Thank you. Go away.

The revelation made me laugh because every time I said "You're welcome," thinking the least she could have done was offer a thank-you. And the whole time, that's what she'd been doing.

I felt used in the best way and sad because there were so many questions I had, insecurities eating me alive, and fear unlike anything I had ever experienced. But I couldn't let her see any of that. Gabby was innocent, and I took that from her. She was the first Jacobson daughter to attend college, and I derailed her plans. Yet, despite all of that, she loved me.

She never gave up on me.

I owed her more than I had to give, but I knew I'd die trying. Of course, I only had four days left to make things right. My parents were uneasy with me driving back to Ann Arbor by myself. But I told them I wanted to visit my friends, including Gabby. And two weeks was the longest I could take off work without losing my job.

With chicken noodle soup, extra crackers, and some sort of lotion to prevent stretch marks, I knocked on her door.

She answered, making her usual face where she pressed her lips together to keep from showing any sort of pleasure over my presence. The mother of my child took my breath away in her black leggings and yellow sweater that hung off one shoulder.

After my heart skipped a beat, I handed her the two bags and sat on her bed while she inspected my gifts. She uncapped the stretch mark cream and applied it to her belly. That made me grin even though she wouldn't look at me. Then, as though I wasn't there, she sat at her desk and ate every drop of soup and all the crackers.

After stuffing all the trash into the bag, she looked at me. Even if the timing was all wrong, pregnancy looked good on Gabby. I understood what people meant when they said pregnant women had a glow about them. My best friend was beautiful, but I'd always known that.

Gabby got that look in her eyes and moseyed toward the bed, but before she could sit down, I signed, "I'm not here to lick your kitty."

She wrinkled her nose and signed, "What?"

I spelled each word, in case she didn't understand, *and* I wanted to show her how good I was at signing the alphabet.

When pink filled her cheeks, I knew she got it.

"Where did you learn that?" she signed.

Aside from the alphabet and a few phrases I practiced for that moment, I couldn't sign much else or understand everything she signed.

"I just started. You have to cut me some slack. Can you do that? Can you continue to write things down until I learn this better?" I asked.

The indecision in her eyes made my heart sink. I still hadn't fully digested the news. Gabby was pregnant. We were having a baby. I tried to feign confidence, but I was terrified. After I lost my hearing, I immediately wanted my mom. How was I supposed to raise a child when I still felt like one?

Gabby sat at her desk and wrote on a notepad.

Why are you learning ASL?

"Because I'm deaf."
She shook her head.

*You've been deaf, but haven't wanted to learn it.
Is this because of Laurel?*

I squinted, slowly shaking my head. "I'm going to be a dad. I have to find a way to communicate in the world. Get a better job. Go back to school. Whatever."

Why did she look so crestfallen? What was wrong with doing exactly what she'd been wanting me to do for months?

She capped the pen and walked to the door, opening it before signing, "Go away."

"I'm not going away. You can't kick me out for doing what you wanted me to do."

She fisted her hands and said something before closing her eyes. In the next breath, she slammed the door and scribbled more words.

*I'll do this on my own. I'll raise this baby with
someone who loves me.*

What was that supposed to mean? My jaw dropped, and all words escaped me.

"Are you serious?" I stood, parking both hands on my hips. "Nobody loves you more than I do. Our friendship has just been various phases of me loving you, from near, from afar, from everywhere. I've spent more of my life loving you than doing anything else. I loved you before I knew the feelings I had for you were love. But they were. They are. And they always will be."

She shook her head and furiously wrote more words.

You're here because I'm pregnant. You're learning ASL because I'm pregnant.

"What's your point?"
She scowled.

I wanted you to come back for ME! I wanted you to learn ASL for ME! But I wasn't allowed to make anything about me. Clearly nothing has changed.

I held out my hands, palms up, before raking my fingers through my hair. "I'll concede that I've been an asshole for the past six months. But before I lost my hearing, my world revolved around you. Whatever you thought or think you feel for Matt, take that times a thousand." I shook my head. "No. Take it times infinity, and that's what I've felt for you. So I get it. The reason I've been so patient with your obsession is because I know what it's like to want someone beyond reason. I know what it's like to wait an eternity for that person to see you. And I know the fear and courage it takes to tell them."

She slowly shook her head as if it wasn't a fair comparison. And she was right. It wasn't. Her feelings for Matt were nothing compared to mine for her.

"Yes. Gabby. *Yes.*" I took her face in my hands. "I told you Michigan was the only school that offered me a scholarship, but I lied. I had three other offers. But I chose this one. Do you know why?"

Tears filled her eyes.

"Because I want to be with you. Even if it means I have to watch you pine for another man, I'll take it. I just want to *be with you*, and I'll take absolutely anything you'll give me."

Gabby blinked, releasing several tears with it.

I rested my forehead on hers. "I'm sorry it took this for me to come to my senses. And I will try so hard to pretend that I'm not scared out of my mind, that I know what I'm doing, and that I won't let you down. And I'll try to pretend that it doesn't hurt to feel like you wish this baby belonged to him."

She stepped back, shaking her head and pointing to herself, then made two fists and crossed her arms in an X over her chest before pointing to me while mouthing "I love you." Then she spelled "Not Matt."

"Because we're having a baby?"

Again, she shook her head and turned. A few seconds later, she held up the notepad.

Despite you knocking me up. When you kissed me, my heart exploded. My dreams died because they couldn't compare to what was real. You are real. We are real.

Her words choked me up, so I swallowed hard. "Do you mean that?"

She nodded, stepping toward me and wrapping her arms around my waist, face buried in my neck for a long breath. Then she pressed her lips to my skin for a soft kiss. I removed her arms from my waist and kneeled at her feet. When I looked up at her, she grinned, sliding one hand into my hair and resting the other on my cheek.

Then I lowered my chin and kissed her belly. She continued to tease her fingers in my hair while her other handed lifted her sweater.

"Hi, baby," I said before kissing her little bump. I could have spent hours on my knees, working through my fears while talking to the life we made, but after a minute, she grabbed my hoodie and tugged it so I'd stand. Then she lifted onto her toes, and I met her halfway for a kiss.

While our lips fused, she unzipped my hoodie, resting her hands on my chest for a few breaths before unbuttoning my jeans. I pulled away just enough to look at her.

"Are you sure?"

She nodded, biting her lip, cheeks stained pink.

I shrugged my hoodie off my shoulders and peeled off my T-shirt. Gabby removed her sweater and leggings. The second my jeans were off, she slid her hands around my neck and we kissed. I unhooked her bra as we stepped closer to the bed. Everything felt different.

Gabby officially felt like mine.

I took my time kissing her where she liked to be kissed— between her legs. When I worked my way up her body and sucked her nipple into my mouth, she arched her back. As I guided my cock between her legs, her hips jerked. And the second I sank into her, she flinched. It wasn't funny, but I couldn't help but smile.

"Our baby will hurt you more," I mumbled.

She grabbed my face and narrowed her eyes, saying so much without saying a word. I kissed her, and we moved slowly together until I couldn't move slowly any longer. I didn't want to hurt her, but nothing felt like being inside of her.

Her lips moving against mine.

Her breasts pressed to my chest.

I was in Heaven.

I found myself breaking our kisses to look at her because I couldn't hear her. It was like I needed to check in, even though her fingernails in my back and her hips lifting from the bed to meet mine were more than enough reassurance that she wanted to keep going.

After we finished, I rolled to the side and tucked her under my arm. My eyes burned, staring at the bunk bed above us. I would never hear her moan or say my name.

Ask for more.

Whisper words of love while having sex.

No contented sighs.

Nothing.

Would I ever stop mourning the loss of my hearing? Would I ever stop thinking of all the parts of life that I could no longer enjoy?

She drew a heart on my chest with the tip of her finger, so I grabbed her hand and kissed her palm.

"I love you, too, Gabriella."

Chapter Thirty-Eight

The Platters, "Only You"

Gabby

IT WAS WEIRD. When I woke the next morning, I no longer recognized the Ben I grew up with.

He stood at my desk, thumbing through one of my textbooks. Shirt off. Jeans on, but not zipped or buttoned. Hair a chaotic mess.

Nope. No sign of best friend Ben.

The guy scratching the back of his head and yawning was hot Ben.

Sexy Ben.

Boyfriend Ben.

I had to think about that. Did it take me nineteen years to get my first boyfriend? And would he be my last? I pressed a hand to my baby bump. Of course, he would be my last.

I sat up and put on his hoodie, zipping it just past my breasts.

He turned and lifted his eyebrows while inspecting me. Then he smiled. "Good morning."

I finger spelled "Only you."

His forehead wrinkled as he stared at my hand. "Slower."

I spelled it again.

"Only you?"

I nodded, pointing to him. Then I padded toward my desk, my body brushing past his to write him a note.

Only You
You're my first and last.
My beginning and my end.
My friend and lover.

Ben read it and lifted his gaze to me. "Gabbs, did you just write me a poem?"

I finger spelled. "A haiku."

He grinned, curling my hair behind my ears while ducking to kiss me. "I love you," he whispered before kissing me. Then he hugged me and swayed.

I wasn't sure what he was doing until he started to sing "Only You" by The Platters.

My heart swelled, forming a lump in my throat. Ben could sing, like really sing. Pitch-perfect. In time. And every step synched to the rhythm. Then I focused on the words, and my emotions multiplied. The song wasn't just poetic; it was beautiful and romantic. It was us.

While Ben serenaded and danced with me, it felt like he could hear. There was nothing tragic about the moment. It was just me and the boy who stole my heart before I even knew it. Perhaps all those years in high school I spent "pin-ing" for Matt were nothing more than searching for my stolen heart. And Ben had it all along.

As he sang the last two lines, he unzipped the hoodie and slid it past my shoulders, leaving me naked before him.

"Baby," he murmured in my ear. "You're so sexy."

I swallowed hard because he called me "baby" and "sexy." For years, I wanted to be someone's "sweetheart" or their "love," and I wanted to be "beautiful" or maybe even "gorgeous." But as Ben cupped my breast and teased his thumb over my nipple, I loved being his sexy baby.

I blinked heavily, staring at my alarm clock. "Oh my gosh! I'm late!" Shoving Ben away from me, I grabbed my previous day's clothes from the floor and wrestled with them.

Ben squinted.

"I'm late!" I yelled, then I tried to sign it, but I couldn't remember the sign for late.

"It's fine. I'm guessing you're late," he said.

I nodded with my back to him as I hopped on one foot and then the other to put on my socks and shoes.

"Sorry. My fault."

Yes. It was his fault. Everything was his fault.

I dry brushed my teeth, swished the melted ice from the previous night's drink, spat it back in the cup, and snagged my backpack on the way to the door.

"That's it. You're leaving me with a boner? No goodbye. No kiss?"

I turned while opening the door.

He crooked a finger at me, and I shook my head.

"You're stubborn," he said.

I grinned.

"Skip your classes. I'll help you study. We'll go to lunch. I'll braid your hair."

I shook my head.

Ben sauntered toward me. It wasn't fair that he was half naked. "You say no, and yet you're still here." He took my bag from me and dropped it on the ground before pushing the door shut. Where was my willpower?

I had none.

No willpower, and less than sixty seconds later, I had no clothes on my body, just naked Ben between my legs.

Why did you finally read my letters?

I HAD SO MANY QUESTIONS, and since Ben convinced me to skip school *and* he fetched me breakfast, I had all day to quiz him.

He sipped a bottle of orange juice, sitting in my desk chair, while I lounged in the bean bag chair I got from Sarah and Isaac for Christmas.

"I don't want to tell you."

I signed, "Why?"

He capped his juice. "Because I'm a stubborn asshole. And I honestly don't know how long it would have taken me to open them had Tillie not opened them the day she cleaned my room." He stared out the window.

Tillie knows!

I panicked because I didn't want anyone telling my parents before I did.

"She won't say anything."

How do you know? That's a big secret to keep. Where are the letters? The ultrasound picture? What if your mom finds them?

Ben stared at the notepad that I held up, and he twisted his lips for a few seconds, then he leaned to the side and pulled his wallet out of his jeans. "Some of the letters were damaged, and the rest are hidden." He slid the ultrasound photo from his wallet. "But I have this."

It melted my heart at first, then I set the notepad aside and rocked forward to pluck the taped-together photo from his fingers.

Ben cringed, scratching the back of his head. "About that ..."

I narrowed my eyes.

"Tillie didn't say you were pregnant. She just told me to read them. So I started to read them in order." Ben shot me a look. "Do you recall what you wrote in your first letter?"

Pressing my lips together, I nodded slowly.

"So I ripped up the letters, but then I stopped when I noticed shreds of the photo. It took me forever to piece it back together. Then I read the letters that I hadn't destroyed. And here I am."

That's not how I wanted him to find out. It left me crestfallen.

"Gabby." He reached for my hand, but I plopped back into the bean bag chair before he touched me.

Were you ever going to read them?

His hesitation answered my question.

Were you going to sleep with her?

"Gabby." His face tensed as he shook his head.

I hurled the notepad at him. "NO! Not *Gabby*! That's not what you say. Oh my—" I cupped a hand over my mouth to muffle my sob.

He was going to have sex with her because we were over in his mind.

"I *hated* my life," he said, stabbing his fingers into his hair. "I hated the pity. I hated the look on your face because you blamed yourself. I hated not knowing if I would ever live up to Matthew Cory in your mind."

I couldn't look at him. And I didn't want to hear his excuses.

"Gabby, you taunted me. Had I opened the first letter from you when you sent it, I never would have opened the rest."

"I was mad," I signed.

He shook his head. "I don't know what you're saying."

"Ugh!" I *hated* that he got to speak his emotions without thinking them through. I had to stop, control myself, and write everything down.

He handed me the notepad, and I jerked it out of his hand.

I was mad! You knew there was a possibility

that I could be pregnant but you still broke up with me.

He frowned. "It was a slim chance."

It was a 100% chance. I'M PREGNANT!

He flinched.

Is that your method? Pulling out? How many other girls have you impregnated?

"None. I wasn't planning on having sex with you. It just happened."

You had no intention of coming here. You're not really here for me. Intention is everything! Just go home.

I stood and shoved the notepad into his chest before opening the door.

"Intention is nothing." He tossed the notepad onto my desk and shoved his feet into his sneakers. "Reality is everything." He stopped at the door, peering down at me. "And here's what is real. I've loved you for *years*. Something really shitty happened to me, and I've had a hard time accepting it. But you're pregnant with our baby, and all I want to do is get my life together and be a good father and husband. *What's real* is I don't care how we got here or how bad the timing may seem. I'm not mad about it. You are my fucking dream,

Gabriella Grace Jacobson. And I'm not letting you go. That's what's real. *That* is everything. So you just think about that while I'm gone."

Chapter Thirty-Nine

Night Ranger, "Sister Christian"

Gabby

"Hey, Gabbs. What's up?" My sister Eve asked, answering my call.

"I need advice."

She laughed. "And you're calling me? Did Sarah die?"

"No. But did she tell you I slept with Ben?" I stared out my dorm room window at the lights illuminating the parking lot a little before ten at night.

There was a silent pause on the line. That was my answer.

"I'm proud of you. Virginity is overrated," she said.

I grunted. "Don't be proud. He pulled out."

"Pulled out of what?"

"Me."

"Oh." She laughed. "Gotcha. That's not all that reliable.

You have to be careful. That last thing you need is to end up pregnant."

I pinched the bridge of my nose. "Do you really think I called you to tell you he pulled out? End of story?"

"Uh ... is this a trick question?"

"Have you heard of pre-ejaculatory fluid?"

She snorted. "Gabriella, are you high?"

"No. But you've had lots of sex, so I thought you would know."

"Yes, I'm the slutty sister. Let's see, I'm guessing just from breaking down the term that it's when a guy dribbles before he shoots."

"What?" I wrinkled my nose.

"When a guy gets turned on, but before he orgasms, a little (I assume) *pre-ejaculatory fluid* comes out. It's like when a girl gets wet because she's turned on. Is this for your anatomy class?"

"I'm not taking anatomy. Ben must have ... dribbled."

"Gabbs, why are you being so weird—holy fuck ... ARE YOU PREGNANT?"

I cringed while pacing my dorm room. "I am," I murmured.

"Who knows? Sarah? Mom and Dad? Have you told Ben? What were you thinking?"

"I was thinking we were going to do that other thing, you know, the dry version. But we only had on underwear, and the next thing I knew, it kind of slipped out. So he asked me if it was okay, and I kinda wanted to, so I said yes. But he pulled out at the end. Then he dumped me. Weeks later, I took several pregnancy tests, but they were all negative. Then I started feeling tired and nauseous, so I went to the doctor, and she said I was for sure pregnant. That's also when I found out that there are sperm in pre-ejaculatory fluid."

There was another long pause.

"Eve?"

"Yeah, I'm still here. I'm just ..."

"How do I tell Mom and Dad?"

"I don't know, but I want to be there when you do."

"Ugh! I knew I should have called Sarah."

"No. No. No. Sorry, that just came out. I'm glad you called me. From my experience, it's just best to tell them when you've done something really bad. Chin up. Shoulders back. And own up to your actions. But have a plan. Like, show them you're an adult. And even if this wasn't part of some grand plan, you're mature enough to handle it and do what needs to be done."

I thought about it for a few seconds.

"Did you say he dumped you?"

"Yeah, but he's here now. And he wants to do the right thing. He says he loves me and he always has, but I don't think we would be together if I wasn't pregnant. And that really bothers me."

"Gabbs, he's deaf. Have you even tried to imagine what he must be going through?"

"No. I haven't because I've been a little preoccupied *being pregnant.*"

"You're going to be pregnant for nine months. He could be deaf for the rest of his life. And pregnancy isn't a disability."

I collapsed onto my bed. "I'm going to have to drop out of school."

"You can always go back later."

"Mom and Dad will kick me out of the house. Then

what? Are Ben and I supposed to live on our own with his salary from working in the meat department?"

"Live with Ben's parents."

"What makes you think they'd let us live there?"

"Because his parents used to let you bring your rescued animals to their place."

"In the barn."

"Well, if it was good enough for Mary and Joseph." Eve chuckled. "You can get married and register for a manger."

"Stop." I laughed.

"You won't know until you tell them."

"It's funny," I bit my thumbnail for a beat, "I've hated keeping this from them, and now that Ben knows, and it's time to tell them, I'm scared to death."

"I'll do it."

"You'll what? Tell them I'm pregnant?"

"Totally. I'll drive back to Devil's Head and whip up a nice dinner. Maybe forage for enough wildflowers to make a beautiful centerpiece. Then after Dad says grace and everyone is passing around the food, I'll say something like, 'What do you think Gabby and Ben are going to name their baby?' Or, maybe something more like, 'Hey, Dad, did you catch the Bulls game the other night? And speaking of dribbling and shooting ... Ben and Gabby had a little pre-ejaculatory mishap. God works in mysterious ways, huh?'"

"Eve—"

"Oh, wait. Maybe I could casually ask Mom if regular crib mattress sheets also work for mangers."

"I'm never calling you again. It's not funny," I said— while giggling.

"Gabby, you're growing a life inside of you. Laugh. Love.

Be happy. Find joy. How am I doing? That's what Sarah would say, right?"

I rested my hand on my belly. "What would Eve say?"

"Oh," she laughed, "Let's see ..."

I prepared for some obnoxious or inappropriate "wisdom."

"Gabby, I'd say to laugh, love, be happy, and find joy."

"Eve," I whispered. One reason I called her was because I trusted her not to make me cry.

She failed.

"Dad and Mom are going to be disappointed and sad that you've somehow *messed up* your future. They're also going to be embarrassed. It doesn't look good for the preacher's daughter to get pregnant out of wedlock. And they might even disown you for the rest of your pregnancy, but there's no way they see your baby and not fall in love with her."

"Her? You think I'm having a girl?"

"Of course. You, Sarah, and I are only having girls. Had you not gotten knocked up like this, I would have said you deserved a boy. But nope. We're having girls who will grow up to be naughty little whores."

"Oh my gosh!" I snorted. "Eve!"

"Well, thanks for calling. Glad I could help."

"Yeah, right."

"Gabbs?"

"Huh?"

"I love you. Congratulations," she said with total sincerity.

"Thank you."

Chapter Forty

Michael Jackson, "Man in the Mirror"

Ben

I RETURNED HOME, and my mom had a million questions written on notecards about the drive, where I stayed, if I wanted to go back to school, how I communicated, and if Gabby was surprised and excited to see me. My dad focused on his dinner, seeing how my mom had all the questions covered. And I felt Tillie's gaze on me the whole time, so I refrained from looking at her.

Then the next morning, we attended church. After the service, I handed notes to my parents and Gabby's.

> AFTER THE CONGREGATION EXITS, I NEED TO
> TALK TO YOU IN THE CHURCH.

All four parents inspected me through narrowed eyes before nodding. Tillie gave me the stink eye when my mom sent her to wait in the car. Then, the five of us gathered at the front of the empty church. It felt like I had God on my side, but I knew better. I was using God and his house as a shield.

"Have a seat," I said to them, but I remained standing.

Pastor Jacobson was the most reluctant. It might have been the first time he sat in the front row of his own church. I came prepared with four notebooks and pens in my backpack, and I handed them to our parents. The uneasiness in their expressions intensified.

The thought of suggesting a prayer before beginning tempted me. I thought, perhaps, asking God to open our minds and hearts and fill them with love, acceptance, and forgiveness might be a nice touch. But I didn't.

"Thanks for staying," I said instead. "I'm sure everyone knows that I've been back at school." I focused on Pastor and Mrs. Jacobson since my parents knew, but I assumed my mom told Gabby's parents.

They nodded.

"I'm in love with Gabriella," I said, wasting no time getting to the point.

Our moms glanced at each other with tears in their eyes and smiles so bright I thought they might explode. Our dads were more reserved.

"I've been in love with her for a long time, and I thought it was a crush that might go away. In some ways, I hoped it would because I didn't think she could ever think of me as more than a friend. Come to find out, she loves me too."

I hoped it was still true.

That's all it took for a stray tear to escape down my mom's face as she squeezed my dad's hand. "I want to ask

Gabby to marry me, and I'd like all of you to give us your blessing and support." I kept my focus on Pastor Jacobson.

He swallowed hard and tiny lines formed along his forehead, then he uncapped his pen and scribbled a response.

YOU'RE BOTH YOUNG. DON'T YOU THINK WAITING UNTIL YOU'RE DONE WITH COLLEGE, AND YOU HAVE YOUR FUTURE FIGURED OUT WOULD BE A BETTER IDEA?

"That," I drew out the word and scratched the back of my neck, "probably would have been the best idea. But," I dove off the cliff, ripped off the bandage, "life rarely goes as planned. For example, I never imagined losing my hearing. And I don't think Gabby nor I imagined having a baby together so soon, but we are, so I hope we can all embrace this exciting moment because there's no going back." Sweat soaked my pits and beaded along my brow.

It felt like a blinking contest, and I didn't know who would win as they sat like statues displaying varying degrees of shock.

"I'm sorry," I continued, forcing my attention to Gabby's parents. "This is my fault. I should have been more responsible. Sadly, it wasn't my first time having sex, and I should have known better."

My mom's shoulders drew inward as she reached for my father's hand, holding it in her lap while squeezing it tightly. She dropped her gaze as if they, too, were in trouble with Pastor Jacobson.

Gabby's mom wrote something, then she scribbled it out. Again, she wrote something, and again, she scribbled it out before setting the pen on the pad of paper with a shaky hand. Then she wiped her tears that no longer seemed like happy ones.

WHY ARE YOU TELLING US THIS INSTEAD OF GABBY?

Pastor Jacobson's jaw muscles tightened as he held up his notepad.

"It's a long story, but she wanted to tell me first, and it took a while for her to get that message to me. She doesn't know I'm telling you this or asking for her hand in marriage. I'm doing it because I don't want her subjected to more stress than necessary. When she comes home for summer, I don't want her scared out of her mind to tell you and risk anything happening to the baby. So if you need to yell at someone, let it be me. I can take the lectures, the anger, the disappointment, but I won't let you dump it on her."

Pastor Jacobson frowned, so I cleared my throat and finished by saying, "sir," so he didn't feel disrespected despite the news that I impregnated his youngest daughter.

When did this happen?

Janet, Gabby's mom, wrote.

"When did she get pregnant?" I clarified, realizing I made it sound like something Gabby did all on her own.

However, "When did I have sex with your daughter?" or "When did I knock her up?" didn't feel right either.

Janet nodded.

"Christmas break," I said. Did that mean the birth of Jesus made us horny?

WHAT ARE YOUR PLANS? HOW ARE YOU GOING TO SUPPORT GABBY AND THE BABY?

Pastor Jacobson wrote.

"Well, Sir, I had a lot of time to think about this on the drive home. And I want to support Gabby in whatever she wants to do. If she wants to stay in school, I'll move to Michigan and work nights and weekends to support us so I can be with the baby during the day when she's at school. If she wants to move back to Devil's Head to be near family, then I will work here."

My dad held up his notepad.

YOU HAVE DERAILED YOUR LIFE AND HERS.

"I know, and I'm sorry about that, but I can't change it no matter how disappointed or angry anyone is about it."

My mom said something to Gabby's mom, and she replied while digging a tissue from her purse. Then Pastor Jacobson's lips moved, but my dad just stared at me with disappointment in his eyes.

I wanted to know what they were saying, but I refrained from speaking until Pastor Jacobson wrote:

WE NEED TO TALK TO GABBY.

"Of course, sir. However, I'd like to let her know I talked to you, so she's not blindsided."

Janet shook her head and scribbled.

She really doesn't know you're telling us?

"No, ma'am." I contemplated sharing more, like how I wasn't sure Gabby would marry me since she didn't even want to speak to me.

I have never felt so disappointed in you as I do right now. Poor Gabby.

My mom delivered her message with a few tears.

Admittedly, it was irresponsible and dumb. But in all fairness, I pulled out.

"Yes, ma'am." I nodded. "But I've always wanted to marry her and have a family with her. I also wanted the ability to hear for the rest of my life. Plans change. Life happens. I can't undo anything even with a million sorrys. So I'm doing my best by taking responsibility. I'm learning sign language. I've bought Gabby books on pregnancy and taken her healthy meals and snacks. I'm going to see if I can get more time off work to be back for her next OB appointment. I'll take all the blame. Just please, don't be mad at Gabby."

Janet stood and stared at me. I half-expected her to slap my face. Instead, she hugged me. I hesitated for a few seconds before embracing her. As I stared at Pastor Jacobson over her shoulder, I didn't get the vibe that he was next in line for a hug.

As soon as we arrived home, I sprinted upstairs and waited for Tillie, who took her sweet time.

"I need you to call Gabby and tell her I need her to listen to me. Then I need you to write down what she says."

Tillie crossed her arms over her chest and scowled at me for a few seconds before brushing past me and sitting at my desk.

Only if you tell me what happened in church.

"I told everyone that Gabby's pregnant. Now I need to tell her before her parents call her."

She doesn't know you were going to tell them?

I shook my head while dialing Gabby's phone number. Tillie returned saucer eyes.

"Just hand me the phone as soon as she says, 'Hello.'"

Tillie held the phone to her ear for a few seconds before quickly handing it back to me.

"Hey, Gabbs. Obviously, I can't hear you, but I need to tell you something, and then you can reply to Tillie, and she will relay your response. After church, I told our parents about the pregnancy because I didn't want you to have to do it and risk anyone getting upset or making you feel bad. That wouldn't be good for you or the baby. I told them it was my fault, and that I planned on doing whatever you feel is best. So I'll move to Michigan and work nights while you go to school during the day. Or I'll get a better job close to Devil's Head if you want to move home and finish your schooling later. It's your choice. And just so you know, when I finished telling them, your mom hugged me. My dad said nothing. My mom is disappointed in me. And your dad might want to kill me. So ... how do you feel? I'm giving the phone to Tillie."

Tillie held the phone back to her ear. After a few seconds, her lips moved. She frowned and hung up the phone.

"Hey!" I hurried and picked it back up.

She hung up.

"What?" I shook my head. "No. You must have gotten disconnected."

I don't think so. She hung up on purpose.

I dialed her number again and handed the phone to Tillie, who rolled her eyes. After a long pause, she hung up.

She's not answering.

"You didn't wait long enough."

It rang ten times.

I scrubbed my hands over my face and grumbled, "Dammit, Gabbs. Pick up the phone."

Sorry.

Tillie set the pen on the paper and patted my shoulder before leaving my room.

Chapter Forty-One

Whitney Houston, "The Greatest Love of All"

Gabby

BEN HAD NO RIGHT TELLING my parents about the pregnancy. Even if it was his baby, too, it wasn't his news to share with *my* parents. So much for holding my chin up and shoulders back to take responsibility like an adult. Ben made me look like a scared child.

He called five times over the following two days, and I hung up as soon as I heard his voice.

Late Wednesday afternoon, while I was trying to study for my psychology test, there was a knock at my door. Despite my anger toward Ben, I wanted it to be him.

"Mom," I said on a gasp.

She hugged me without a word, and just like when Ben showed up unexpectedly, I broke down in tears and stated the thing that she already knew, "I'm pregnant."

"I know," she whispered, hugging me tighter.

It was hard to release her and look her in the eyes, but I did while wiping my tears. "Where's Dad?" I asked, closing the door.

"Home." She glanced around my room.

"I'm sorry Ben was the one who told you." I sat on my bed and tucked my knees under a large T-shirt.

Mom returned a slight nod while looking out my window, arms hugging herself. She had a nervous disposition that felt like my own. "You didn't have to keep it."

I squinted. "The baby?"

She nodded, leaving me speechless.

"When you were almost twelve, I got pregnant." She turned toward me, displaying a vulnerability I had never seen. "I was done raising babies. It felt like it was anything but a blessing, a gift from God. I felt weak and hopeless. And I just ..." She shook her head. "I didn't want to do it. I *couldn't*." She wiped a few tears. "So I took a bottle of pills. And I was gone for a few days. Your dad told you girls I was having some routine testing. And that was it. No baby."

I cleared my throat. "You took the pills to kill the baby?"

Mom's face tensed while she averted her gaze.

She took the pills to kill herself.

"Gabriella," she sat next to me and squeezed my hand, "I know your dad preaches that God doesn't give us more than we can handle, but ... I don't know if that's true."

She blew up my world.

I wanted to be my mom—hard-working, a loving mom, and loyal wife. I had always admired her strong faith and commitment to our family. Of course, I knew she wasn't perfect, but I thought she was awfully close.

I released my legs from the confines of my T-shirt and

leaned to the side to hug my mom. "I'm so glad it was just the baby, and not you."

She pulled away, blotting her red eyes and nodding. "Me too."

"I wanted to tell you. And I'm so mad at Ben for doing it first."

"I think this baby saved him, Gabby. I think he felt lost without a purpose, and now he has one. And I hate saying that because I don't know what that means for you. The last thing I want is for you to feel thrust into motherhood when you're not ready."

I grunted a laugh and rested my hand on my belly. "I'm not ready, but I want this. I'm scared, but I want this. I hate Ben for a hundred different reasons, but I love him."

Mom smiled. "Ben's willing to support you, no matter what. And your dad and I want to support you, no matter what."

"Dad?" I asked with skepticism. "He's not livid that I'm pregnant at nineteen, out of wedlock?"

Mom rolled her eyes. "Well, he's not elated."

"When Sarah and Eve disappointed him, he was ready to kick them out and disown them," I said.

"Oh," she laughed. "He's ready to disown you, young lady. But he wants what's best for your innocent child. So you can stay in school or come home. Either way, we'll do our best to support you."

I dropped my head and murmured, "I don't know what I want. Not anymore. I'm still in a state of shock that it's Ben."

"What do you mean?"

I stood and stepped toward my desk, staring at the picture of Ben and me, arm in arm at our high school graduation. Could I tell her about Matt? I financially strapped myself to thousands of dollars in debt to be at the University of Michigan *just* for Matthew Cory, but my infatuation (coveting) felt like a greater sin than getting pregnant. If I stuck it out and finished school, then it wouldn't all be for nothing.

"I came here for Matt," I said.

"Matt? Matt Cory? What do you mean?"

With my back to her, I grunted a laugh and shook my head. "I've had a crush on him since before he was with Sarah. I've written poems about him, imagined our wedding, and little things about our life together. I'm"— I stared at the ceiling—"embarrassed. *He* was my dream. He was the reason I refused to go to college anywhere but here. I had never felt so determined about anything or anyone as I did about him."

When I looked at my mom, her face corkscrewed as if I wasn't speaking English.

"Then he kissed me," I murmured.

"Matt?" she asked with a tone of distaste.

"Ben. He kissed me and ruined me for Matt or anyone else. I knew it was him, and it broke my heart because I also knew it meant we would have to be everything to each other or nothing. There was no going back, no middle ground. I couldn't kiss my best friend and *just* be friends. But the feelings that surfaced dumbfounded my heart, and I was scared because I came here for Matt. And my mind was like, what does this mean? What does this say about me? Then he got sick, and I was ignoring—" I choked, cupping a hand to my mouth. Would I ever stop feeling responsible?

Pressing my fingers to the corners of my eyes, I blew out a slow breath. "I avoided Ben after the kiss. And that's when he got sick. Had I not been so stubborn and immature, I would have known he needed to go to the doctor. And he might still be able to hear."

"Gabby—"

I shook my head. "I hated him for making me love him. I hated myself for not seeing it sooner. And now I'm pregnant, but I still feel the hate. And there's all these insecurities that I can't get past. Does he blame me for what happened? Even if he does, he will never say it. Had I not gotten pregnant, would he be with me? Would he be with Laurel instead? If my foolish heart led me in the wrong direction towards Matt, isn't it possible that Ben's has led him in the wrong direction towards me?"

"My dear, Benjamin Ashford is head over heels in love with you. He didn't go in the wrong direction. Every path in that young man's mind was going to lead to you."

"He was interested in Laurel. He only came back here for the baby."

"And you came to Michigan for Matt, yet you're having Ben's baby."

I frowned.

"Listen," she held out her hand, and I took it, sitting next to her, "Life is an interpretation of our dreams. You dreamed of falling in love, and life gave you Ben." Mom grinned before resting her head on my shoulder with a soft sigh. "I want to be nineteen so I can fall in love with a Benjamin Ashford. He's so dreamy."

"Stop." I giggled.

"Well, he is," Mom said.

I rested my head against hers. "Yeah. I know."

My mom stayed for three days. She took me out to dinner one night and to see *Pretty Woman* the next.

"I can't believe you took me to see a movie about a prostitute," I said, feeling overjoyed that my mom decided to just be my friend for the night.

"Don't you dare tell your dad." She laughed, unlocking the doors to the rental car.

"I'm glad you came. I was so nervous about going home at the end of the semester, but now I feel relieved that you and Dad know."

"Thanks to Ben."

"Yes. Thanks to Ben, I'm pregnant. Did you and Dad thank him for that?"

"We didn't go that far."

When she dropped me off at my dorm, I leaned over and hugged her. "Will I see you before you fly out tomorrow?"

"Not unless you're getting up at five in the morning."

"Oof! Nope. I won't. Love you. Thanks for coming."

"Love you too," she said. "Call me more than once a week. I need updates. And let me know what the doctor says after your next appointment."

I nodded.

"And don't stress over deciding about your schooling right now. It's okay to take some time. It's okay to take a year off and go back to school the following year. Once you hold this baby in your arms, you're not going to want to let her go for a single second."

"Her?" I squinted.

"Yes, dear. It's a girl. I just know."

I laughed. "We'll see about that." I opened the door.

She blew me a kiss before I closed it.

Chapter Forty-Two

Keith Whitley, "When You Say Nothing at All"

Ben

I HAD to quit my job to get time off to make it to Gabby's next OB appointment. Joblessness seemed counterintuitive to my goal of supporting us, but working in the meat department wasn't a long-term solution anyway.

After a thirteen-hour drive, mostly through the night, I arrived in Ann Arbor. It took three knocks on Gabby's door before she opened it. At first, her eyes widened, and a smile tugged at her lips, but she quickly corrected her reaction with a scowl.

She signed something. I caught the "what," but not the rest.

"Too late. I saw you smile. You're happy to see me."

Gabby crossed her arms over her chest, and I grinned. She looked irresistible in her pink nightshirt, bare legs, and messy hair.

"Come on, Gabbs. I drove all night to be with you. In fact, I scrolled every radio station just to find Cyndi Lauper's song, 'I Drove All Night.'"

Again, she fought her grin. "You're deaf," she signed. That one I caught.

"Don't rub it in."

She went for the eye roll, so predictable. Then she turned her back to me, grabbing her robe and toiletry bag while shoving her feet into white slippers.

"I missed you," I said, sliding my arms around her, bringing her back to my chest while nuzzling my nose in her hair at her ear. "What time is your appointment?"

She signed, "three," then peeled my arms from her waist and left the room.

I made her bed and tidied up her desk. A pen was sticking out of a journal, and I fell prey to the temptation of peeking inside.

I don't trust my instincts anymore. Everything I thought I wanted feels like an outdated fashion trend. How am I supposed to think about my future career when I'll be a mom in five months?

Before reading the entire day's entry, I flipped back a few pages.

My mom showed up, and I didn't know how much I needed her until she hugged me.

I smiled. When my mom told me that Janet had flown here to visit Gabby, I knew everything would be okay.

Again, I thumbed back through earlier entries, not taking the time to read anything in full because I knew she'd be back soon, and I had no business reading them.

Today I heard my baby's heartbeat. There are no words to describe how that felt. I wish Ben would have been there. I wish he would respond to my letters. It's funny how I used to dream of marrying Matt and the look on his face when we heard our first baby's heartbeat. I just never imagined he'd be holding my hand, but the baby wouldn't be his. Life continues to surprise me. I want this unexpected turn in my life to be a good one, but I don't know yet. The uncertainty steals my joy.

I jumped, closing the journal and turning. Gabby narrowed her eyes, gaze flitting between me and the journal.

"Him? You took *him* to your appointment? *He* heard my baby's heartbeat? *He* held your hand?"

She nudged me out of her way and wrote on a notepad.

Why were you reading my journal?

"It doesn't matter. Why did you take Matthew Fucking Cory?"

My journals are private!

"I was straightening up a few things, and I went to pull the pen out and my curiosity got the best of me." I shook my head a half dozen times. "It doesn't matter. Why him, Gabby? Do you hate me that much?"

She winced, then reached her hand toward my cheek, but I batted it away.

I dropped my head, rubbing my temples with the heels of my hands. "You gave him something I will never have. Why? Why would you do that?"

Because you wouldn't read my letters! And I had no one. So he offered to go with me. I wasn't thinking about getting to hear the heartbeat. I was lonely and scared!

I read her words, but they didn't help, so I wadded up the paper and threw it toward the trash can, missing by several feet. After so much time spent contemplating ways to make this work, telling our parents so Gabby wouldn't have to, and looking for better jobs and places to live, I didn't stop to think of everything I would miss. But her journal entry hit me so hard, it made my eyes burn with painful emotions and my heart deflated like someone had a tight grip on it.

She reached for the pad and started to scribble again.

He was here when you weren't

I yanked the pad away from her and heaved it at the trash bin, and I did everything to keep from crying in front of her. But it hurt like hell.

With the back of my hands, I roughly wiped my eyes. "I will never hear our child's heartbeat. Their cry. Taking their first breath. Giggles. Squeals. First words. My ..." My voice cracked. "My name, Gabby. I'll never hear them say 'Daddy.'" I shook my head, rubbing my fist in circles over my heart. "And that really *fucking* hurts."

She threw her arms around my neck, holding me tightly. It broke me, and my body shook with a sob. When would I stop seeing all the things I was missing? When would I forget that sound ever existed?

After I contained my emotions, she released me and pressed her hands to my chest, guiding me to sit in the desk chair. She stood between my spread legs and covered my eyes. Then she uncovered them, wearing an obnoxiously big grin. Then she covered them again. When her hands left my eyes for a second time, she was squinting with her tongue out.

Again, she covered them, and again, she removed them. This time, the tip of her tongue reached for her nose while she crossed her eyes.

I laughed, and her face relaxed into a soft smile. She took my hand, holding it palm up while her other hand feathered along my skin. It kinda tickled. Then she slowly ran her fingers through my hair. I closed my eyes because it felt so good.

In the next breath, her lips ghosted along my cheek. When her touch vanished, I opened my eyes, and she was tearing open an orange package of Reese's peanut butter cups. After pulling one from the wrapper, she held it to my nose, and I inhaled. Then she held it to my lips, and I took a bite.

It was our favorite. The perfect mix of sweet and salty.

She didn't have to write a single word or sign anything. I got it. We experienced the world and the people in it in different ways. Joy was a smile, a funny face, a soft touch, the aroma of something sweet, and the mouthwatering marriage of peanut butter and chocolate.

I held up my hand with my middle two fingers folded in. *I love you.*

She nodded and smiled while returning the same sign before framing my face and kissing me.

THE MIND WAS self-destructive if left to its own devices. Lucky for me, Gabby had a way of interrupting those thoughts. As I held her hand during the OB appointment, she'd occasionally lift it to her lips and kiss it. When the doctor listened for the heartbeat, Gabby released my hand and pressed hers to my chest. Her index and middle fingers tapped, and I realized she was letting me feel the rhythm of our baby's heartbeat. I covered her hand with mine and mimicked the rhythm until we were in perfect sync. And when I closed my eyes, I could piece together memories of sounds, and I heard it with my mind instead of my ears.

And it was beautiful.

On our way to my car, I squeezed her hand. "I gathered our parents in the front of the church and told them I knocked you up. I thought God would protect me."

Gabby giggled, shaking her head.

"I think I'm going to stop learning ASL. I kind of like it when you're forced to be my captive audience, and you can't talk back to me."

She hugged my arm while playfully shoving me to the side.

"Careful, I might just tickle you until you pee your

pants." I reached for her sides, and she tried to wriggle out of my hold, bending forward.

I scooped her up in my arms, and her mouth opened. Again, I could hear a faint noise, but my memory remembered the way she released a blood-curdling shriek when I tickled her, and that memory was enough.

Chapter Forty-Three

The B-52's, "Love Shack"

Gabby

BEN COULDN'T STAY until the end of semester because he needed to look for a job, but he did the one thing I had wanted him to do since he lost his hearing—he sent me letters.

DEAR GABBY,

HOW ARE YOU? PASSING YOUR CLASSES? ANY JUICY GOSSIP ON YOUR FLOOR? ARE YOU KEEPING YOUR PLANT ALIVE? WHAT ELSE DID I WANT TO ASK YOU??? OH, YEAH, HOW'S OUR BABY?

I FOUND A JOB. IT'S NOTHING I EVER IMAGINED DOING, BUT FOR NOW IT'S GOOD PAY. I'M A RANCH HAND FOR DON O'NEILL, THE RANCHER WHO PURCHASED MOST OF THE CORY LAND. HE SAID AS

LONG AS I COMPLETED MY TASKS PROPERLY AND ON TIME, NO ONE WOULD SAY ANYTHING TO ME. I SORT OF LIED ABOUT KNOWING HOW TO RIDE A HORSE, SO YOUR MOM CONTACTED ISAAC, AND HE'LL BE HERE NEXT WEEK TO GIVE ME A CRASH COURSE BEFORE I START MY NEW JOB.

I'M MASTERING ASL, SO WATCH OUT. WHEN I SEE YOU, YOU'LL NO LONGER BE ABLE TO SIGN THINGS I DON'T KNOW. MY INSTRUCTOR SAID HE'S NEVER SEEN ANYONE CATCH ON AS QUICKLY AS ME. ALSO, I'M WORKING WITH SOMEONE ON LIP READ-ING. BUT I'M NOT PLANNING ON READING YOUR LIPS. I HAVE OTHER PLANS FOR THEM.

LOVE,
BENJAMIN ASHFORD, BABY DADDY IN TRAINING

AT THE END OF MAY, my parents drove to campus to move me back home. Despite everyone's reassurance and having talked to my dad on the phone, I still felt nervous seeing him because I officially had a noticeable baby bump, even though it was hidden under my oversized T-shirt.

"Hi, darling," was all he said when he hugged me, and I sank into his embrace.

Fourteen hours and three stops later, with my parents taking turns to drive, we arrived home. It was just before eight on Wednesday morning. I covered my mouth to muffle my squeal because Ben's car was in the driveway.

"Whoa, let me get the car stopped," Dad said as I

jumped out and ran toward Ben's blue Monte Carlo just as he stepped out.

"Hi." He grinned as I threw my arms around him. "Careful, Pastor Jacobson is watching."

I released him and signed, "I missed you."

Ben signed and spoke, "I missed you more."

I shook my head and took his hand, pulling him toward my dad's car to unload my things.

"Pastor Jacobson," Ben greeted my dad with a respectful nod.

My dad returned an uneasy look, and a less noticeable nod, but my mom hugged Ben.

After we unloaded everything and hauled it to my room, my dad stood in the doorway as Ben sat on the end of my bed, watching me sort through my things on the floor.

"The door stays open, young lady," Dad said.

I narrowed my eyes at him and bit back my smirk while slowly nodding. "Yes, Sir."

Once he headed down the stairs, I snorted and looked at Ben.

"What?" he said and signed.

I loved that he was making an effort to sign everything he said.

I signed, "My dad said door stays open."

"Fine," Ben said, sliding off the side of the bed. "But I want to see my baby."

I giggled when he guided me to lie back amongst my sorted clothes and the rest of my junk. Ben lifted my shirt, and my heart soared when his face lit up at my noticeable baby bump.

"It's me, your dad," he said, kissing my belly.

Listening for any sign of my parents, like the creak of the

stairs, I weaved my fingers in his hair and playfully tried to guide his head lower.

Ben stiffened, shooting his gaze up to mine. "What are you doing?"

I smirked.

"Gabbs, I'm not licking your kitty on your bedroom floor with your door open and your parents downstairs."

I laughed because the way Ben said "licking your kitty" was so matter-of-fact, not seductive at all.

Still, maybe it was too many weeks without him, maybe it was the letters he wrote me, or maybe it was second trimester hormones, but my need for sex was almost painful.

I sat up and signed, "I need," giving extra emphasis with my face to the *need* part.

Ben sat back on his heels and shook his head. "Don't do that." He adjusted himself. Ben was so sexy in his white T-shirt, black jeans, messy hair, and scruffy face.

Pre-pregnancy Gabby was a romantic, a dreamer. The idea of a chaste kiss and holding hands was everything. Second trimester Gabby needed to orgasm.

No chaste kisses. Only hard kisses with lots of tongue. And when I thought about Ben holding my hands, I imagined him pinning them next to my head as he hovered above me, hips thrusting into mine.

I crawled toward him, and he fell backwards, crab crawling away from me until his back hit the side of my bed.

He shook his head as I straddled his lap. "Gab—"

I kissed him while guiding his hand up my shirt to my breast. He moaned.

"Gabby? Is Ben staying for breakfast? I'm making pancakes," Mom called upstairs.

I quickly stood and straightened my bra. Ben narrowed his eyes.

I signed, "My mom is making breakfast. You hungry?"

After a second, as if his comprehension had a slight delay, he smirked and nodded.

I turned my head. "Yes, we'll have pancakes," I yelled.

Ben stood and closed my door partway so that we were standing behind it. "Quickly and quietly," he said, unbuttoning and unzipping his jeans.

I nodded, doing the same to my shorts.

Were we really going to remove our pants and have sex behind my partially closed bedroom door with my parents downstairs making breakfast?

Yes, we were.

He impatiently kissed me before either of us got out of our pants. I started to slide my hand down the front of his briefs.

"Gabby? We're out of eggs. Your dad is going to run and get them. He wants you to ride along. Ben can stay with me."

They were punishing us on purpose.

I pulled back, breathless and shaking my head while zipping my shorts. He did the same before peeking through the space between the door and its hinges for someone coming.

I wasn't sure how to sign everything, so I hopped over my sorted piles on the floor to my desk.

I have to go with my dad to get eggs and my mom said you're staying here with her.

He frowned, taking the pen from me. Ben rarely wrote

his words, perhaps he didn't want to risk my parents hearing him.

LET'S GET MARRIED. WE'LL RENT A LITTLE HOUSE OR EVEN A TRAILER. THEN WE CAN HAVE SEX ALL DAY AND THERE IS NOTHING YOUR DAD CAN DO ABOUT IT.

I snorted.
He wrote:

I'M SERIOUS.

I took back the pen.

You want to marry me just to have sex?

NO. I WANT TO MARRY YOU BECAUSE I'VE LOVED YOU FOREVER!!! ALL DAY SEX IS JUST A BONUS.

"Gabby? Are you ready?" Dad called from downstairs.

"Yes," I replied. "Just a sec!"

"Dad is ready to go," I signed, nodding toward the door before walking that way.

Ben hooked his arm around my waist, hand on my little baby bump as he hugged me from behind. "Marry me, Gabby," he said next to my ear. "I don't have a ring, yet, and I know this is all out of order and not the fairy tale you always dreamed of. Still, marry me."

I pulled away from him and stepped into the hallway, then I glanced back and rolled my eyes.

"Wow. Thanks for that," Ben said, deflating.

"What?" I signed.

"I just asked you to marry me, and you roll your eyes like it's a joke? We're having a baby."

I wrinkled my nose at him and finger spelled, "S T U P I D."

"Stupid? You think I'm stupid?"

I nodded while grinning, but Ben didn't find humor in my reply, so I stepped back into the room and nudged him aside to reach my desk and the pad of paper.

You got your preacher's daughter pregnant. Of course you have to marry her, STUPID! I rolled my eyes because you asked me as if you think either of us has a choice.

"Gabriella!" my dad called.

"Yes. I'm coming!" I jerked my head toward the door.

Ben kept his frown, even after reading what I wrote.

When I reached the bottom of the stairs, I slipped on my sandals and followed my dad outside. As we pulled onto the main road, he cleared his throat.

"I know you don't understand why I'm forcing you to abide by house rules, but just because you and Ben did something you should not have doesn't make it right to keep doing it."

"I know. And just so you know, he asked me to marry him. And I kind of assumed that was the obvious next step."

Dad nodded. "I think the sooner the better."

"Because you're embarrassed that I'm pregnant and not married?"

He winced, shooting me a quick sidelong glance. "No, Gabriella."

"Come on. There's no way you're not a little embarrassed. You preach to everyone in this town about the importance of honoring God in all we do, and your nineteen-year-old daughter gets pregnant her freshman year at college. That totally doesn't feel like a 'praise God' moment."

"Darling, I'm human. Of course, it's not what I wanted for you or our family. There is a long list of things in my life that have not gone as planned. We are all sinners."

"But you had higher hopes for me. After everything Sarah and Eve put you through, I was your last chance to feel fatherly pride."

Dad barked an unexpected laugh. He was a somber man of God with a practiced smile for his congregation, but he rarely laughed out loud.

"Gabriella, I never thought of it like that." He continued to chuckle.

I crossed my arms over my chest and stared out my window. "Why is sin so tempting?"

"No one is completely immune to desires of the flesh. When we give in to such pleasures, it's a symptom of our separation from God. When we allow that separation, sin steps in to fill that void."

"Dad, please don't say 'desires of the flesh.' It sounds perverted. And I don't want to look at my child and think of him as the result of *desires of the flesh*."

"When you look at your child, what do you want to think?"

I shrugged. "I don't know, but I don't want to feel like they're a mistake. Bob Ross says there are no such things as mistakes, just happy accidents. This baby is a happy accident."

He hummed. "Perhaps."

That was as good as it got. "Perhaps" from my dad was synonymous with "yes." When my sisters and I were younger, we'd bug him for things like letting us spend the night with friends, going to the local carnival, or opening one Christmas present on Christmas Eve. And every time he gave us a "perhaps," usually followed by "I'll think about it," that was a yes.

Chapter Forty-Four

Chicago, "Will You Still Love Me?"

Ben

AFTER GABBY and her dad left, I checked with Janet to see if she needed help in the kitchen. She was on the phone, so I returned to Gabby's room to tidy things up after she dumped everything into piles on her floor.

I emptied her backpack, stacking notebooks and folders onto her desk, accidentally scooting her Bible off the edge. When I picked it up, I shook my head at the weathered leather cover and limp, broken binding. The margins on every page were filled with her handwriting. Poems and doodled hearts. For years, I sat beside her in church as she poured her young heart onto the blank spaces, but I never focused on the actual words.

Blue-eyed boy
Best at baseball
Bashful smile
Berry red lips
Be mine

I cringed on her behalf as I turned page after page. There was no big, brilliant, bearded, baritone, brooding best friend Ben anywhere in sight. I asked myself if I could ever love another like I loved Gabby after pining for her the way she had for Matt. The answer made me nauseous.

I was easy, comfortable, familiar, accepting, her teacher, her safe place, and the father of her child. But was I the man who made her heart skip a beat? Did her palms get sweaty when I walked into the room? How many sappy, ridiculous, yet romantic dreams about her future involved me as her husband?

She told me she loved me, and that the kiss in the stairwell changed everything. I wanted to believe her, but I wasn't immune to insecurities.

Doing a double take, I caught her out of the corner of my eyes, shoulder resting on the doorframe, hands crossed over her chest. Once again, she caught me snooping in her personal things.

"I'll never be him," I said, closing the Bible and setting it next to the stack of folders and notepads from school.

She signed, "No. You're not him. You're more."

"I don't know, Gabbs." I laughed, staring at the Bible. "There's *a lot* of him in there. Years of him. I don't know if there's room for anyone to be *more*. Don't get me wrong, I'm okay with loving you more. That would make your Grandma

Bonnie so happy. But I can't help but see him inked in the margins of your whole world and not feel like there's no room for me."

She reached for my face, and I shook my head.

"It's fine, Gabby. You don't have to make me feel better. I don't know if you can. I'm just working on accepting it. Ya know? We'll be fine. We'll have a good life. We'll laugh like we've always done. We'll be there for each other. Raise a family and all that comes with that. I'm just ..." I ran my fingers through my hair. "I guess I'm still young and *stupid*, and I want to be the muse for all your poems. I selfishly want my name to be in the margins of your books. But I'm not, and that's fine. I'll grow up and focus on more important things like our baby. But right now, I'm struggling to be the man you need instead of the boyfriend you didn't want."

She flinched, and that wasn't my intention. In fact, it wasn't my intention to tell her that I looked inside her Bible. But she caught me, and I couldn't lie.

Before her tears escaped, she blotted the corners of her eyes while squeezing between my legs and her desk, resting her backside on the edge while I leaned back in her desk chair and laced my fingers behind my neck. She stared at me for the longest time, like I was a riddle she needed to solve. Then she grabbed a pen and notebook and started writing ... and writing.

> For the record, I wanted you first, but you were
> with Susie, and you told me we could only be friends.
> And that, Benjamin Ashford, was just how long it
> took me to get the nerve to ask you to be more than
> friends. You were my first crush long before that,

and I want you to be my last. And because you're so STUPID, you didn't think to look at the beginning. Genesis Chapter 1.

I lifted my gaze from the paper to her straight face, then I opened her Bible to Genesis Chapter 1.

After the first three words "In the beginning," she drew a caret symbol and inserted "there was Benjamin Ashford" with a heart behind my name.

Well, damn ...

I scooted the chair back and got on my knees, holding her left hand with mine. She grinned as I took the pen and drew a heart on her ring finger, then I drew a circle around her finger connecting the heart—a temporary ring for a forever promise. When I looked up, she nodded a half dozen times.

There was no room in my mind or my heart for regret. Gabriella Grace Jacobson owned every inch. I lifted her shirt and drew a heart around her belly button. When I glanced up, Gabby rolled her eyes.

"Your mom said yes." I kissed her belly.

Chapter Forty-Five

Pete Townshend, "Let My Love Open the Door"

Gabby

"WHERE ARE WE GOING?" I signed when Ben gave me a sidelong glance as he drove us in the wrong direction.

He took the morning off to take me to my OB appointment the week before our wedding, but he was supposed to take me home before going back to work.

Ben shrugged as he always did when he knew I said something but didn't want to answer. We pulled onto the long drive where his boss lived, but instead of heading to the gray two-story farmhouse, he veered right where cars were parked around a trailer I hadn't seen before. I recognized my mom's car right away.

"What is this?" I signed.

Ben jumped out and ran around his car, opening my door. "Welcome home, my soon-to-be wife." He held out his hand.

I stepped out of the car and straightened my green sundress. "Home?" I signed.

"Yes. For now. Mr. O'Neill said as long as I'm working for him, we can stay here. If there's a tornado warning, he said we could take cover in his basement."

It was a beige mobile home with white trim and a makeshift set of wood stairs to the front door.

Nothing big.

Not a dream home.

It screamed accidental pregnancy and shotgun wedding.

I threw my arms around Ben because I loved it. One day, we would remember it as our first home. Ben's parents offered to let us live with them, but we wanted our own place, and Ben delivered.

"It's small," he said.

I released him and shook my head while signing, "It's perfect."

The hesitation on his face vanished, leaving nothing but pride. "Get going. I have to get back to work." He nodded toward the trailer.

I narrowed my eyes.

He kissed me before sauntering toward the barns on the opposite side of the drive. Benjamin Ashford looked sinful in Wranglers and boots.

When I climbed the stairs and opened the door, the living room of women yelled, "Surprise!"

I stood still, wide-eyed and grinning.

"Welcome to your shower," Mom said, hugging me. "It's a wedding shower, baby shower, and housewarming party all in one."

When she released me, I didn't know what to take in first. It was my house, so I wanted to see it, but there were family and friends, party decorations, food covering every surface of the kitchen counter and dinette table, and a mountain of gifts piled between the sofa and television.

As everyone bombarded me with warm hugs and sweet greetings, I wormed my way through the trailer to peek into the back two bedrooms separated by a bathroom. The nursery already had a cradle and white baby dresser. A queen bed with a light blue striped comforter occupied most of the other bedroom.

I bit my lip to hide my grin. That's where Ben and I would sleep and do other things that didn't involve sleep.

For the next two hours, the women who loved me the most showered me with gifts and advice on marriage and parenting.

"Do you want us to stay and help get everything put away, or do you want to do that with Ben?" Sarah asked.

"I bought her lingerie," Eve said. "It's safe to assume she'll want to be alone with Ben."

"Not until your wedding night." Mom said, tying the top of the last trash bag.

Sarah snorted and Eve rolled her eyes while I sat in my rocking chair, fanning myself with one of the cards.

"Mom, do you know how Gabby got pregnant?" Eve asked.

"It's neither here nor there. That's in the past. They've waited this long since being home from school, what's another few days?" Mom asked.

Sarah and Eve looked at me. I shook my head, lips pressed together. My parents lived in their own world, and that was fine. Ben and I were respectful of their rules. But just because we hadn't been allowed in his room or mine with the door shut didn't mean we were abstaining.

Quite the opposite.

The barn.

The garage.

His car.

By the creek.

We had so much sex.

"I'm not staying here until our wedding night," I said in my sweetest voice, which earned me an approving smile from my mom as she set the trash by the door.

Eve and Sarah synchronized their barely restrained snorts which only made my innocent grin double. I even batted my eyelashes for extra emphasis. Was I pregnant out of wedlock?

Yes.

Was I still the favorite child?

For sure.

"Are you having dinner with us tonight or are you eating with Ben's family?" Mom asked, wiping her brow with the back of her hand.

I drummed my fingers on the arms of the rocking chair. "Hmm, I think we'll be at his house for dinner."

"Okay. Then we'll see you after dinner."

I rocked forward and stood, hugging my sisters and then my mom. "Thank you for everything."

"You're welcome, honey." Mom never made a big deal of it, but I loved the way she discreetly pressed her hand to my belly at the end of our hugs.

As soon as they closed the door behind them, and the place was quiet, I turned in a slow circle, inspecting all the gifts. Then I squealed and jumped up and down.

I had a house with furniture.

I was getting married.

We were having a baby!

As a little girl, I loved playing house. Part of me still felt like that little girl, so I didn't wait for Ben before organizing my kitchen and stacking new towels in the linen closet. After I put all the baby clothes and diapers in the dresser and folded the blanket Grandma Bonnie crocheted the baby, I put my lingerie in our dresser.

My belly seemed a little big for sexy lace and satin, but the red nightie was so pretty, I couldn't stop myself from trying it on. After I stepped into the bathroom to look in the mirror, the front door opened.

I quickly shut the bathroom door.

"Gabby?" Ben called.

Gah!

He couldn't hear me. And my clothes were in the bedroom.

"It's fine," I murmured to myself, blowing out a slow breath, while inspecting my reflection. My boobs were so big. I looked ready to shoot a porno. And the lace didn't hide my nipples at all. The crotch of the matching panties crawled up my butt. There was nothing sexy about me. "Ben won't care," I said, closing my eyes.

"Gabbs?" He knocked on the door.

With my shoulders back, I bit one side of my lip and then the other, testing which one felt most sexy, then I opened the door.

"Oh my gosh!" I gasped, slamming the door shut.

"Uh, sorry about that. I'll just give Gabby the gift and tell her it's from you and Mrs. O'Neill," Ben said to *his boss!*

"No. No. No." I covered my face.

A few seconds later, Ben opened the door, forcing me to take a step backward.

His gaze landed on my boobs before slowly inspecting the rest of me.

"Your boss saw me!" I signed.

My dramatic hand movements brought Ben's attention to my face.

He scraped his teeth along his lower lip and slowly shook his head like Mr. O'Neill didn't see me. But he did! Or Ben was dismissing the incident like it wasn't a big deal. But it was!

I crossed my arms over my chest to hide my nipples poking through the lace.

Ben smirked, balancing on one foot and then the other to remove his dirty socks. "Baby, don't do that."

I swallowed hard and shook my head. We weren't having sex after Mr. O'Neill saw me.

"Ya think that little red getup is dry clean only?" he asked, unbuttoning his dirty gray shirt. "Because I need a shower, but I need you more."

"Your boss saw me!" I signed. "Do you understand me?"

Ben's grin doubled as he shrugged off his shirt and unbuckled his belt. "Yeah, I understand. I'm sorry. Did you try to tell me?" He stepped closer.

When his jeans slid down his legs, he cupped the back of my head and kissed me.

Every time we had sex, but most especially after Ben got off work and needed a shower, I thought of the girl who was saving herself for marriage—the girl who imagined a white canopy bed and a husband who wore a suit and had a clean-shaven face. That girl no longer existed.

Rebel Gabby slid her hand into Ben's briefs and stroked him until he groaned.

Rebel Gabby knew she wasn't rebellious enough to mess up the new bedding, so she made Ben lie on the floor.

He grinned up at me while pushing his briefs down his thighs. I slid off my uncomfortable panties and started to take off the nightie.

"Leave it on," Ben said.

I paused for a second, eating up the way he looked at me like I was the most beautiful person in the world. His hands slid up my legs as I straddled him, and they gripped my hips when I guided his erection into me.

We were young and stupid.

Wild and free.

Figuring out life one day—one *happy accident*— at a time.

Chapter Forty-Six

The Cure, "Just Like Heaven"

Gabby

THE SUN SHINED on our wedding day.

My father walked me down the aisle and took his place at the front of the church to marry us. I would never love my father as much as I did that day. His pride and happiness never wavered, despite the polite smiles and whispers of judgment from people around town.

We had a small reception at our house with a two-tiered cake. Then I threw my bouquet straight into Tillie's anxious arms just before everyone threw rice to send us off as Mr. and Mrs. Benjamin Ashford.

"Wife," Ben said and signed while holding open the car door.

"Husband," I signed back to him.

We drove off with cans dragging from the back of his Monte Carlo.

Sarah and Isaac gifted us two nights in St. Louis for a short honeymoon in a fancy hotel with a stunning view of downtown. Ben carried me into the room, and I giggled when he deposited me onto the bed.

"I have something for you," he said. "I don't know if this is the right time, but when I was packing my things yesterday, I came across it."

I nodded slowly, then signed, "I didn't get you anything."

"Gabbs, you're everything I need. That's why I want you to have this, in case there's ever any doubt." He pulled his journal I gave him for Christmas from his duffle bag and handed it to me.

There were pages and pages of entries. I glanced up at him.

Ben shrugged, removing his bowtie. "I didn't send you letters, but I wrote them. You were always on my mind."

"Benjamin," I whispered to myself, opening to the first entry. He was wrong. I didn't need the journal because I no longer doubted his love for me. Still, my heart melted.

DEAR GABBS,

MY MOM MOVED HER PRECIOUS MOMENTS OFF THE TOP OF THE PIANO YESTERDAY SO I COULD LIE ON IT. THEN TILLIE PLAYED IT FOR NEARLY AN HOUR. SHE SAID I MOANED SEVERAL TIMES, AND IT MADE ME THINK OF YOUR TINY MOANS WHEN I BRAIDED YOUR HAIR. I LIKE TO THINK THAT SOMEDAY I WILL FIND MY WAY AGAIN, AND IT WILL LEAD ME BACK TO YOU.

DEAR GABBS,

I HAVE A CAVITY. IT'S MY FIRST. I BLAME YOU
BECAUSE I'VE BEEN EATING ALL OUR FAVORITES,
BUT SINCE YOU'RE NOT HERE TO SHARE THEM WITH
ME, I'M EATING TWICE THE AMOUNT OF SUGAR. DO
YOU REMEMBER WHEN WE STARTED BUYING SNACKS
THAT CAME IN TWOS? IT WAS THE FIRST TIME WE
RODE OUR BIKES INTO TOWN AND LOADED UP ON
JUNK FOOD AT THE GAS STATION. IT STARTED WHEN
I GRABBED A PACK OF REESE'S PEANUT BUTTER
CUPS. YOU SAID YOU LIKED THEM TOO, SO I SAID
WE COULD SHARE. THAT LED TO PACKS OF
TWINKIES, DING DONGS, TWIX, POP-TARTS, AND
TWIN POPS. I MISS THE TWO OF US.

DEAR GABBS,

I CAN'T STOP THINKING ABOUT WHAT WE DID.
I'M SURE YOU REGRET IT SINCE I TREATED YOU SO
BADLY. I'M SORRY IT HAPPENED. YOU DESERVED
BETTER. I TOOK SOMETHING FROM YOU THAT I
CAN'T GIVE BACK. IT'S WEIRD REGRETTING THE
GREATEST MOMENT OF MY LIFE, BUT I DO. THE
OTHER NIGHT, I DREAMED YOU WERE PREGNANT.
CAN YOU IMAGINE?

I LOOKED up at Ben as he watched me read his journal, his white button-down shirt completely unbuttoned. He narrowed his eyes and leaned forward to see what page I was reading.

Then he smirked. "Uh, yeah. I bet you *can* imagine."

Epilogue

Sixpence None the Richer, "Kiss Me"

10 years later
Gabby

"Once upon a time, a young girl who dreamed of fairy tales, while scribbling poems about love, met a boy who heard music in everything around him. I call them the poet and the composer. What do you think?" Seren said while signing.

She sat cross-legged on the floor at the end of our bed, and Ben braided her hair.

It calmed both of them.

I, however, was anything but calm, unzipping my dress for a third outfit change.

"It's perfect, sweetheart. But we can't forget Aunt Sarah," Ben said to our daughter.

Our whole family was being interviewed on a nationally televised morning show because Sarah, Ben, and I won an

Obie (Off-Broadway Theater Award) for our musical *The Preacher's Daughter*.

Seren thought they would ask her what the play was about, so she was practicing her explanation.

She wasn't wrong. It was inspired by our love story, a dramedy that ended with the birth of a child, a girl named Bobbie (a nod to Bob Ross) because she was a happy accident. In real life, Bobbie was Seren, inspired by the word serendipity, which also defined a happy accident.

The Preacher's Daughter stood a good chance of transitioning to a Broadway musical with its success and awards. We never intended on staying in New York City forever, but our life was the epitome of unplanned.

"Seren, get dressed," I said when Ben finished her braid.

"I'm going," she said with a little sass before carrying her brush out of our bedroom.

"Baby, take a breath," Ben said, looking handsome and unfairly calm, perched on the end of our bed, hands folded between his spread legs.

Benjamin Ashford looked sinful in a black suit and tie. My best friend got more handsome every year. And the world was about to get a good look at him and hear how he didn't let his disability deter him from pursuing his passion.

After two years of working on the ranch, Ben went back to school and earned his degree in music composition. We rented a tiny apartment near campus, and I worked evenings and weekends waiting tables while Ben stayed home with Seren and studied. During the day, when Seren napped, I worked on my writing. Sarah convinced me to write my and Ben's story. Then she and Ben wrote the lyrics and music. With her connections in the industry, our little story came to life as a musical.

I turned so Ben would zip my black dress that covered my knees, shoulders, and cleavage. Dad would be proud.

But before he zipped it, Ben kissed my bare back. "I love you. I think it's what I do best."

After he zipped it, I pivoted toward him, resting my hands on his clean-shaven face for a few seconds before signing, "You try. And I appreciate that. But you didn't love me *in the beginning,* chapter one, like I loved you. But—"

"That's bullshit, and you know it."

"Ben!" I squealed when he tickled my sides. "Stop." I giggled and squirmed. "I'm going to wet my pants."

"Sorry. I can't hear you. Did you say I'm a stud, and I've always loved you more than you love me?"

I tried to push him away.

"For goodness' sake. Mom, just say he's a stud!" Seren called from her bedroom.

It wasn't the first time she heard or witnessed Ben's childish behavior. I wasn't sure Seren knew what a stud was, but Ben loved that our playfulness amused her.

I grabbed his hair, and he stopped, our faces an inch apart as I caught my breath. There was something special about the moments when we weren't moving our hands or lips to speak. There was a stillness, a magic, an exchange of something more than words. When I opened my mouth to speak, to break the silence, he kissed me.

Also By
Jewel E. Ann

Standalone Novels

Idle Bloom

Undeniably You

Naked Love

Only Trick

Perfectly Adequate

Look The Part

When Life Happened

A Place Without You

Jersey Six

Scarlet Stone

Not What I Expected

For Lucy

What Lovers Do

Before Us

If This Is Love

Right Guy, Wrong Word

I Thought of You

Sunday Morning Series

Sunday Morning

The Apple Tree

A Good Book

Wildfire Series

From Air

From Nowhere

The Fisherman Series

The Naked Fisherman

The Lost Fisherman

Jack & Jill Series

End of Day

Middle of Knight

Dawn of Forever

One (*standalone*)

Out of Love (*standalone*)

Because of Her (*standalone*)

Holding You Series

Holding You

Releasing Me

About The Author

Jewel E. Ann is a *Wall Street Journal* and *USA Today* bestselling author. She's written over thirty novels, including LOOK THE PART, a contemporary romance, the JACK & JILL TRILOGY, a romantic suspense series; and BEFORE US, an emotional women's fiction story. With 10 years of flossing lectures under her belt, she took early retirement from her dental hygiene career to write mind-bending love stories. She's living her best life in Iowa with her husband, three boys, and a Goldendoodle.

Receive special offers and stay informed of new releases, sales, and exclusive stories:
www.jeweleann.com